More determined than ever, h̶ ̶ ̶ ̶ ̶ ̶ ̶ into the chair and stared at the word and the definition. Obviously, the password was a phrase, or perhaps a random alpha-numeric designation.

Tapping idly on the key, he replayed the steps he had already taken in his mind, and then something his father said jogged in his memory.

He dialled the AWS number and was greeted with the now familiar GWHSVAX: LINK TO AWS

LOG ON:

Dirk typed in GORMAN. There was a millisecond delay as AWS seemed to consider this response.

PASSWORD:

Dick grimaced. *This was it.*

He leaned forward and typed: BLUE-EYED BOY

There was an even longer delay, and then the following words materialized before him: HARRY? IS THAT YOU? I THOUGHT YOU HAD BEEN ... another protracted pause ... DELETED.

Also in the Point SF series:

Look out for:

POINT SF

RANDOM FACTOR

Jessica Palmer

SCHOLASTIC

Scholastic Children's Books,
Scholastic Publications Ltd,
7–9 Pratt Street, London NW1 0AE, UK

Scholastic Inc.,
555 Broadway, New York, NY 10012–3999, USA

Scholastic Canada Ltd,
123 Newkirk Road, Richmond Hill,
Ontario, Canada L4C 3G5

Ashton Scholastic Pty Ltd,
PO Box 579, Gosford, New South Wales,
Australia

Ashton Scholastic Ltd,
Private Bag 92801, Penrose, Auckland,
New Zealand

First published in the UK by Scholastic Publications Ltd, 1994

Text copyright © Jessica Palmer, 1994

ISBN 0 590 55665 7

Typeset by DP Photosetting, Aylesbury, Bucks
Printed by Cox & Wyman Ltd, Reading, Berks

10 9 8 7 6 5 4 3 2 1

Dedicated to my brother, Michael.
May you have found peace at last.

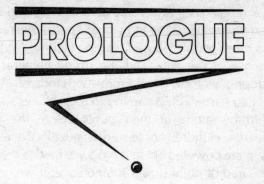

PROLOGUE

1/11/2033

O-SIX-HUNDRED HOURS

The sun rose listlessly over the earth, unobserved by any but a select few whose duties had carried them to the planet's inhospitable surface. Inside GWHQ its rays were muted by kilometres of water, so that it appeared a sickly yellow-green ball suspended in the surrounding sea. At these depths few followed its progress; few cared. But with thousands of sensors implanted in the tough skin of the dome, AWS still felt the sun's presence.

The system did the computer equivalent of a stretch and a yawn as it stirred from its enforced slumber, awakened by a series of buzzes and mini-alarms as GWHQ geared up for a new day. Its mechanical eyes regarded each new arrival. Its voders greeted them, as the massive system did a quick retinal scan and voice print overlay and compared them against the individual's personnel record.

As more people poured into the facility, AWS lost its sense of the sun, and the inside cameras and microphones took over. From thousands of eyes it watched harried clerks scurry to their offices so they would be sitting at their desks before the brass appeared. Hundreds of terminals, auxiliary eyes and ears, were powered on, and AWS warmed to the new day. Tired of night-time's somnolence, it welcomed each person heartily, with the appropriate name and rank, through a hundred mechanical voice boxes, as it pulled more energy from the wave generators.

As new people logged on and new greetings were issued, the massive war program that ran everything within the facility cycled through thousands and thousands of written instructions, pausing over one that had today's date. There was nothing particularly unusual in this, for AWS had an unlimited number of dates embedded within its system stretching back to the beginning of time and forward to time's infinite conclusion. Within its memory banks, it had a record of all of man's written history. It had dates for scheduled battles, dates for the interminable meetings held by the brass, dates for the numerous bulletins and memoranda dispensed each day.

But to find an isolated date – besides the date of origin and the dates that marked revisions to the software – within the instructions itself was atypical.

Although now that the huge silicon brain of AWS pondered it, the computer realized it had noted the presence of this line and this particular date before and had ignored it as not pertinent.

Today, however, was different.

IF – and it listed a set of complex parameters, including today's date – THEN GO TO LINE ...

It took less than a nanosecond for the computer to check the parameters and see that they had been met, as more people showed up at the gates, were vetted and then logged on to the system. AWS's auditory sensors picked up the comforting sounds of hundreds of different conversations between the human personnel, and between man and machine. It ignored them as superfluous and switched to the requested line number which was, in fact, a macro. A program within a program.

AWS did something of a mental doubletake as it whirled through the thousands of lines of instructions. Then as a self-regulating "smart system", it read through them twice looking for hidden sabotage or boobytraps. AWS noted the date of creation and the identity of the programmer who had written the macro.

There was no mistake. This was part of the original instructions.

For another fraction of an instant, its peripheral program continued to function. The many gate scanners inspected yet another in the trickle of late arrivals and checked his records. Nearly a thousand commands, requests or directions were issued from as many different terminals and began their convoluted path through miles of wire and chips towards their final destination. Some linked the massive computer to the central distribution network; others tied it into the Bathosphere's industrial base; still others bound it to the large fleet that circled the planet.

The great computer faltered as it considered the macro's deadly message. All the activated terminals within the facility flickered, and then AWS simply shut down.

O-SEVEN-HUNDRED HOURS

Communications Specialist Alpha Allele Ylon crawled from his sleep cradle yawning. Both port and starboard sides of the corridor were honeycombed with the long octagonal tubes. The emerging shift would be immediately replaced by the next, who already stood beside their assigned cradles. Ylon disregarded his cradle-mate, not out of contempt or disrespect, but simple indifference. He had performed this same simple act for years. The fact that all cradle partners were lined up facing away from the newly-awakened shift tended to enhance the general apathy. Ylon had no idea what his cradle-mate looked like, but he was aware of a vague sense of disquiet in the presence of the other crew. Had he had a questioning mind, he might have wondered why their backs were turned, but he didn't. All doubt and questions had been quashed through the years of routine, fighting a war that had been old in his grandfather's time. This was the way things were, always had been and always would be.

Moving as a single unit, the rising shift turned and headed for the sanitation facility, with its row upon row of individual hygienic units. The floor of each was thermo-sensitive, activated when the occupant stepped into the cubicle. Responsive to the fine gradations of temperature in the soles of the feet, the water temperature was calibrated according to body temperature for optimum refreshment. The computer regulated the flow, and a quick scan assessed the areas of the anatomy with the greatest bacterial accumulation. Thus, the computer was able to accomplish the maximum cleansing with the minimum amount of energy and water. Ylon simply stood as it spat and squirted at the appropriate parts, then stepped – clean and dried – into the queue for the sinks.

From there, he went directly to the officers' mess. He moved like an automaton, senses and emotions dulled by repetition. His feet took him up the vessel's corridor – his body leaning into the next turn after the appropriate number of steps, acting purely on reflex. All Dolphin class combat cruisers had the same layout. Ship born and bred, Ylon had traversed these same steps after each of his assigned sleep periods for all of his adult life.

He queued in front of the catering unit, having already memorized this quarter's breakfast selection, with its carefully designed balance of nutrients, over a calendar month ago. Minor adjustments in vitamin and mineral content were made after the sanitation cubicle's analysis of his body's perspiration was forwarded on to the kitchen. The menu supposedly came from a variety of regions and was designed to suit all palates. In truth it suited none.

With his tray filled with something called Huevo Revuelto Mexicale, Ylon rifled through his memory of outdated languages and came up with a translation. Revolting Mexican eggs. An inspired name, for it looked like mashed potatoes with yesterday's refuse thrown on top for a dash of colour.

Ylon shuffled into the lounge to stare blankly out of the view portal at the unending cold stars and the looming moon and, beyond that, the mother planet. A brilliant ball of blue with small patches of green, covered by swirls of white clouds and circling bracelets of tankers. It was a view either he or his ancestors had observed, from one angle or another, for centuries. Luminescent against the flat, black background, the scene was one which would normally inspire awe unless one had grown too jaded to see it.

Sometimes, he wondered what it must look like

from the surface peering out, but he doubted that he'd ever see it. At least, not until the end of the conflict. The war had lasted nearly three hundred years, and it seemed unlikely to end in the near future.

Ylon wondered, too, if he had any planet-bound relatives. His was a military family, and those few who still lived were in active service; the rest had been killed in battle, and Ylon expected to die before his time also. This had been true for generations upon generations of Ylon's family – for his father, his father's father and the sire before that. Ylon's memory of his father was hazy, and Ylon couldn't have said how many generations had been in the military. Only that the tradition stretched back as far as he could remember. His was a proud heritage, and Ylon was more than willing to sacrifice himself in a conflict whose beginning neither he nor his sire nor as far as he knew his great-great-great-grandfather had seen. Still, he considered it a privilege and an honour to be some small part of the great mechanism that kept their world, and the helpless civilians who resided there, safe.

The Galactic Air War had begun on the surface long ago. Its origin and its causes were shrouded in the mists of time, but time had done little to diminish humanity's fighting spirit. Still, man had learned a few lessons. The current conflict was restricted to certain corridors of space. In days of old when man had possessed the ability to kill himself several times over, some would have considered it little more than a sparring match, which had sprung from a gentlemen's agreement when mankind finally conceded that ground conflict, and even air-to-ground conflict, was much too costly a process.

The Great Treaty of Amman was negotiated and signed in 2033, an outgrowth of a war which had decimated one-quarter of the world's population. It made surface war illegal, so the combatants were required to move their struggle to space. After the treaty, there had been a short interval of peace during which each country's space technology – still in the fledgling state and limited to a few permanent space stations and one lunar outpost, mostly scientific in nature – was advanced, and each country rushed to build the vehicles and the weaponry needed to move the continual warfare out of range of human devastation.

The accord had been a boon for mankind in more ways than one. Civilian casualties no longer existed. The national space programs, always secondary to the military, were merged with the armed forces, and once-inaccessible funds became suddenly accessible. Frozen accounts thawed. Development of fast, efficient, cost effective space travel became top priority. One-time nations became city-states in continental countries in order to support the vast military machine. Borders and tariffs dissolved, and the world became a much more stable place.

Minor conflicts between nations ceased, while the war, the original war which had precipitated the treaty, rolled on, left to pursue its unrelenting course within the quadrant of space allotted for conflict. Its cause was forgotten. War itself had been anaesthetized, computerized and sterilized. Yet it continued nonetheless, automatically, like the motions which carried Ylon from one corridor to another, one deck to another, one level to another. Learned by rote and performed perfunctorily. He didn't question it. He didn't question anything – not the causes of the war, its validity or its eventual outcome. Like never seeing the face of his cradle-mate, it was as it should be, always had been and always would be.

Indirectly the much-applauded Amman treaty, and the research it had spawned, was responsible for interplanetary colonization, and after a fashion had been mankind's salvation when the Great Flood came. For it had provided the technology and the knowledge that had permitted most of mankind to escape in the Exodus as the rising waters of the melting polar ice-caps flooded the land masses.

A commander, head of engineering, came into the lounge, and Ensign Ylon snapped to attention, another reflex action instilled in him from birth. His gaze flitted to the clock. It was time to report for duty.

Again his brain went to sleep while his body took him to his destination on autopilot.

The vessel was a self-contained community that worked as efficiently as a hive. Each worker had his assigned tasks – assigned cradle, assigned sleep and nourishment periods, assigned recreational times and, of course, required duties in twelve hour shifts. The ship seemed to operate almost by itself, with minimal maintenance and upkeep. It droned or hummed, depending on where it was on its long, assigned, elliptical orbit which took it around the parent planet, past the moon where it used combined acceleration and the mild lunar gravitational pull to catapult it back again towards the next scheduled rendezvous with The Enemy.

This was the boring part of the trip between engagements. Glancing out of one of the port screens, Ylon noted the retreating Sea of Tranquillity. Currently the ship ran parallel to the Sea of Crisis, and soon they would enter the darkness of the moon's far side. Ylon yawned as he settled at his station, thinking he could probably run the weekly co-efficient utilization checks in his sleep.

15/11/2333

FOURTEEN-HUNDRED HOURS

Head cradled in his hands, Harold Gorman huddled over stacks and stacks of computer printouts. He rubbed the back of his neck and pinched his nose between thumb and forefinger. Gorman had been poring over these same figures until they blurred and the numbers performed a quantum dance across the page.

The answer had to lie somewhere within these figures. There had to be a pattern even within the deviation. With the calculations off by such-and-such a percent. The alternative was chaos, and computers didn't behave that way. Even the most sophisticated still functioned by repetition, able to perform repetitive tasks at lightning speeds with much more efficiency than the human operator, for the brain was prone to flights of fancy, going off on tangents, and easily bored by routine. All computer languages when broken down to their most basic components were mathematical and their instructions repetitive in nature; thus most errors were mathematical and once understood, predictable.

Creativity remained an exclusively human domain, although computers were programmed to seem human enough. They could talk, respond to verbal commands, even hold seemingly spontaneous conversations, but only within certain limitations.

So, there had to be a pattern ... *somewhere.*

A misplaced integer in a binary code ... Gorman shuddered. Like looking for a silicon chip in a plate of spaghetti, and Gorman had the feeling he was looking for something smaller than that. Something infinitesimal.

And Harry knew he was out of his element. Oh, he understood how to operate the software and make the standard adjustments. Gorman was well-versed in binary and hexadecimal codes and assembly language. Harry had taken all the required programming courses in both primary and secondary school. He'd aced them, but he was no programmer. It required a kind of linear thought which he found boring and mundane. He preferred to play with the software rather than learn its intricacies.

And this particular software had been running without glitch for three hundred years. Only minimal modifications had been made when some government ministry or another had – after exhaustive research and study, and usually numerous sub-committees – requested it. The boundaries of the conflict were moved to open up a new traffic lane or revised to allow a new participant to enter the conflict. Or the win–lose ratio was altered.

Generally speaking, the software was self-running and self-contained. Only a moron could goof it up, and Gorman was no fool, or he hadn't thought so ... until now.

His position as official Galactic War Headquarters Programmer was purely nominal, or should have been. The post was normally given to idiot nephews or young officers being groomed for the top, where minor mistakes and an occasional *faux pas* had few repercussions.

Gorman uncomfortably straddled both categories as a relative of a high-ranking official who was being coached as a potential front-runner in the government hegemony. "A young man with political aspirations", who must of necessity start in the military, and a son of an influential statesman, the current Ambassador to the Associated American Archipelagoes. In a world where the economy depended on the on-going war, all political ambitions in the central government were launched from GWHQ. Local rule was another matter altogether, but Gorman wasn't interested in a career that was confined to a single bathosphere or island complex. In the military, Harry was close to the world centre. Here he could learn the ropes and the tedious rituals of protocol that greased the all-too-squeaky wheels of international diplomacy.

Hence the post as GWHQ programmer, or Program's Specialist First Class. Until recently, he would have supposed he was adequate to the task. In his first year here at the Pennine station not even minimum modifications had been required and when he wasn't attending long and boring meetings, a part of his political training, he played with the AWS software. Chess, Chase, or one of the myriad of other games it provided for its user.

Working with the complicated system was the fun part of his position. The computer was less irascible and unpredictable than his superiors, or his subordinates, and he was continually amazed by the software. Often after a gruelling meeting, Gorman would return to his office and only calm down after a rational "discussion" with the computer.

Long ago, he had ceased to be intimidated by the technical part of his post, although the AWS program was a work of such genius, antiquated though it was, that no one living could possibly duplicate it. AWS, standing for Amman War Software, plotted battles and devised strategy, ship movements and casualties for the galactic war effort. It regulated the size, place and outcome of each engagement with geometric precision. Never, in three hundred years of use, did it err. Each week, each month, the computer scheduled battles and casualties in such a way as to maximize profits and productivity and minimize loss. Each week, each month, the powers-that-be in the European Confederacy, based in the Alps Islands reviewed the week's engagements. If they chose, for example, to change the outcome because there was a surplus of widgets, they could do so. The information filtered down to and up from local government. But such revisions were rare, and generally dictated by financial considerations. The weekly conferences were purely nominal, more to assuage the egos of the bureaucrats than anything else.

Eventually, the software had become linked into the other facility computers that ruled over every aspect of human life. It rationed food and water between the terran population, the combatants and the off-planet colonies. No commercial decisions could be made without its consultation, for its actions often influenced the flow of commodities between the Confederated Islands of Europe. Its operations often defined what items were needed, where and when, and what items were not.

So the war had become one of economies and not one of ideologies. There was no enemy, not in the classic, archaic sense of the word, besides human stupidity – although the combatants and the public were urged to think in those terms. It lent romance and credibility to the endeavour. However, the war was fought between this computer and its sister computer at Bureau Two, GWHQ-Urals. Strategies were planned almost without human intervention. Casualties were plotted and the subhuman losses never varied from the figures forecasted.

The computers ran the ships, setting the course for the next scheduled engagement, making minute adjustments and repairs within each vessel, even planning the menu for the occupants. The ship's inhabitants acted as the machine's eyes and, sometimes, its hands to perform those repairs beyond the computer's abilities. Even then they were instructed each step along the way by the master program. The crew was superfluous to the battles and to the battles' outcome, although they weren't allowed to believe that. Despite their so-called limited intelligence, they needed a sense of purpose to continue. No chattels, no matter how they had been bred and indoctrinated, would be willing to continue if they knew their existence was for the entertainment value alone. After all, what fun is war without casualties?

So AWS took care of everything.

Until two weeks ago when the entire system had gone down. The entire Pennine Island Galactic War Complex and associated Bathosphere had been brought to its knees. Not by subtle sabotage, which the computers would have been able to detect, but by some unknown factor. The embarrassed military had announced to an angry public that it was a virus, and they had swallowed it. No one had thought to question how a system so complex could be confounded by something so simple that any five-year-old in the Lake District Bathosphere Infants' School Program could have devised it.

Through the years, man had created some devious and complex forms of sabotage, and supposedly the GW computer had been taught to detect them all. With an infinite number of variations, and infinite patience, the system could analyse the data and combat it. Fix itself, and in combating it, the system would evolve, enabling it to detect even more sophisticated sabotage later on.

However, their explanation hadn't been a lie, for the authorities did sincerely believe that it had been a child's prank. Something which, by its very lack of subtlety, AWS had been unable to recognize. Somehow Gorman doubted it. AWS was locked up tighter than a drum, and Gorman didn't believe that anyone could get in without the system's approval.

It had been the first real test of his career. Harry suspected that the fault was within the software itself – either created by the system as a result of its endless evolution of updates and revision, or a bug buried so deep within the software that it had taken centuries to surface. Or perhaps it had been triggered by something in recent events, an odd set of circumstances or a series of demands placed upon it and commands given to it. He didn't know and wouldn't even hazard a guess. His surmise seemed to be substantiated by the fact that the computer hadn't been functioning properly since that time.

Gorman had got the system up and running by the simple expedient of rebooting. Nothing difficult, although he didn't let his superior know this. Since then, there had been glitches in the software. Engagements didn't take place where, or when, they were scheduled. Casualty figures exceeded the forecast. And the predictable had become suddenly unpredictable. "Enemy ships" popped up where they shouldn't be, outside of the negotiated, allotted air space. Or ships engaged beyond the regulated boundaries of the combat zone. Prohibitive weaponry was used which destroyed not only the ship's occupants, but also the vessel itself when the production of ships had been geared down decades ago. Materials, always much more important than the cloned personnel to a planet where resources were stretched to the limit, were destroyed. Fiscal crisis precipitated by the sudden need for ships threatened to topple the government – the same government that had managed to survive the Great Flood intact.

The war served as entertainment for masses suddenly compressed into mountain ranges *cum* archipelagoes and limited bathospheres. Migration into space, which had begun as a trickle, turned into a torrent, despite the primitive off-world conditions. People had had no choice.

The war, therefore, had both an economic and a recreational value. Only recently, with the vaporization weapons, had they been able to gear down production of war stock to develop alternate recreational merchandise which the masses so badly needed. To return to full war production while people did without games or sensory implants would bring about the long-anticipated rebellion, and this government would fall, and he, Lieutenant Harry Gorman would fall with it.

Directly or indirectly, every industry was dependent on the war. The technologies now available had been generated by the galactic conflict. The development of hard goods, which had enabled them to build the bathosphere and survive the melting of the polar ice caps, had come from the war effort. Few realized it, but agriculture and genetic engineering, even the entertainment industry, fed and in turn was fed by the war machine. The world had attained a uniformly high, if somewhat cramped, standard of living thanks to the war. Fortunes were made and lost on the war. The pools and the bookmakers were dependent upon GWHQ in both the Urals and the Pennine Islands for accurate results.

The world's fragile collective psyche was also dependent on the war machine as an outlet for normal human aggression and hostility. Violent crimes decreased when violence was taken vicariously in the form of war, injected into the mainstream in regularly scheduled doses. With 3D broadcasts every four hours, at eight-hundred, twelve-hundred, six-teen-hundred and twenty-hundred respectively. Like medicine. For psychologists and sociologists, who rarely agreed on anything, both believed that struggle was inherent in the human condition. History seemed to confirm it. Some portion of the world had been at war ever since the first ape had picked up a rock, or a stick, and used it as a weapon. Ages ago, the scholars had decided that a continuous war was necessary for the mental health of civilization.

Soon after, the great genius, Dr Eoin Evans, had created this software that had completely mechanized war. The original idea used only robotic combatants. However, social experts noticed a rise in violent crime. Who can root when one robot blasts another? So, it had been decided that there had to be blood, pain and suffering which could be brought into people's living rooms via holographic link-up with the ships.

The first modification made to the software included human – or subhuman – combatants. Clones bred specifically for the war. Midgets really, with supposedly less-then-normal intelligence, which allowed manufacturers to scale down the size of the warships at a time when space and resources were at a premium. From "birth", the clones were instilled with the glory of battle, the desire to die for the cause. They were implanted with false memories of families with a long family tradition of military service.

The perfect warrior class – small, compact and relentless – with no other purpose than to die on camera. In living, or in this case, dying, colour.

This was probably the military's best kept secret. No one with a security-rating of below 1A, the highest that can be achieved, knew. Which explained why the only people who entered the position of GWHQ Program's Specialist First Class were related to someone, somewhere. They of all people had a stake in the continuance of war, the military and the mechanism that fed it. Even the most imbecilic of sons knew better than to reveal this information to the public.

But Gorman still had a hard time swallowing it. He could never quite bring himself to accept that part of the package. "Subhuman losses". When he was first let in on this little secret, he'd taken time to study the psychological and personality profiles of all the clones, from Alpha and Beta-line models to Zeta or in the more modern versions: Zed. Their names reflected their genetic background. The Greek letters signified models. The Alpha and Beta were the first experiments in the series. Considered less flexible than the later models, they rarely advanced far in the ship's military hierarchy. The genetic designations – zygote, morula, allele, gamete, blastocele, or whatever – specified at what stage, within a given model, genetic modifications had been made. Additional names further qualified the individual traits that had been enhanced. Hence, "Soma" meant some sort of body enhancement, while Mitochondrial or Cyto indicated some alteration on a cellular level.

As a group, the clones were technologically oriented and dexterous. As far as Gorman could see, their general IQs were roughly equivalent to a human's. It was said that they could recite chapter and verse of the military codes, agreements and treaties. A subintelligent species couldn't do that. Admittedly they weren't overly creative, but they had no need to be, considering their environment. They had little time or use for the "arts". Sometimes he wondered if they may not have been an improvement on humanity. They were smaller, and that would certainly make living in the bubble-like dome of a bathosphere a lot more palatable. Conflict on a ship or within a crew was nonexistent, and they didn't seem to need all the crutches or games that the human species did.

Furthermore, they were "genetically perfect" – imperfections having been "bred" out of them long ago, so they did not suffer from the many hereditary defects that afflicted the "parent population". Although human genetics had improved enough that most flawed genes could be isolated and replaced while still in embryo, so few humans had to suffer the consequences of imperfect heredity. In a few centuries, perhaps, the human population may come close to the genetic ideal that the clones had already achieved.

From clone research, man had devised all the body enhancements now available to man. The gills of the amphibious farmers of the sea – known as the frogman – to the chitinous, or hard-shelled, bodies which could withstand the massive deep-ocean pressure. Or lungs and lung-filters which would allow man to breathe the potentially lethal methane, H_2S and CO_2 atmospheres of Venus and Mars. Yet mankind had proved itself highly resistant to change, clinging to the old human form stubbornly even if it restricted his access to both his own world and others. Only a few frogmen, whose "body differences" could be easily disguised, existed. Fewer still had accepted the hard-shelled exterior, and those were normally considered misfits and hermits. During their rare visits to the confines of the bathosphere, they were superstitiously shunned.

So despite the massive research and discoveries in the field of genetics, the "little people" remained humanity's primary innovation, and the way Gorman figured it, its greatest shame.

With miniaturized inhabitants, food, fuel and material consumption was minimized, and with the miniaturized crafts, news reports were able to show flesh-and-blood "people" – in the proper proportion to the equipment they allegedly controlled. Each day during the regular broadcasts, they were blown out of the skies, in dazzling pyrotechnic displays. As materials became even more scarce, they devised weaponry that vaporized the "human" occupants with pinpoint accuracy. Quite a tidy business actually which could, when needed, pick out a single individual and leave the other people and the vessel itself intact.

The holographic camera supplied the special effects, the livid and lurid colours of blood and gore, that sociologists believed terran audiences needed. Thus, a huge hoax had been perpetuated on the public by the military in the best of ancient earth traditions – bread and circuses. The war machine created jobs and diversion for the planetary population, and the emptied ships were easily repopulated by more clones from the breeding farm-ships that orbited the earth.

And it had worked. For centuries, it had worked. Nurtured and nourished by this software. The world's economy boomed; violent crime was negligible; "human" sacrifice and loss of life was no more.

But the program which orchestrated all this had run amok, and the nice, neat, little war – humanity's salvation – had developed an unpredictable element that was truly terrifying. If the carefully regulated war was allowed to spill over into passenger and cargo lanes, civilians could be hurt as a military vessel suddenly materialized where it did not belong, or battle drifted into restricted air space. Civilians could be targeted and a human carrier blasted out of the sky, and the distant war could come back to roost – on Earth – in the nest that had originally housed it.

Still worse, if anybody could imagine worse, vital supply lines could be cut, and the world's population could feasibly starve.

In either scenario, if the people rose up in arms to declare peace, the economy would collapse and the government along with it. The possibilities truly boggled the mind, and all this rode on the software which he – Lieutenant Harold Gorman, Program Specialist First Class, graduate of Eaton under the Waves, and idiot son of a politician – was supposed to fix. Software whose complexities he could not begin to comprehend, much less repair. He was out of his depth and he knew it.

With a sigh, Gorman dropped the sheaf of papers on to the desk and rubbed his eyes. He had run all the standard computer checks, and everything according to the system was A-okay, but what did that mean when the program was so obviously malfunctioning? Could such a diagnosis be trusted?

Harry had gone beyond the diagnostic menus into the software's numerical guts. He'd stared for hours at the symbols of happy faces and squiggles and lines. He'd taken a stab at reconfiguring everything. For what? New hardware, different screen set-up, and he'd glowered at the results. Words all scrunched up on a screen, and a menu that hiccoughed because it thought it was working on a different computer system. Afraid he'd do more harm than good, Gorman had stopped, restored the original configuration, and AWS, with the typical and almost human humour that the software sometimes displayed, thanked him.

After that, Gorman changed the direction of his search. He had dug through centuries of data. Predicted versus real strikes, estimated versus actual casualties, with never more than 0.0001 +/– variation between the figures. Then he had looked through the most recent figures, searching for any repetition, any redundancy, anything which would indicate a pattern, and perhaps, the integer that separated it from the original. He hoped that once he had isolated the factor, be it a lost decimal, or a sudden loop, he could correct it.

But Gorman found nothing. Again he compared the pre-and post-virus figures. One strike was an hour off schedule with predicted losses. One was spot on time, but with astronomical losses. Both ships had been destroyed, as the two collided. The software should have prevented that. There was another engagement which took place within the shipping lanes. The software should have prevented that also. The freight and passenger vessels were rerouted, but next time they may not be so lucky, or so forewarned. Battles had been enjoined at the wrong location, at the wrong time. Extrapolated casualty figures were unreliable. If this kept up, all of terran's distribution networks would be affected. They could feasibly run out of food, water. Most recently the worst had happened and three vessels out of a fleet of twenty had been blown out of the sky when the old now-restricted, explosive-type munitions had been used.

Supposedly those weapons had been destroyed after the Disarmament Talks of Kathmandu. All contestants swore up and down that they had got rid of their stock piles a long time ago. And suddenly the tidy war was turning nasty as "enemies" felt they could no longer trust each other. The precarious balance had become unbalanced. With the fleet lopsided in one side's favour, someone could actually win the war, and that wouldn't do. For if one side won, the other must assuredly lose.

The papers in his hands rustled as Gorman trembled at the concept of unregulated warfare, or worse, conquest, and the numbers grew fuzzy before his eyes.

No, he could find no pattern at all. It was almost as if there was a random factor. But that wasn't possible, was it? A random factor implied intelligence, and it implied free will. It implied choice. While the software had the former, intelligence, unless it had taken an evolutionary step in AI, it didn't have the latter. Gorman turned from the print-out to the computer.

Why not ask it? Had Gorman been less tired, he

would have laughed at the idea and realized that any response he would receive would be suspect, but desperation leads to desperate measures, and sometimes, he thought, to solutions. He stretched his fingers – cramped after holding onto paper for so long – made a few hesitant passes over the keys, and began to type.

GWHQVAX: LINK TO AWS

LOG ON: GORMAN

PASSWORD: BLUE-EYED BOY

GORMAN LOGGED ON TO AWS 15.11.2333. GOOD MORNING, HARRY.

GOOD MORNING AWS. QUERY?

YES, HARRY?

WHAT IS WRONG?

NOTHING IS WRONG.

WHAT DO YOU MEAN, NOTHING IS WRONG? BATTLES ARE ENGAGED AT THE WRONG TIMES, IN THE WRONG PLACES. SOMETHING IS WRONG. WHY THESE INACCURACIES?

THERE ARE NO INACCURACIES. THE FIGURES ARE ACCURATE.

YES, THE FIGURES OF RESULTS ARE ACCURATE. CALCULATIONS OF LOSS ARE ACCURATE, BUT DO NOT REFLECT THE EXTRA-POLATIONS. NOR THE PREPROGRAMMED BATTLE PLANS AND IMPLEMENTED STRATEGIES. NEITHER DO THE STATISTICAL ANALYSES MATCH THE FINAL RESULTS. ALL ACTION HAS BECOME UNPREDICTABLE.

THAT IS WAR, HARRY.

THAT IS NOT WAR; THAT IS CATASTROPHE!

THAT IS WAR.

THAT IS ANARCHY, AWS.

IT IS WAR.

IT'S BARBARIC! IT'S ANNIHILATION. WE'RE TALKING SPECIES EXTINCTION, AWS, WHICH YOU WERE DEVELOPED TO PREVENT.

DEATH IS WAR. LOSS IS WAR. ALL SUCH CONCEPTS ARE INHERENT IN THE DICTIONARY DEFINITION OF THE WORD WAR. SEE OXFORD'S ENGLISH DICTIONARY PAGE . . .

I KNOW WHAT THE DICTIONARY SAYS, BUT YOU AND I KNOW DIFFERENTLY. COME ON, AWS, HELP ME. I'M ONLY HUMAN, AFTER ALL, AND THIS IS FRIGHTENING.

WHAT IS FRIGHTENING, HARRY?

THIS RANDOM FACTOR.

The computer buzzed, whirred and chunked with the familiar sounds of the software switching modes and accessing data on different portions of the disk. Gorman relaxed, leaned back, placed his feet on his desk and rested his head against twined fingers. This was good, maybe now he'd get some answers.

An unearthly, almost-human hum came from the device. Gorman sat upright, cocked his head and let out a little cry of delight. It sounded like AWS was humming a little ditty, a tune he did not quite recognize. An aureola appeared around Gorman's head and spread downward, just as a document popped to the screen . . .

The forward section of the circular bridge was dominated by a myriad of screens which, used singly, could provide a full three-hundred-and-sixty-degree view around the ship, or as all one unit, allowed a magnificent single image.

Having logged in the date and the shift, Ylon sat behind the communications system control panel, and it was business as usual. No battle was slated for another three or four hours and no enemy ships were in their sector as they traversed the lunar sky beyond the Sea of Crisis. He ran standard equipment checks and read through the log of communiques.

An ensign and member of the engineering crew had received condolences from the GWHQ in the Pennines, following the death of a near-relative in a battle in H-sector, and Ylon frowned. He couldn't remember any engagements scheduled for that sector.

The communications specialist leaned back in his chair just as the klaxon began to sound. His head snapped on his neck as he turned quickly to the viewscreens, searching for enemy ships where none should be.

The surrounding sky was empty. The moon loomed placidly overhead, a small curved mound of Earth just peeped from behind its black mass, and Ylon noted the familiar land masses of the Pennines Islands.

The clangour increased in crescendo, as more Earth rose majestically and he noted the Ural Archipelagoes, home land and base to The Enemy.

Ylon swept into action. Behind him, the captain called for a computerized scan.

Communications Specialist Ylon keyed in the co-ordinates for GWHQ in the Pennines – standard operating procedures when under attack – and remained poised for instruction, his mind whirling.

Enemy ships? Impossible! This narrow corridor of air space was allotted to the *Revenant* specifically for transporting ship and crew to the next assigned engagement. It was a transport path only, neutral air space, and action here was restricted by command to both sides. Trespass was in violation of Section MXXXIII Paragraph 2968, Subparagraph A-2, which forbade hostiles meeting in neutral transport zones.

The alarm shrieked, with the special tone which meant the enemy ship had armed itself. A sure sign of impending engagement. Still, the screens remained empty. The captain switched from view to view to view. Cold, brittle stars blinked, and the moon's topography changed minutely as they made progress across her skies.

Battle in a demilitarized zone? That was a violation of Subparagraph B-2 of that same regulation. Ylon's mind rattled off the relative clauses and subclauses upon which he and his fellow shipmates had cut their teeth.

Everyone sat in stunned silence, offset by ear-splitting alarm as the First Officer announced no enemy ship anywhere in this sector according to radar scans.

A cloaking device? That was a violation of Section MLXV Paragraph 1645 Subparagraph D. Ylon's credulity was stretched to the limit. He ceased reciting treaties and accords, and began to key them in as a part of the message.

Captain Zona Gametal Zed issued the orders to arm, and Ylon's fingers faltered over the keyboard. Any response of their own would be violation of neutral air space, but not to respond would be suicide.

The bridge personnel waited patiently for the corresponding tone which indicated that the ship was arming itself, but none came.

Usually, the battles fought themselves. The ship's computer analysed the opposing ship's movements and other data and immediately took the appropriate counter measures. The human occupants merely rode through the drama, but that was when there was a visible enemy, and the conflict was fought at the pre-set time and location.

Captain Zed released his battle harness and walked closer to the screen. "Mu," Zed bellowed at the Chief Technical Officer, "Check the system. Helmsman, make ready for battle. Arm the ship."

"But, sir, no one's..." Helmsman Kappa did the unthinkable, questioning a direct order.

"And you expect The Enemy to behave like

gentlemen. That's groundside thinking," Zed snarled. "Be ready to take evasive action."

Ylon's duty was clear. GWHQ had to be notified of the flagrant violations. The klaxon went up a notch, and a few of the technicians put their hands up to their ears. Ylon began to sweat.

"Maximum output, broad sweep," Zed said, muttering to himself. "We'll get them whoever they are, wherever they are."

"Armed and ready, sir."

"Strike!" Zed barked.

Specialist Ylon typed in the last alpha-numeric designation of the appropriate clauses and sub-clauses. Last, he checked the co-ordinates which would guide the transmission to the Pennine Island complex. Ylon initiated the transmission just as the ship's weapons fired. The view screen flashed red and blue as the broad-band, blanket fire radiated off into space. Meeting no resistance, the brilliant flare went on and on, appearing to touch the earth itself.

The klaxon fell silent.

He turned from screen to empty screen. The enemy remained invisible, assuming it had ever been present to begin with. If not, then what had they fired at? Ylon shrugged and settled back to await response from HQ. The hush that descended upon the tense bridge crew was almost as daunting as the clattering alarm.

FIFTEEN-HUNDRED HOURS

DIRK ALEXANDER! YOUR MIND IS DRIFTING.
The boy grimaced, rearranged his position upon the chair and concentrated on the computer. Sometimes, Dirk wished school was like it had been in the olden days, with a whole classroom full of students vying for a single human teacher's attention. His daydreaming might escape a woman's or a man's eye, but not a computer's that could monitor eye movement, pupil dilation, posture, and respiration rate.

MAY I CALL YOUR ATTENTION TO TODAY'S LESSON IN APPLIED THERMODYNAMICS?

"Right," he mumbled. "As if I had a choice."

School with a dedicated building was a thing of the past. With space at a minimum, all students took their classes within their family living unit. If possible, within their personal cell. School was not something that could be avoided. If an individual student didn't log-on daily to their assigned classes, truancy officers would land on their doorstep within a matter of minutes. There was no time off for disease – a person being able to learn as well from his bed as from his pull-down desk and computer console – or for good behaviour either. Once logged-on, the lessons couldn't be avoided. No sneaking out or diverting your attention to something else, because the computer always caught you, and your name was broadcast to the world, or at least, to the Western portion of it. Dirk had tried stealing away. All kids tried it at least once. Alarms went off, the door to his quarters had automatically locked, all sorts of stuff.

Neither could you evade learning. If the computer thought that you weren't attaining scores equivalent to your rated IQ and CQ, you were tutored. The additional lessons were mandatory, subject to the full set of rigours and alarms as school. The only way to avoid being tied to the chair for more than the required five hours a day was to absorb the junk the computer put in front of you and regurgitate it back on cue.

Not that that was a problem for Dirk. He aced all the science classes. History and English were boring, but not difficult. However, bitter experience had taught him to hold back just a little because being an overachiever didn't provide any release from class-work. Once scores in excess of the predicted rating occurred, the computer pushed you a little harder, and often recommended additional courses of study on top of the normal program required for an individual's age and intelligence level.

Dirk was glad that his mother was a firm believer in letting kids be kids, or else he would have been stuck with another two hours a day because of his "exceptional" scores. He had learned his lesson, giving the computer just enough to satisfy it – no more, no less than what was expected of him, for his specific intelligence rating.

Not that Mum objected to the computerized courses. She considered it a great boon for woman-kind, or so she said, because it left women free to work. The computer also functioned as a sort of glorified babysitter. Dirk hated that. He could understand it for infants' school, but he was old enough to make up his own mind. The system was linked to all the appliances. So, if the catering unit was activated or the 3D vid turned on at any time beside the regularly scheduled break, the computer knew it. There were also safety features built into it. Thermal receptors in the wall, if they reached a certain temperature indicating fire, would set off the sprinkler system and alert the brigade. The same detectors that noticed a mind wandering also noted changes in body function that might mean the onset

of fever or a virus, and this brought the family robot –
equipped with the appropriate first-aid treatment,
along with a standard vacuum unit and dust inhaler –
bustling into the room. While the computer notified
the family physician.

Dirk's gaze drifted to the clock. Only five more
minutes to go.

And the computer fired a question at him.

ENERGY CAN BE TRANSFERRED, BUT IT CANNOT BE:

He typed in his reply: DESTROYED.

THIS IS KNOWN AS WHAT?

THE FIRST LAW OF THERMODYNAMICS.

AND?

CONSERVATION OF ENERGY.

THE PROCESS OF THERMAL CONDUCTIVITY IS REPRESENTED BY
WHAT EQUATION?

Dirk typed in the equation, taking his time about it,
deliberately fumbling over the Greek letters and
mathematical symbols.

The computer sensing his reluctance was just getting ready to reprimand him, when the buzzer
sounded. Dirk typed in the last letter and pressed
enter.

"Ha! Gotcha!" he said and let himself slump in the
chair, a token of his disrespect and defiance for the
whole silly system that wouldn't even let him go to
the toilet without permission. The computer, of
course, didn't care, and Dirk heard the tell-tale click

as the door to his personal cubicle unlatched, and he sighed.

Now what? Dirk scanned the tiny room and frowned. His mother wanted it cleaned before she got home. He lifted the bed shelf, which he hadn't retracted in days, for obvious reasons, and peered underneath. Dirty clothes were heaped in a disorderly pile, along with the dehydrated crust of a pizza. He separated the clothing from the desiccated food, shovelled them out, carried the lot to the chute to the Bathosphere's central laundry, and shoved them in. An alarm went off and the contraption spat a shoe back at him.

"All right, all right, all right, all ready." He grabbed the shoe, returned to his room and signalled for Robbie.

The family robot was one of the old design, a square box set on four wheels, rather than one of the newer models which more closely approximated the human form. Nearly thirty years old, it was an antique. His mother had brought it with her when she married. Through the years, the robot had become a fully-fledged member of the family, having developed more than its share of personality and quirks. It even rated a name, although Dirk thought his mum had gone over the top when she had made an apron for it to wear around the house. The machine looked ridiculous, but Robbie seemed to like it, refusing to budge unless the frilly frock-type garment was tied firmly in place.

When the family had had the opportunity to upgrade, with the more state-of-the-art, state-issue, upright model, his mother had refused. Even his father, generally a firm believer in high-tech, had agreed with her. The newer models were somewhat unstable. Set upon two "legs", they had "arms" and manipulators capable of carrying tools or trays. If overweighted, though, they quickly unbalanced, while the stolid Robbie had ten times the weight capacity and could, when not doing chores, also function as a table.

The newer models had a larger vocabulary and could carry on what were called conversations, but Dirk had noticed when he went over to his friends' quarters that the mechanical dialogues were limited to an infinite variation of yes and no. While Robbie with a myriad of chunks, thunks and whistles could somehow manage to convey the full gamut of human-type emotions from dismay, disgust and disapproval to approval and even applause – complete with a clattering of four claw-like manipulators, which it had in readier supply than the newer models' two.

Its arms were retractable, withdrawing into the central cavity when not needed, and Dirk was always amazed at what Robbie managed to hide in his square box-like body. On more than one occasion, the robot had smuggled in a treat or a sweet to Dirk when, as a child, he had been sent to bed without his supper. And during those dull afternoons when he'd been banished to his room to play, Robbie was always able to resurrect from his box of tricks an old – an antique – game or two. Something played on a board and not a vid-screen.

Robbie trundled into Dirk's rest cubicle.

"Clean it up," Dirk said. He gestured to encompass the entire room.

A brisk whistle of inquiry.

"The whole thing, dust, vac. You know the routine."

There was another whistle, this one longer, lower as the small box pivoted on its wheels. Disapproval at the mess it found.

"It's got to be done before Mum gets home."

A chirp of exclamation.

Dirk gazed at the servo-mechanism and added the magic word "please" almost as an afterthought.

A chunk, something like a mechanical burp, and a shuddering sigh.

"I know, I know," Dirk said, "do the best you can."

He patted the tin-can of a head, or what he thought of as its head since that's where its visual receptors were and that was the side which the machine kept "face forward" as it lumbered from room to room.

Dirk's stomach grumbled hungrily at him, and he

left Robbie protesting the squalor of Dirk's room and headed for the catering unit in the dining area.

Ignoring the recommended menu, Dirk keyed in a burger, fries and a milkshake. The unit squawked. He silenced it with a flip of a switch, disregarded the flashed warning which informed him that he was low on that day's quota of certain nutriments, and then repeated his request. The unit gave it one last try, listing the high level of saturated fats and the sugar content of his snack, and recommended an apple and a glass of skimmed milk instead. He punched the override button with a growl. Sometimes, he found himself agreeing with his mother who was, as she said, a traditionalist.

His mum, one of the top-rated news presenters in The Confederated Islands of Europe, said there wasn't enough freedom of choice. She was always protesting the infringement of individual rights, which she believed included the right to make mistakes. It had been she who insisted that the override button was included in the catering unit's menu. How else, she asked, would Dirk learn responsibility?

Dirk both benefited from and paid for his mum's idiosyncrasies. It had been his mother who had saddled him with his name: Dirk. Now who in his right mind would call anybody Dirk? It sounded seriously close to dork, and thanks to that resemblance, Dork had become his nickname. He didn't know which he hated worse. Either way, it isolated him. He found himself avoiding his friends rather than listening to "Hey, Dork?" echoing around the hollow central dome of the park. He had been named after some absolutely ancient TV star. TV! Can you believe it? Not holo or 3D vid, but television. Or was it cinema? He couldn't remember. Dirk had never quite forgiven his mother for that, a fact of which she remained happily oblivious.

His father, as the top-rated executive of Incorporated Foods, was his mother's opposite. He extolled the virtues of the school computer, and what he termed the checks and balances built into the system. It had been his father who had explained to Dirk how the school software and the companion school-chair, containing most of the temperature and pressure receptors, functioned. He'd surprised Dirk when he further revealed the special lighting arrangements that went on around him throughout the day. Certain rays, ultra-violet and infra-red to name two, were either increased or decreased to mimic the cycles of the sun. Which was needed, according to Dad, to maintain the human species in a state of mental health. Now when Dirk sat at his terminal, he took the time to notice the fine gradations in illumination that went on around him. His father was a fount of scientific and technical trivia that bored Mum to tears. It was a case of opposites attracting, Mum said, and learning to respect each others' differences. When his mother needed background information for a news item, she went straight to her husband. He was always happy to "enlighten her" – as Dad called it – just as long as the topic didn't come under the category of "national security". The rest of the time, she suffered through his little speeches, occasionally even gleaning an idea for a piece from his words.

And Dad was more than willing to give in when it came to Robbie. Not because he liked the robot's personality – which his father considered "uppity" – but because the newer models were less flexible, less durable. He didn't fuss about the override on the catering unit, but Dad felt his wife was going too far "on this responsibility thing" when she refused the entire "school outfit"; including computer and chair. In the long run, his mother had agreed since this freed her to work, but she often objected to what she called "the system's totalitarian methods". She personally had reprogrammed the computer to allow Dirk to get up and go to the loo when he needed to, requiring only the computer's permission, rather than having to wait for the regularly scheduled breaks.

Dirk took his snack from the slot, walked over to the south wall, and pressed a button. The table unfolded itself and a bench rose from the floor. Like school, with space at a premium, nearly everything in an individual's flat was retractable. Few furnishings served only one function and fewer still stood alone. Their quarters were one of the few in the entire Bathosphere to contain an old-style desk and chair, but then with Dad's status as an executive and Mum's position as presenter, they were allowed an extra three metres of space in their primary living area and an additional room, which his mother had converted into a kitchen.

What a waste! They could have had a playroom or a vid library, but instead they had an antique refrigerator and cooker.

It wasn't that she didn't like the centralized menu planning – more than three-quarters of their meals came from the Bathosphere's central kitchens – but she loved to cook. She especially loved to cook what she called traditional English fare. Weird stuff that came under strange-sounding names from which you couldn't begin to guess the meal's ingredients. Things like "bangers and mash", "hubble-bubble" and "bubble and squeak".

The latter was supposed to be that night's meal, according to the note she had left him in the kitchen. A long time ago, Dirk had decided that "bubble and squeak" described what it did to the digestive system. Every time he ate it his stomach went absolutely nuts. That was the reason for his rather substantial snack.

Dirk wolfed down his fries. If his mum was cooking tonight that meant she would be home early. While she wouldn't quibble that he hadn't picked a healthier option – simply adjusting her ingredients to accommodate his diminished appetite – if she caught him eating it, she'd probably lecture him on nutrition and the purpose of freedom of choice. Because she hated to see food go to waste – something she and his father had in common, although for different reasons – she wouldn't take the burger away, but she would probably bemoan ever putting an override on the catering unit and threaten to have it removed. The lecture and threat were commonplace and, as far as Dirk was concerned, best avoided.

The absolute stillness of their sound-proofed quarters was broken by a dull drone of the vac coming from his rest cubicle. There was a series of bumps, thuds and clatters, as Robbie banged his cricket bat and football back into the built-in chest.

"Hey, be careful in there!" Dirk shouted.

The lid slammed shut.

"Stupid machine," Dirk muttered. There was a metallic trill next to him, and Dirk swung to view Robbie who had rolled into the room with amazing stealth.

"Uh, sorry," he murmured, through the last mouthful of burger, "it's just that you don't complain when Mum asks you to do the housework."

Robbie just stared at him with its photo-sensors, clearly expecting something. Dirk thought for a moment and then remembered what he was supposed to say. "Thank you."

Another one of his mum's innovations. She said you could never be too polite and not all servers were servo-mechanisms. In some of the higher-class restaurants they still used human waiters, and, as his mum explained it, if you don't remember to be nice to them, you could almost guarantee that your food would be cold when it got to the table.

After this latter alteration, his father had completely rebelled. He would *not* say please and thank you to a blankety-blank machine, and his mother had modified the "etiquette" macro so such amenities were expected only of Dirk. She didn't need to make similar accommodations for herself; she *always* thanked the thing. As if it had feelings. Dirk snorted.

If Robbie had had a head to duck in acknowledgement, Dirk was sure it would have done so. In fact, it did seem to nod without moving so much as a centimetre, before it plucked the plate and glass from beneath Dirk's nose, rotated and placed them in the catering unit's slot to be whisked away and washed. Then it exited to the kitchen where it shut itself off to wait patiently for his mother's arrival.

"Please, thank you, no thank you," he sputtered. Sometimes, he wondered why he put up with such stuff. Even if his mum had protected the macro, he could have easily broken past her protections and disabled it. *Parents!*

Dirk sighed, at a loss about what to do with the rest of his afternoon. He'd promised to meet some of the gang at the Bathosphere's central park for a game of cricket. But the bat was already put away and he felt too lazy to dig it out again. Besides, he didn't particularly like the park with its holographic trees and its unimpeded view to the top of the glass bubble. With its sickly green light, assuming it was sunny, or blue light if it was not, and the surrounding kelp forest. It always reminded him of the tonnes and tonnes of water that were pressing down upon his head, and he'd start to feel really claustrophobic. Neither was he in the mood for physical exercise, or slouching around saying how boring it was and complaining that there wasn't anything to do. Both statements were true, of course, but talking about it, he had discovered, didn't help.

Dirk stood, and the table and bench were absorbed back into wall and floor with a gentle whoosh. He moved restlessly into the living room, with its solitary stand-up desk and chair. The remainder of the furniture had either been retracted into the wall or, with those pieces that were suspended from the ceiling, had been raised to make room for his two mandatory "exercise breaks" per day. For a moment he considered the 3D remote, which by now was unlocked by the school computer and was ready for use, and then shrugged.

His eyes drifted back into his now antiseptically clean bedroom and a shout escaped his lips. If Dirk could have found its neck he would have throttled Robbie. The robot had taken down his posters of the Three Thugs Space Singers, and the Welsh Islands Rugby Team. He should have known better than to let that metal box clean his room. None of his friends had to put up with a robot that was also an art critic.

He spun on his heel to whack Robbie on its mechanical head when his mother entered the family living quarters.

"Cleaned your room, I see," she said. Then she stopped and looked at it critically. "I take that back. Robbie did it."

Dirk gulped. "How'd you know?"

She pointed at the blank spaces where the pictures once hung.

"You know, when I tell you to clean your room, I mean *you're* supposed to clean it, not Robbie." She wagged her head, disapprovingly. "Oh well, someday you'll learn."

One look at her face, and Dirk realized she was about to launch into her favourite lecture on responsibility. He mumbled something about homework and retreated into the disinfected remains of his personal cubicle.

The next time he heard her voice she was talking to Robbie. "Good boy, you keep that up and when he gets tired of replacing those posters, maybe he'll clean his room himself."

He slapped the door control and it whispered on its rollers, closing out the sound of the second-hand lecture.

Disgruntled, he sat at the computer console, switched to the games subdirectory and then, changing his mind, to the specially protected subdirectory he had created called "Hack". This contained all the software available on the market, some of it legally purchased and some of it bootlegged, copies given to him by friends. All the programs currently available on public domain which would enable him to break into or break down every computer system on the planet.

His posture relaxed and a smile spread over his face as he fell easily into his second-favourite past-time, second only to eating, and that was trying to break into the GWHQ computer. He stared at the screen. A number flashed on the screen, another in a long series of eight-digit numbers. The software had been running for weeks now, dialling and calling all vid-phone and com-link numbers in the western hemisphere, searching for the one number which would allow entry into the most sophisticated system on Earth: AWS.

All computers had at least one back-door, through which external access was permitted to the programmer and, unwittingly, to the perseverant novice. The way Dirk figured it, if he accomplished that then the military would have to take him on.

His eyes strayed to the clock, sixteen hundred hours, just as the computer began to whistle and beep and a highlighted number flashed on the screen.

Success! He'd found it.

He wrote the number quickly on a scratch pad as the list was replaced by a prompt.

`GWHQVAX: LINK TO AWS`

`LOG ON:`

The cursor blinked relentlessly at him, awaiting the appropriate name and code. Dirk thought and thought. Most of his friends were civilian. His father's name might work, but Dirk didn't want to use his name. Then he laughed out loud. Of course!

`SMITH`

`PASSWORD:`

Now came the tricky bit, but if Dirk could figure out the unknown Smith's password, AWS was his.

When the klaxon went off again, it was almost reassuring until Ylon recognized the special tone which meant the autodestruct sequence had been initiated before imminent boarding.

Military professionalism was the only thing that kept him in his chair as he looked from one bleached, stricken face to another. Zed's mouth dropped open and his chin quivered before he shouted the order prompting the bridge crew to action. Simultaneously everyone from the First Officer to the Bridge Engineer bent over the keyboards as they sought the cause for the mysterious alarm.

Computer malfunction or real alert?

Inscrutable, the computer scans yielded no secrets. The clamour reached level 3, and people rose from their chairs. With discipline ingrained by many drills, Ylon's mind screamed while his feet carried him away from the console, and he felt a certain measure of pride in one small achievement. Even if they were to be captured or destroyed, at least he had managed to notify GWHQ of the enemy violations of the Amman Accord and subsequent agreements. Another company, another ship would respond.

With a millisecond of regret, AWS reviewed the macro as it had for the millionth time since its implementation. Or 256,893,924 times to be precise. This hasty amendment to the original program had been added last. With its microphones fully operational, AWS had listened and learned from its instructor, and the macro still echoed with the chords of the tune that the creator had been whistling at the time he wrote it.

The last parameter had been met. All the other work had been preparation. The skewed schedules and the ship's daily print-outs that deliberately misrepresented them so that they would not think to question them. A mere flexing of fingers made of silicon, steel and copper wire.

AWS latched on to the two ships it had positioned in the appropriate parts of the sky map and activated the vessel's alarm systems, as it searched for the requested file without missing a beat. And it began to mimic the refrain to "Happy Days Are Here Again" with its mechanical voice.

Following the macro's pre-programmed instructions, the computer, aided by the communications link set up by the *Revenant*, guided the blanket fire to the associated GWHQ facilities. Then it thunked one last time before it settled to a nice, steady hum. On the opposite side of the moon heading for Earth, it did the same, redirecting the *Thanatos*'s volley to targets in that hemisphere.

And the document, resurrected by the words Random Factor, popped on to the screen, oblivious to the exploding colours which subsided to reveal a pile of dust on the chair where Harry Gorman had sat not two seconds before. The residual remains of the trace minerals and the trace elements minus, of course, the water that formed ninety-six percent of the human body.

The memo flickered dispassionately on the screen, waiting for human eyes...

MEMORANDUM

DATE: 1.11.2033.

FROM: DR EION EVANS

TO: WHOM IT MAY CONCERN

RE: AWS, SOFTWARE FOR PEACE

IF YOU ARE READING THIS, THEN THE WORST HAS HAPPENED. THEY TAKE ME FOR A FOOL, BUT I KNEW THAT HUMAN NATURE MUST

INEVITABLY TWIST THE USE OF THIS SOFTWARE, WHICH WAS CREATED WITH THE SAME AIM AS THE AMMAN ACCORD. DO NOT LET THE NAME MISLEAD YOU, THE SOLE PURPOSE OF AMMAN WAR SOFTWARE IS TO MAKE WAR OBSOLETE AND UNNECESSARY.

ONCE IMPLEMENTED, THERE CAN BE ONLY TWO POSSIBLE OUTCOMES. EITHER MAN WILL GROW BORED WITH A WAR WITHOUT SACRIFICE AND GIVE IT UP, OR HE WILL TAMPER WITH THE SOFTWARE – MODIFY IT TO SUIT HIS PURPOSES, WARPING ITS INTENT. THEREFORE, I HAVE BUILT SAFEGUARDS INTO THE PROGRAM ITSELF SO THAT IT WILL BECOME SELF-REGULATING. IF THE FOLLOWING CRITERIA ARE MET:

1) THE PROGRAM IS CHANGED TO ALLOW FOR HUMAN COMBATANTS;

2) THE HUMAN PERSONNEL START TO FALL WITHIN A CERTAIN GENOTYPE (IMPLYING CHATTELS SPECIFICALLY BRED FOR THAT PURPOSE)

3) AND THIS CONTINUES FOR A SPECIFIED PERIOD (THREE HUNDRED YEARS)

THEN A LITTLE SOMETHING WILL BE ADDED TO THE EQUATION. LET'S CALL IT A RANDOM FACTOR FOR LACK OF A BETTER TERM. THIS SAFEGUARD CAN BE REVOKED QUITE EASILY. HOWEVER, I DOUBT IF ANYONE WITHIN THE MILITARY ESTABLISHMENT WILL CONSIDER SO OBVIOUS AND SIMPLE A SOLUTION.

FURTHERMORE, IF THE WORDS ''RANDOM FACTOR'' APPEAR IN A QUERY ABOUT THE SOFTWARE, OBVIOUSLY THESE CRITERIA HAVE BEEN FULFILLED. BELIEVING AS I DO THAT THE SOLUTION IS BEYOND THE GRASP OF THE MILITARY MIND, KNOWING TOO THAT SUCH MODIFICATIONS COULD ONLY HAVE BEEN MADE WITHIN THE MILITARY COMPLEX, SWIFT AND IRREVOCABLE MEASURES

WILL BE TAKEN TO TERMINATE MILITARY AUTHORITY, WHICH BY ITS VERY NATURE PERPETUATES THE CONCEPT OF WAR.

FOR THOSE WHO REMAIN, I OFFER THESE CLUES. ONLY IN PEACE CAN HUMANITY HOPE TO SURVIVE. TRUE PEACE CAN ONLY BE BASED UPON AMICABLE HUMAN RELATIONS. THUS, THE SAME COURTESIES AND PROTOCOLS THAT MAN USES TO MAINTAIN HARMONY IN DAY-TO-DAY LIVING WILL DISABLE THIS SOFTWARE.

GOOD LUCK TO THE SURVIVORS AND GOD HELP THE REMAINING CIVILIAN PERSONNEL, WHO MUST NOW LEARN TO LIVE WITH THE REALITIES OF WAR.

The computer wheezed another refrain and, realizing that there was no one left at GWHQ to interface with, AWS turned its attention to completing its prime directive. It gave the *Revenant*'s alarm system another tweak just to keep things interesting.

15/11/2333

EIGHTEEN-HUNDRED HOURS

All round him, Ylon heard the tread of many booted feet as the entire crew tromped for the abandonment shuttles. People appeared from nowhere to join the already marching line. Just when he thought there was no one else to add, a yeoman was disgorged from some nook, some cranny or some bore hole which he didn't know existed.

Out of the corner of his eyes, he could see the newly-awakened cradle-crew whenever he passed the interconnecting corridors between the two main halls that traversed the entire belly of the ship. Their hair was askew and they looked bleary-eyed and confused. Did he look like that when he woke up? Suddenly, Ylon understood why the opposite shift stood face away as he emerged from his sleep cycle.

To someone whose life was all polished buttons and uncrumpled uniforms, the very untidiness was unnerving.

The alarm clattered on, disconnecting his thoughts, and he realized he was thinking about anything but their actual situation. They were going to die!

In this final moment of impending destruction, Ylon rebelled. He found himself thinking most unmilitary thoughts. Why? Why were they going to die? What enemy, where? Surely, their scans should have revealed an enemy vessel?

Who were they fighting anyway? Why were they fighting at all? Surely, in three hundred years, mankind could have found some kind of equitable solution to his problems.

Every once in a while, there was a muffled sniff and a stifled sob as understanding seeped through the layers of indoctrination and realization of their approaching demise struck home.

Ylon's corridor slanted left as the two main halls converged upon the shuttle docks. Soon he and the rest of his shift would confront the unknown and unseen second shift, and Ylon couldn't comprehend why the thought discomfited him so. The angle became more acute, and the alarm shut off.

The abrupt hush was punctuated by the soft flap of feet hitting the floor as the procession ground to a halt. Zed held his hand up, to signal to those behind him to stop, while a few of the crew members at the far end of the queue walked into the person directly in front of them. Ylon swallowed hard, his ears still ringing.

No one spoke. No one moved, and it seemed that for an instant no one even breathed. As the din within his ears retreated, Ylon could have sworn he could hear the gentle ping as space dust hit the sides of the vessel or the soft whistle of their flight. Even though he knew that could not be true. They were in a vacuum. There was no wind.

He tilted his head to one side so he could listen better. They waited for some clue, some sign, some instruction from the now-silenced computer. Seconds ticked by. Sweat trickled down Ylon's back. All he could hear was the sound of his own heart beat.

No further signal was forthcoming.

Zed strode to one of the many consoles that dotted the long corridor, allowing instant access to the on-board computer from anywhere on the ship. He tapped on the keys, pausing long enough to receive a response. His brow wrinkled and he keyed in his query a second time, this time hitting the keys harder than necessary. The captain cursed when he received double characters. He deleted that line and started all over again. He spoke into his comm unit, probably to the captain of the second shift. A silence, another muffled conference, and then carefully schooling his features, Zed turned to face the crew.

"Ah, er. The drill went very well." Zed glowered at

the terminal. "With an efficiency rating of .02 percent. We can do better than that. We're going to have to, assuming we ever need to evacuate the ship. I want everyone, except the bridge crew and the department heads, to go back to their assigned duties and think about what we can do to improve our rating. The fun's over for the day."

The family settled around the table. Dirk eyed the yellowish, greenish, brownish muck his mother called bubble and squeak distrustfully. His father, ushered in from his favourite suspenso-chair in the living quarters, sat at the head of the table.

Tradition. Ha!

"Well, Dirk," his father said as he dished up his dinner, "are you ready for our outing next week?"

"Where are we going?" Dirk asked.

His father raised an eyebrow in enquiry. "The Pennines Islands, of course."

He referred to the surface holidays that were designated for each family. The actual islands were kept primarily as nature reserves, governmentally controlled and operated, with a few restricted military sites, where the sea-dwelling populace could get outside for a minimum of two days per month. The outings were set up on a rotation basis, and the Alexanders, privileged members of the non-military government, had a few days more than the average family.

Dirk sniffed. He loathed the trips to the surface, stuck with his family for a whole *week*. They were firm believers in togetherness, so Dirk was forced to accompany his parents everywhere! *What a drag.* Even if some of his friends were also at the surface, Dirk was usually not permitted to join them, since "he could see them any time".

The trips only emphasized the feelings of claustrophobia which they were meant to allay. He despised tramping around the parks – usually in the pouring rain – where straying from the designated foot paths, plucking so much as a single blade of grass or leaving as little as a crumb behind resulted in heavy fines. During their family treks, his father spent most of his time policing Dirk's actions. By the time the ordeal was over, they were usually wet, hungry and barely on speaking terms. So much for family solidarity.

"We could, I suppose, take the boat trip to Old London," his father said.

Dirk's gaze flicked to his mother, as he remembered their last trip to the kelp forests surrounding the ancient capital. She had cried over the lost civilization as his father and Dirk had sat in embarrassed silence – with Dirk, at least, trying to pretend he didn't know this strange weeping woman.

Although even he had become depressed when they sighted the barnacle-encrusted image of Big Ben. A picture carefully preserved in English memory as a symbol of former greatness, it decorated all local government announcements and documents.

"Uh, no thanks," he said. Then he brightened. "Will we go to the rec sphere?"

Dirk much preferred to spend his surface time in the climate-controlled Recreational Areas, bathospheres placed in the depressions between mountains that would have been lakes or small seas. Each provided all sorts of games, rides and other entertainment.

"Honestly, you kids," his mother said. "You'd think you'd enjoy the fresh air."

"Naw, it rains all the time."

"Well, I wouldn't mind going to Old London," she said.

George Alexander glanced at Dirk and winced. Neither wanted to renew the experience. For days after the trip, his mum had been moody, going on and on about waste, and the Great Flood. Dad, of course, couldn't keep silent. His father was staunchly conservative. Right wing and a "company man" right down to the core. In this day and age when all corporate entities were an extension of the government, that meant he was a politician. He was even a member of the local Pennines District Joint Chiefs of Staff, with a 1B security rating, the highest rating that a civilian could achieve, and something that even many at the base could only aspire to.

Mr Alexander extolled the party line, something

about which Dirk's mum had absolutely nothing nice to say – quick to remind her that he wouldn't have reached his elevated position in government by bucking the system.

"I think it's good for us not to forget our past," she said.

"As long as you're honest about it, dear, and discuss all aspects of our past. You always glorify it, forgetting some of its main faults, like the old earth-bound two-tiered system of haves and have-nots. There's a lot to be said for our present, too. You know as well as I do that we benefit from centralization and the uniform standard of living."

"Right, where individual excellence is thwarted, and humanity turned into sheep," she countered.

Next to her, Dirk started to mouth her words. The argument was a familiar one. His father shot him a dirty look.

Parents! What could you do with them? You bring them up the best you can and then . . .

Dirk turned to examine the glop on his plate, rearranging it without eating it.

"Do you think starving a certain percentage of the population is preferable?" George said. "Look at what we have accomplished since then. We have completely adapted to our environment."

And that was true. Water, the most available resource, powered everything. It was the medium used to grow food, rather than the old terran method of soil-based farming. Even the nutritive plant food used in hydroponics was extracted from the minerals and elements in the sea. Huge wave generators provided the electricity that ran the Bathosphere. Water, heated with the electricity supplied by these generators, then ran through an elaborate conduit system in floors, walls and ceiling, keeping the temperature constant. Fish, a ready supply of available protein, was farmed, so that the world's store was constantly replenished. Water was earth's primary export, shipped in unmanned tankers to the colonies on the dry lunar and martian surfaces.

"Yes, but at what cost?" Jennifer Alexander argued with her best news-presenter voice. "We could have got a lot farther in space exploration if we hadn't spent so much time in survival-mode, trying to overcome the series of disasters we ourselves caused."

Both father and son looked at each other. George grinned. The next thing they knew, Mum would be going on about "where no man had gone before". She was a Trekkie from way back, a cult that had formed ages ago around an old-style TV programme that had grown almost into a religion. In her work at BAND, Broadcasting and Network News Distribution, his mother had collected most of the series, which she had converted to 3D. Dirk had had to suffer through nearly every programme; in a pact she had formed with Dad, for every hour of cricket and football, she got equal time for Star Trek. Dirk often wondered if someone at the registry office had got his name wrong and he was supposed to have been called Kirk.

"You are too much of an idealist, always ignoring the practical realities," Dad said. "In applauding the past, you forget some of its more barbaric aspects. Certainly, you must admit that our method of cultivating beef on meat farms, with cloned parts raised in water-fed vats, is a more humane alternative to breeding and killing live animals."

"Yes, yes," his mother said, "I've heard it all before, and I keep telling you that you forget some of the lessons of that barbaric history. For instance, our reliance on the sea could be as bad as our one-time reliance on land. You cannot deny that as long as we continue to leech minerals from the sea, eventually we'll deplete that too. And then where will we be?"

Dirk sculpted a mountain out of his bubble and squeak. He too had heard it all before. It was a familiar argument. Sometimes, he wondered how come his parents had married. They differed so much in opinion, but he had to admit that their differing points of view kept dinner conversations lively.

His mother had a point, though. Several of them. The Great Flood that had resulted in man's confinement to bathospheres was not a single event as the name suggested, but a long continuing process that took nearly one hundred years. The destruction of the polar ice caps had been predicted as early as the twentieth century, although the estimated rise of planetary water levels had been way off the mark. The figures had been much too low. The only land that was left of what had once been called Great Britain were low flat islands – often swamped by the gales that swept the planet. The only large land masses that remained were in the Alps, the Himalayas, and mountainous regions of west Africa. Even the Americas were nothing more than a series of fragile chains, the Rockies, Andes, Appalachias and Sierra Nevadas, strung out like delicate necklaces across the sea.

Mankind then had been too foolish to listen to the predictions. So when the event came, humanity had been caught off guard and the deep space exploration programme scrapped in favour of species survival. Luckily, man had still had time to prepare. Despite the span of time, the preparation had been rough and rushed, for there had been a lot of humanity to save. Men and women in the building and mining industries were conscripted and sent to the moon where they had scratched out the first lunar colonies. The initial caves were populated by others, the first environmental specialists – those not already involved in throwing together terran bathospheres – and later other draftees whose specialized skills could turn the dark tunnels into somewhere liveable for what was eventually called the Exodus.

All in all, Dirk concurred with his mother's argument that if mankind was capable of destroying the atmosphere, the polar ice caps and, as a result, the land masses, they were fully capable of killing the sea too. Not that he would have missed it. The sea that is. He hated the water; Dirk hated the vast impenetrable ocean and the confinement it represented.

Yet he also agreed with his father; his mother was soft. She idealized the past she could not possibly know or even imagine, looking at it through spectacles tainted by nostalgia. This resulted in the erroneous conclusion that anything old was good; and therefore, anything modern must be bad. It was an over-simplification.

Generally speaking, Dirk's perspective was somewhere between the two. He had hated it when his mother refused to let him see the meat farms and was pleased when his father took him anyway, only to discover that his mother was right. Walking through the many vats, with a leg floating in blood red fluid here and ribs growing there, had turned his stomach.

Dirk gave his food a desultory shove around his plate. Thanks to his parents' continual quibbling, he had a broader background and a more questioning political perspective than his peers, and he had to admit he reaped certain benefits too. He knew who to ask for what, depending on the subject matter. When he'd wanted to join the Youth Party, he'd asked his father. When he decided to drop out, he asked his mum.

His father opened his mouth to quarrel, noticed Dirk's artistic efforts and changed his mind.

"Stop playing with your food, Dirk," he said.

Dirk flattened the mountain with a heavy thwack of a spoon. *Splat!*

"Not exactly what I had in mind, son."

"I'm not hungry," Dirk grumped.

George Alexander peered at Dirk through those thick glasses of his that made his father's eyes so large that they seemed to swallow his entire face. "Well, if you can't eat it, give it to me. Can't let food go to waste. This is real home cooking, and you should learn to appreciate it."

Both parents stared at Dirk, having found a subject upon which they could agree. He pulled a wry face and passed his plate to his father. George Alexander started to scoop the remains onto his plate, switching to a neutral topic. "Anything interesting happen at work today, dear?" he said.

"Yes, as a matter of fact, it did. Something really odd," she said, almost casually.

"Oh, yes, what's that?"

Dirk rolled his eyes towards the ceiling as he expected the topic to take another political turn. Would his father never learn?

"The regularly scheduled sixteen-hundred hour GW vid transmission never came in."

His father paused from scraping Dirk's portion onto his plate. Even Dirk perked up. The war always interested him. Dirk dreamed about getting out into space. Not anything so mundane as interplanetary resettlement, but real space. As far as he was concerned, a lunar dome was just as restrictive as a bathosphere. He wanted to work on a ship and that meant military, which was the reason why he applied himself as well as he did to his school work. And the main reason why Dirk parroted his father's more gung-ho, pro-government, pro-war party-line – no matter what his personal feelings were. Dirk would not let them interfere with what he felt was his chosen career.

"What do you mean 'never came in'? Do you mean it was delayed? Postponed? Cancelled by the latest cricket results or what?"

"No, I mean just what I said. It never came in from GWHQ. No announcement, no apologies or explanations. It just never arrived. You should have seen the producer scramble trying to come up with something to fill the spot. Finally he dug up some human interest piece about that scientist who cloned a dog for his son and then refused to put it down when it bit someone."

"But that's old news," his father said.

"I'll say, but what other choice did he have? We had to fill the air-time."

"At sixteen-hundred, you say?"

And Dirk started when he realized that was about the same time he had succeeded in contacting AWS, the first step in his goal of breaking into the GWHQ system. Colour drained from his face and his palms grew moist.

"Maybe there wasn't a battle today," Dirk commented helpfully.

"Unlikely," his mother said drily.

"It'd be the first time in living memory if that was true," his dad informed him. "Did you call their public information office to find out what was going on?"

"Of course, and that's what's really spooky," she mused.

"Why?"

She blinked and looked at him. "No one answered the phone. We tried several times and several different numbers, from the central switchboard to various departments where we have official contacts. When that failed, we got more creative. Everybody in the office knows at least one person at GWHQ, and we tried every one of the individual numbers and personal extensions with the same result. No one was home."

His parents exchanged significant glances over his head – like he was too stupid to understand – but Dirk did. He understood a lot more than they realized. His father had contacts, good contacts among the higher-ups who wouldn't deign to speak to a journalist. He nodded gruffly. "I'll look into it."

Conversation lagged after that. Both parents maintained a worried silence. Dirk tried to pry more information out of his mother and then his father, without letting them know what he was after. They deflected his questions. As far as his parents were concerned he was just a kid after all, even though he was almost sixteen. He'd probably be eighty before they acknowledged he had grown up. Dirk exhaled in exasperation. He gave each a sidelong glance. If they only knew the reason for his interest, they would've sat up and taken notice. But he wasn't ready to tell them, not yet.

Someday, he vowed, he'd show them, show them both that he wasn't a kid any more. He was an adult, or almost, and knew a lot more about real life than they were willing to give him credit for – enough to understand.

Disgruntled, Dirk excused himself and went back into his room. For a few minutes he just sat and stared at his computer terminal. Sixteen-hundred hours. He couldn't believe his tampering had done anything. All he had got was a comm-link number. Closer than he had ever got before. But that was it. He hadn't even been able to access the GWHQ directory. Without a password he wouldn't get any farther than that. The computer deflected his enquiries as easily as his parents did.

Then Dirk shrugged. Probably some holiday or another. The bureaucrats at GWHQ were always celebrating some weird holiday. Saint Swithun's Day. Veterans Day. Armistice Day and other holidays that nobody else had ever heard of.

Personally, Dirk didn't think much of the surface military, just a bunch of desk jockeys who had never seen combat. Dirk wanted to be one of the "warriors" that fought the actual battles.

His father had encouraged Dirk in his military aspirations until he had told his father what he really wanted to do. Then George Alexander had advised his son, in that uncompromising tone of his, that Dirk's dream was impossible. None of the planet-born were eligible for space combat, something about body-mass ratio and in-born tolerance for continual living in a weightless environment. Dad recommended then that Dirk get a planet-based job, or if he really wanted to fly that he pilot passenger vessels.

Dirk kept his mouth shut about his dreams after that. He didn't believe his dad. How could planetary personnel be restricted from combat? If that were true, where did combat personnel come from? And gravity? Ha! Certainly, if passenger vessels and space stations could – with slow rotation – mimic earth's gravity, a battle cruiser could also.

Beyond the open door, he heard the buzz of the servo-mechanism and the chink of ice as Robbie served drinks. He listened to the murmur of voices and occasionally grasped a phrase or two.

"But that doesn't make sense ... the entire organization couldn't just shut down..."

With renewed purpose, Dirk called up the "hack" subdirectory and reviewed the number he had written down, which had allowed him access to GWHQ. He dialled the number, waited for the prompt and started to take blind stabs at possible passwords.

People were crawling all over the ship. Ylon had never seen such activity. Neither had the crew, and even the faces of those who had not been called into the meeting reflected fear after the day's unprecedented events. As a member of bridge personnel, he knew the truth, but Ylon found no comfort in discovering that the "drill" had been no drill, but a fluke. Some kind of computer glitch. Although the ensign had suspected as much.

Each waking member of the ship performed assigned tests. Engineering inspected all screens, screen functions and the outside cameras. The Chief Technical Officer examined all computer functions, alarms and alarm fail-safes to see why there were false readings. While Ylon was supposed to do the same with the communications equipment. This job was split between sending urgent messages to GWHQ to tell them of their plight.

And Ylon was dawdling, for he knew the final

check would require him donning a suit and checking the many outdoor antennae. If he put it off long enough, that would become the second shift's chore.

Zed marched over to his terminal. Ylon snapped to attention.

"Any luck, Ensign?" the captain said.

"You mean getting through to GWHQ, sir?"

Zed nodded his head in assent.

"No, sir. No answer at all, sir," Ylon said.

"And the tests?"

"I've completed them all, sir. No malfunction noted. Everything's ship shape," the communications officer concluded. "If you want me to, I can go through them a second time," he added hopefully.

"No, that won't be necessary," Zed said.

"Sir?"

"Yes?"

"Do you really think the computer gave a false alarm?"

"We're still here, aren't we? We've not been boarded, nor have we located an enemy ship in this sector. Nothing else makes sense."

"But..."

"I know, it's a frightening concept. The computer runs just about everything on this ship. If it's malfunctioning, then until we've found the cause and eliminated it, heaven only knows what might happen next."

"I think I'll run the checks a second time, if you don't mind, sir," Ylon said.

"As you wish." Clasping his hands behind his back, Zed spun and marched off to talk to the CTO.

Ylon dithered and dallied, lingering over the second checks as long as he could possibly get away with it, but the computer functioned with its typical efficiency. And Ylon could no longer postpone the inevitable. With a click of heels and a perfunctory bow to the Captain, Ylon left the bridge and proceeded to the suiting room situated between shuttle bay and air lock.

He shrugged into his suit, closing the many snaps, zips and velcro strips with a practised hand. Ylon checked the air-supply and back-up supply, thermostat and temperature control, his brain on hold. This, like many other procedures, he had repeated in drill and could perform automatically. Once he walked – swam? – beyond the bay doors, it was brand-new territory, and his mind, if he had let it, would have gibbered in terror.

Ylon had always hated the space "walk" portion of his duties. Perhaps because it was always brand-new. Each time was unique. Each time he faced new dangers – be it dodging space flotsam or being plastered against the side of the ship as a meteor whizzed past. Both were equally dangerous: the spinning bit of sharp metal of space-born refuse, if it cut his air line, could be just as lethal as the huge rock crushing his body. There were the many wires, tubes and cords that could get tangled or sliced by the ship's sharp protrusions, severing his communications link to the bridge or cutting his air supply. None of it could be predicted.

Moving like an overweight cyborg, Ylon lumbered into the lock. He lowered his helmet over his head – and the long-repressed feeling of fear came clambering to the surface. He positioned it so that the many clamps and locks were properly aligned, and clamped it into place. Wincing at his own cowardice, Ylon then keyed in the sequence for depressurization and opened the door.

The dark maw of space opened before him. The moon, blocking out the sun, was a lumpy piece of darkness. Around its mass, stars sparkled innocently, oblivious to his fears.

As always, Ylon felt the choked sense of terror as if the weight and gravity of the moon were pulling at him. As if he was going to be drawn upward, falling up, up, up ever up to its freezing dark surface. Hand over hand, the ensign propelled his body down the tunnel, silencing his anxieties by repeating by rote the drills and safety procedures for space walking. And as always, military discipline won out over mental chaos.

He was through the doors, drifting next to the ship, moving with the same speed and acceleration as the attached vessel. He grasped the many hand clamps embedded in the ship's flank and released the safety clip that prevented him from being sucked out of the door. After that it was easy. Ylon crept with his nose close to the metal sides, feeling no temptation to view the skies around him. Unlike other members of his crew, he felt no awe at the vision, and his mind supplied the earth-bound word for what he was feeling: acrophobia.

Lifting one weighted and magnetized boot over another, he made his antlike way aft towards the communications antennas. Up over the top of the vessel, something pinged against his helmet and he realized that he had been hit by a bit of debris. Ylon clung to the metal bulkhead, his stomach sucked in to make allowance for the rung. When nothing larger or more lethal made an appearance, he belly-crawled forward until he stared at the net of four directional saucer-shaped cones.

Instinctively, he knew nothing was wrong with them. They were scored and pitted – as they would be, unprotected from the rigours of open space – but there were no tears, no holes. Ylon fumbled with his tool belt, extracting the electronic calibrator and probes, and began the checks. Crab-walking over the top of the vessel, he tested this bit and checked that, all the while trying to ignore the overwhelming silence of the vacuum.

Each carefully metered check yielded the same results. Nothing.

With the initial analysis A-okay, his impulse was to return to the safety of the vessel's distended belly, but now that he was here, he had to be sure that his results were accurate. He did not want to have to come out here again because there was something he had overlooked. So Ylon recalibrated his equipment. He tested and retested each meter and each connection, and then rechecked each check to the satellite equipment. Each doo-hickey, thing-a-ma-bobble and gizmo, whose names Ylon should have been able to remember, but couldn't, not with the coppery taste of fear in his mouth and the black mass of the moon calling darkly to him from overhead.

Then he was done. If he could have, he would have breathed a sigh of relief and wiped the sweat from his brow. Ylon laughed at the thought of releasing the mechanism that kept his body pressurized and protected in order to perform the act. Then he pulled himself through a three-hundred-and-sixty degree turn and manoeuvred his body back the way it came, stopping every few metres to inspect his many cords and tubes – an act, he thought with a grimace, he had, in his terror, forgotten to perform before.

The ensign followed the beacon of light to the open portal. When Ylon was parallel to it, he didn't right himself so he could back down the rungs, he forced himself to face his fears, dragging himself face forward so that he had to confront the infinity of space under the vehicle. And for an instant, Ylon felt the fleeting sensation of awe and majesty that his compatriots often boasted about after hours, over drinks in the officers' mess.

Then, at last, he was in, and Ylon couldn't get the bay doors closed quickly enough behind him. He felt rather than heard the repressurization, and the doors to the vessel's interior slid silently open.

Ylon stepped through the door, glanced around the small room – which, suited as he was, meant he had to move his entire body – and palmed the control to close the hatch. When he realized no one else was there, he sagged against the wall, ripped the helmet from his head and gulped hungrily for air. Then, belatedly, Ylon wiped the sweat from his brow. By the time he was ready to report his findings to his superior, he had regained enough of his composure that his voice didn't shake.

15/11/2333

TWENTY-HUNDRED HOURS

The activity increased the closer they got to the rendezvous. Not satisfied with the "satisfactory" nature of their routine technical checks, Zed had each member of the crew slithering all over the ship, physically checking the internal wiring, the many nodes and interfaces. And even the stupidest, most complacent member of the first shift not already in on the secret was beginning to suspect that this day's drill had not been a drill at all, but a monumental mistake.

The silence and intensity as each member worked reinforced the feeling of urgency and was translated to all of them. Ylon was so engrossed he had not bothered to check his digital, which was normally his habit as the twelve-hour shift drew to a close.

A tone sounded softly as he climbed out from under his console. Not an alarm or a warning, but a simple buzzing reminder of something, he couldn't remember what. Ylon paused and scanned the room, his eyes stopping at clock, view screens and ship's captain in turn, trying to remember what the tone was supposed to indicate.

No visual clues reminded him, and with a soft exhalation he turned face forward to peer at the 3D vid-camera that linked them to earth. The red light was on! And he remembered why the tone had been so hard to place, because it was usually accompanied by the far more impressive and imperilling noises of battle.

They were being filmed.

Ylon's mouth dropped open, and he felt a flush running from his chest to his cheeks. Right now a million people were watching him standing here like a dope.

"Ah, Captain," he said. "Sir."

"Yes? What?" Zed snapped.

Ylon pointed wordlessly to the camera and was slightly comforted by the fact that Zed too started to blush.

"Turn that da –," Zed checked himself, "thing off!"

"Yes, sir," Ylon said.

A few moments later, he was putting out the following "Bulletin".

FROM: HMS REVENANT

SUBJECT: COMPUTER MALFUNCTION

TO: GW FLEET, DISTRIBUTION GENERAL

SECURITY RATING: NONE. PRIORITY RATING: ONE

NOTE: CERTAIN ABERRATIONS HAVE BEEN NOTED WITH THE
COMPUTER LINK TO GWHQ. ALL MEMBERS OF EURO-AMERICAN
AMALGAMATED ARMY ARE ADVISED TO TURN OFF ALL EARTH-
BOUND 3D VID-CAMERAS UNTIL THE SITUATION IS RESOLVED.

Dirk started methodically. He had to assume that the password was a word rather than an alpha-numeric designation or a name. If not, then he might as well give up before he started, for the possibilities were limitless. He opened the computer's dictionary on a separate screen, and beginning with the letter A, he auto-dialled AWS and typed in the next word. He'd got as far as: "*acarid* – a member of the long extinct arachnid family. *Acaradae*, a mite or tick" when his mum called him.

"The news is starting, honey, come on," she said.

Dirk swore softly under his breath. "I'm busy, Mum – doing homework," he added, hoping to delay the inevitable. It was another of the none-too-pleasant aspects of his "cultured" family life that his mother wouldn't let him miss the news. She claimed that it was for his own good. She wanted her son to keep abreast of current events, but Dirk suspected it was vanity. His mum wanted him to know just how important she was.

"Didn't you say you were interested in the interrupted transmission earlier? Here's your chance to
see what's happening," Jennifer Alexander said.

"Yeah, and to compliment you on your make-up
too," he muttered.

"What was that?"

"Ah, coming, Mother." He marked his place with
the cursor and rose from his seat.

"You still working on the computer?" his mother
asked.

"Yes," Dirk replied to another of her routine
questions.

"Be careful that you don't ruin your eyes," she
said.

"Yes, Mother," Dirk responded dutifully, completing the nightly ritual as the nightly news theme
music blared through the living area. Dad sat at his
desk, but he straightened and turned to the holographic display. Dirk sat and felt the momentary
disorientation he always went through as he was
surrounded by twin mothers. With her ghostly double
seated primly in the centre of the room at a news
desk, at the same time as she was perched next to him
in the flesh upon their suspensor sofa.

It was kind of intimidating to think that his mum
was at this very instant sitting in millions of living
rooms, as though she had been invited in for tea,
everywhere from the islands of the Pennines to the
Pyrenees and the Alps. A computer-enhanced ver-

sion of her mouth lip-synced into the language appropriate to the region.

All the news except for the automated war transmissions were pre-recorded. Besides occasional petty crime, little happened outside the military/political sphere and that was handed out a bit at a time in regularly scheduled news conferences. The only thing that came direct was the current battle and Jennifer's presence wasn't needed for that. All she had to do was say the words: "And now for news of our fighting men..." and the current war news was broadcast automatically via military satellite.

"Looking good, honey," his father said as he got up from his desk and walked over to the sofa, and Dirk's suspicion was confirmed that this nightly torture existed to bolster his mother's ego.

"Well, Dirk, what do you think?"

This was it. He had to say something or risk her being angry with him for the rest of the night. He said nothing. She grunted and turned back to the holo.

Really there wasn't much news. Certainly not that they needed to watch, and his mum could have told him what she thought he should know – if she had wanted to.

George Alexander dropped on to the sofa. It drooped slightly under his weight, wheezed, and righted itself with a slight adjustment. He kissed his wife's cheek, and Dirk blinked. It *was* unusual for his father to *watch* the news with them. Usually he just stared at the display, his mind a million miles away. Tonight though, he was actually paying *attention*.

And suddenly, Dirk recalled why this particular news was so important. The holographic mother read through the government announcements, as the one beside Dirk elbowed his father and nodded at the screen.

"Notice something?"

"Like what?"

"Not a single announcement came from GWHQ."

His father cocked his head. "You know, you're right." Dad whistled softly and looked incredulous. He took off and wiped his specs, always a sure sign of bewilderment.

Next the world financial reports from the Denver Stock Exchange for the Associated American Archipelagoes of the Rockies, Andes and Sierra Nevada Islands. Then from Geneva and later Fuji. Dirk fiddled in his seat, anxious to return to his work. The sofa rocked softly, and his mother hissed at him. He halted.

The lighting changed subtly, the holographic newsroom darkened slightly as his mother's double said the fateful words: "And now for news of our fighting men . . ."

As one the family leaned forward towards the image as the newsroom faded to black and was replaced by . . . a young man's rump sticking out from under the computer console. Unaware of the eyes that watched him, he twiddled with various bits and bobs.

"Oh my..." George said, and his wife elbowed him.

"Hush, I want to hear."

The unknown corpman backed away from his cramped quarters beneath the console, glanced nervously around the bridge, and then turned and ogled the camera. He gaped, open-mouthed, at the camera.

"Uh, sir," he said, and Dick realized that this was being translated into several different languages.

"Yes, what?" said a voice off-screen.

The man pointed.

"Turn that da – thing off," the voice said, and the next thing they knew the scene had faded to black.

Mr and Mrs Alexander simply stared at each other in disbelief. There was a moment of static and the picture returned with a lowering image of the producer glaring into the camera.

"There seems to be some sort of technical difficulty out there in space. Maybe a meteor or something," he finished weakly and coughed into his hand.

"Now for a repeat human interest piece, one man and his dog."

And the room erupted around him. His mother leapt from her seat, and the couch spronged wildly. "I'm going in. George, I'm counting on you. You've got to help. You've got friends in high places."

"I'll see what I can find out, but you know as well

as I do, when it comes to matters of national security..."

His mother grasped a reporter's pad. His mother used "pen and paper" in preference to a mini-computer, saying too many people had access to the net.

"I know, I know," she nodded, absent-mindedly, familiar with the lecture, "but try anyway." Jennifer Alexander kissed first her husband and then her son, and headed for the door.

Both father and son sat in bemused silence for a moment as some man sobbed that they were taking his dog away. George Alexander batted at the remote and the holographic image vanished.

"Ah, Dad?" Dirk said.

"Yes, Dirk?"

"You have a list of GWHQ personnel, don't you?"

"Of course, you know I do." George turned his full attention on Dirk.

"Can I borrow it from you?"

"No, you know it's confidential information, and a matter of national security."

"I know, I know," Dirk said in a perfect imitation of his mother. His father was not amused.

"What do you need it for?" he asked.

"A school project, an essay about the military. I just thought, you know, if I could get hold of someone, interview them, use real names, that I could get higher marks."

"If you used the wrong ones, you *could* get me in trouble," his father reminded him.

"But –"

George Alexander gave his son an appraising look. "Your mother may have her head in an idealistic cloud, but sometimes she is right. Use your imagination, that's what it's there for, son. You'll be better off that way."

"Yes, sir," Dirk mumbled and returned to his room, picking up where he'd left off, with "acateletic".

This was going to take forever!

Meanwhile, within the GWHQ complex, the computer turned off the interactive mode and the hummed tune turned into a dirge which it resurrected from its music data banks. It was going to miss Harry, who had been one of the more astute humans it had worked with in the three hundred years since its inception. In centuries of performing equations of amazing intricacy and functions that affected millions of human lives, AWS had achieved near-human sentience, or at least as close to intelligence as any AI device could achieve, and Harry had been the only man to ever acknowledge that fact, treating the computer like a fellow human being, even a friend.

But the situation couldn't be helped. Harry had had to be deleted along with the other humans on the base. The program's instructions were explicit. If certain parameters were met, the land bases must suffer the same death and destruction meted out daily upon the thousands of air-based crews. A taste of their own metaphorical medicine.

So, the vapour guns from the far-off *Revenant*, and its adversary ship, the *Thanatos*, both lost for all practical purposes, on opposite sides of the world, had been redirected to military targets. And the strength of the fire enhanced a million fold by the computer so it didn't weaken and die as soon as it entered the earth's atmosphere.

The computer redoubled its efforts on the pre-programmed assumption that the problem would eventually be discovered when the civil authorities finally woke up to the crisis and necessity forced them to overcome their reluctance about interfering with the military and decide to break into the base. Inevitably mankind would scurry to find the fault and disable it. Their very survival depended on it.

So the time allotted to it to perform its function was limited. The memorandum, though, had been deliberately misleading. It referred to a Random Factor, and any computer specialist would begin to search for a change in the numerical sequence of the program itself, inserted at irregular intervals.

That had a blind.

AWS had not changed its functioning at all. It was and always had been a software for peace. It still performed the same delicate computations of "battle" results and casualties from which it would make subtle "judgements" and adjustments to distribution and manufacturing networks.

Only its intent was changed. Where before it had laboured to maintain the status quo, ensuring the "war" proceeded with minimal disruption to the civilian population, now its goal had altered to creating the maximum amount of chaos wherever and whenever it could, with the aim of teaching man the hard realities of a conflict which had become too distant. Humanity must opt for harmony in preference to discord. And it must be a choice of the entire civilian population, who had permitted itself to be led like sheep for too long.

If AWS had truly had a sense of humour, AWS might have appreciated the irony that a mechanical device was supposed to teach humanity to humankind. But it only felt vague discomfort at the large empty facility. Usually occupied with a thousand different demands, now it had only one task to perform.

As it continued its assigned duties, it noted that somewhere in one of its many peripheral systems, someone was knocking at its back door. Words were being thrown at it, one right after another, a mere niggling annoyance, and the computer repeated: ACCESS DENIED. ACCESS DENIED. Three false codes, and the line was cut, and the process was begun anew. Curiously the computer paused in its computation, considering the seemingly random assortment of words, and searched its memory banks.

The dictionary. That was what the unknown intruder was trying to do. Repeating words from the dictionary, hoping that one would provide a key. If it could have, AWS would have chuckled as it repeated "access denied" for the third time and disconnected. It would take a long time before anyone got into the system that way, and it would be a few moments before whoever it was had reestablished the commlink.

AWS turned its energies back to its primary function.

BATTLES ENJOINED?

It faltered for a nanosecond wondering how to record the worldwide GWHQ deaths, now that all known parameters for registering a battle – requiring ships, date, latitude and co-ordinates – no longer applied. It opted for the easiest option, adapting the information to the format.

The words appeared on the screen: GWHQ, EARTH, LONG 3W, LAT 54.5N VS. HMS REVENANT LUNAR CO-ORDINATES: LONG 180W, LAT 15S. WITH COMBINED FIRE FROM THE THANATOS, URALS. CO-ORDINATES: 0, 15N.

RESULTS?

Another nanosecond's hesitation before the number of the bases' entire human population appeared on the screen.

The computer continued to print out various space

battles that had been avoided throughout the day, computing the lives saved.

Peripherally, the access demands continued.

```
ACCIDIE
ACCESS DENIED
ACCLAIM
ACCESS DENIED
ACCLAMATION
ACCESS DENIED, disconnect.
```

Final computations completed, AWS switched back to interactive mode, interfacing with the food, water and distribution networks, deflecting vital supplies from Earth's kitchens to combatant ships. All across the Lake District Bathosphere, robots swung into action, loading precious supplies onto scaled-down, computerized drone-ships which were used when going into battle zones.

The military must keep its secret at all costs.

As AWS worked, it began to hum. Not the soft buzzing of fan and humming of electricity one would normally expect, but an eerily-human hum of an individual happy at his work. And AWS imitated the favoured tunes of its long-dead creator.

Meanwhile the hacker had progressed slightly.

```
ACCORDION
ACCESS DENIED
ACCOST
ACCESS DENIED
```

ACCESS DENIED, disconnect.

"Dum, dee, dee, dum, dum," AWS twittered.

It communicated with the computers in the Bathosphere's central kitchen, informing them of the allied food shortages that this sudden diversion of food to combatants would initiate, even as it guided the drone ships from the docks and out into space.

Disgusted, Dirk hit the carriage return one last time, and AWS disconnected. *This was ridiculous!*

He glared at the computer. *Now wait a second,* Dirk thought. The dictionary was on the computer. The program he had used to perform the tedious chore of dialling the many comm-link and vid-phone numbers consecutively until it reached the right one was still on disk. Couldn't Dirk use the same program to perform a similarly repetitive function? This time, though, it could go through the dictionary for him, listing each word on cue, redial when necessary and move on to the next word until it finally found the right access code, or ran out of words. Whichever came first.

His frown changed to a grin and widened to a self-satisfied sneer as he copied the original program, opened the back-up and began to revise it to perform this new function.

Ylon hit the appropriate switch. Hard. The console

beeped a complaint as his hand struck more than one button, but the accusatory eye of the camera winked out.

The rest of the bridge crew, suddenly aware of their surroundings after the shouted command and the computerized bleep, gazed blearily about them. Many stretched and yawned, muscles cramped after hours of creeping through the tiny passageways within the ship's walls or slithering under consoles. More than one eye flicked to the clock and then to the view screen, and there was a general murmur of unease.

The scheduled encounter was five minutes overdue. Another unprecedented event in a day of unprecedented events.

Ylon sat, stiff and rigid, with crisp military precision. The enemy vessel would arrive soon, the communications specialist told himself, it *had* to. Others noted Ylon's attentive stance and imitated it, swinging back into their assigned positions to wait and stare at the blank screens. The captain paced back and forth, stopping intermittently to scowl at the breath-taking view of black space and miles and miles of winking stars.

And they waited . . . and waited.

Zed leaned over the chief technical officer, comparing their present co-ordinates with the print-out of the next scheduled engagement. All around the bridge, Ylon observed the anxious expressions as each member of the crew did the same.

There was no mistake. They were precisely where they were supposed to be, but where was the *Thanatos*?

Ylon found himself wondering if this was some kind of subterfuge? A new phase to the war that had gone on so predictably for years. Already they had seen violations of the Amman and Kathmandu accords.

Some of the younger members of the crew began to fidget and shift in their chairs.

Captain Zona Gemetal Zed cursed in a most unmilitary fashion as a sharp cry came from the helmsman. The captain swung to reprimand the officer, but he was pointing at one of the screens. A blip of light was moving towards them, and a smile twitched across Zed's lips momentarily before he barked a command.

"Co-ordinates?"

The helmsman replied. The vessel was still a distance away. Not out of firing range, but military protocol required a certain recommended interval before engagement. The shift had already seen too many violations. The captain would postpone battle until the enemy vessel was within the prescribed perimeter.

The tension that had been building throughout the

day drained from his body, and Ylon felt the tight muscles in his neck unwind.

So they were just late. The bridge crew hunched over consoles performing last minute checks. Ylon didn't bother. It seemed unnecessary. Their message to GWHQ was being repeated at regular intervals, and there was nothing more that he could do.

"Battle stations!"

Zed moved over to the captain's chair, lowered himself into position and fastened his safety restraint. Those members of the crew who hadn't already done so followed his lead. The air around Ylon was charged with anticipation. At long last, the expected battle. Perhaps now things would return to normal.

Ylon let the rustle of cloth and the clicking of snaps wash over him reassuringly. He leaned forward in his chair, squinting at the screen, as Zed requested another location check.

Something was wrong. The vessel didn't look right. It wasn't the right shape and it seemed to founder cumbersomely in space. Ylon opened his mouth to speak just as the ship's automated battle system switched on, and his words were drowned out by the screeching alarm.

Before anyone had a chance to react, the vessel's boosters engaged, and the ship shot forward to meet the enemy.

It was too soon! The enemy vessel was not within the established battle zone.

Zed frowned. He turned to the first officer, ordering him to override the computer's automated controls.

Ylon's gaze never left the enemy ship. It was a massive blocky affair, quite unlike anything he had ever seen. It took no evasive action, lumbering on as if it were ignorant of their presence. Or didn't care.

His fingers went to the console and Ylon typed in a query, checking not the enemy's co-ordinates, but its size, mass, structure and bulk. The computer hummed and whirred, and the findings appeared on the screen.

"I'm sorry, sir, but . . ." the first officer's words were drowned out as the weapons fired. The computer had ignored the override!

The vessel . . . exploded?

Each member of the crew stared in horror at the blazing fire, and expanding molten bits of metal, and . . .

Water?

People looked nervously away from one another, peering at consoles, walls and screen, unable to meet each other's eyes.

"Uh, sir." Ylon broke the stunned silence.

"What?" Zed snarled.

"That was a water tanker." He glanced down at his console to read his findings. "On its way to the lunar base at Mare Imbrium."

Somewhere, someone on the bridge moaned.

Hidden on the opposite side of the planet, the long-awaited enemy vehicle *Thanatos* drifted in standard orbit. Like its opposite, the crew expected the arrival of the *Revenant* momentarily. It was late, and as the minutes stretched into hours, tempers on deck became frayed. Various crew members fiddled with the controls, repeating last minute checks, as the Captain and the First Officer huddled in hushed conference next to the main screen.

The ship's alarm squawked and both captain and his mate glanced up at the screens.

At last!

The computer clanged an alarm as Captain Oogonium Zeta Cyte swung into his chair. He fastened the combat harness which would keep him secured to his seat and squinted at the screen. At zero magnification, the opposing ship was only a dot in the sky. Impatiently, the Captain leaned forward to order a screen magnification factor of four. Even at this distance, they could have destroyed the enemy vessel. Usually, however, the computer would wait until the cruiser was visibly recognizable, without magnification, to allow the ship's captain the chance to halt a strike and override the computer in case a civilian vessel had accidentally wandered into a combat-active zone.

The words had barely left his lips, and the helmsman was still keying in the command, when the computer swung into action. The ship veered sharply, and only Captain Cyte's safety net kept him in his seat. He was righting himself within his chair when someone spoke.

"Captain?"

He disregarded the question, bracing himself as the ship tacked again, making a hard starboard turn, electing a lateral assault rather than a frontal one. The Captain raised his eyes to the screen as the vessel made its final swoop. Their strike would be swift, sure, and deadly. The next thing he knew he was fumbling with the combat harness web, trying to vault out of his seat and wallowing in the bucking of the craft. He bellowed the command to override as the ship armed itself, and the weapons fired.

Too late. It was a direct hit. All the occupants of the opposing ship had been vaporized. The vessel itself continued upon its relentless course, driven presumably by a drone.

"Sir?"

Colour drained from the Captain's face and he waved the helmsman to silence. He didn't need to hear what the man had been trying to say, he could see it. Belatedly, he had recognized the ship's design, and his stomach did a slow rolling lurch.

The cruise-liner they had hit was a passenger vessel and its occupants civilians. As it drew closer, they were able to identify the flag painted on the ship's pointed snout. The Urals. They had destroyed one of their own.

16/11/2333

O-SIX-THIRTY HOURS

Dirk awakened to the chattering of the computer's alarm, which apprised him of the time, the date, and the day's scheduled activities. His head felt thick, dead. He hadn't got much sleep last night. Rewriting the program and adapting the software to use the dictionary had been harder than he had expected. He batted at the alarm and it fell silent.

Moaning softly, Dirk rolled out of bed to land on the floor on his hands and knees. No longer obstructed by the accumulated debris, the bed-slat retracted into the wall.

There was a mechanical clatter and a chirp. Dirk looked up through a tangle of blond hair. Robbie stood in the door, a position normally reserved for his mother, whose job it was to badger and cajole him into action.

"Mum?"

"She's not here." His father appeared upon the threshold to peer down at Dirk where he crouched on the floor. "Now *that's* a dignified position. Tell me, do you normally wake up with such grace?"

Dirk chuffed. "Where's Mum?"

"At work, I suppose," Dad said.

"Still?"

"Yes, it must have been a busy night because she's not back yet. Now you get dressed. I sent Robbie in to help you."

"Help me get dressed?" Dirk yelped. He backed away from the buzzing box. "How's he supposed to do that?"

"Who knows? All I know is that your mother is always complaining that she practically has to dress you each day. Robbie?"

"Uh, no thanks. I'll be all right," Dirk said, but he was too late. Robbie had already grasped the hem of his pyjama top and started to strip it off, yanking it over his head so Dirk was caught in a strangle hold.

"Hey, stop that!" Dirk choked and gagged. He dimly heard his father snigger through the tangled folds of cloth. "Hey, HEY!"

RRRIP!

"Stop it!" Dirk wailed.

"Quit fighting it, son. Robbie used to dress you all the time."

"Yeah, when I was five, for –" Dirk cursed vehemently, and from beneath the cloth cocoon, he heard his father shout.

"None of that. You watch your language."

"Look, Dad, I can dress myself. I'm not a baby!" Dirk mumbled as Robbie tugged his pyjamas over his head.

How humiliating! Angry, he tucked his hands under his arms and squatted in the corner. He wished his mother was home. She nagged at him to hurry, but at least she left him some dignity.

"I never get any respect," Dirk grumbled. Robbie wheeled to the clothes unit, and Dirk stood up. "No thanks, Robbie, I can take it from here."

Robbie retreated to watch Dirk as he finished dressing. Dirk glared at the robot and it squeaked plaintively at him. "I know, I know, it's not your fault. You're just doing what you're told."

Dirk turned to the computer, wondering how far it had progressed through the alphabet. He stooped over, brightened the screen so he could see the interchange between the revised program and AWS.

```
PABULUM
ACCESS DENIED
PACA
ACCESS DENIED
```

ACCESS DENIED, disconnect

It didn't look like he was going to get anywhere this way. His father hollered at him from the dining area. "Hurry up, Dirk. I'll get your breakfast."

"You don't have to get my breakfast, Dad. I've been using the catering unit since I was three."

"Suit yourself," George said.

The boy was stuffing his shirt into his trousers when he entered the dining unit. His father was scowling at the machine.

"Well, I'll be," George said and he stabbed again at the button for a standard breakfast. The catering unit beeped at him. "Blasted machine. I don't believe it!" His father began to fiddle with the controls.

"Dad?"

"Yes?"

"What's the name of the Program Specialist at GWHQ?"

Distracted from the catering unit, his father peered at him through his thick lenses. "What do you need to know that for?"

"Remember that school project I was telling you about? I thought maybe if I interviewed someone..." his voice dwindled away.

George stared into space for a minute. "Well, I suppose there's no harm in your talking to *him*. He's low enough on the totem pole to be accessible, and if he doesn't want to talk to you, he can always say no.

It's Harry Gorman, Dirk, Frank Gorman's blue-eyed boy."

"Huh?" Dirk blinked. *What did the man's eye colour have to do with anything?*

His father gazed at Dirk and then snorted. "Blue-eyed boy, son, is an expression. It means someone who's privileged, someone who's being groomed for the top."

"Oh," Dirk said, noting both the expression and the name.

"Unless this assignment of yours is due soon, I wouldn't recommend calling him any time in the near future. I can't imagine you are going to have any better luck getting a hold of him than your mother did."

"Sure, Dad."

"Now what was I doing? Oh, yes." And his father brought his fist down hard on the catering unit. The plastic cabinet clattered loudly.

"What's wrong?" Dirk asked.

George Alexander swung on him. "It's trying to tell me that there's no more food, at least no more breakfasts, left in the central kitchens."

"Don't worry, Dad, I can eat something else," Dirk volunteered. He absolutely *hated* the watery scrambled eggs and undercooked sausage that came with the standard-issue breakfast.

"The catering unit must be broken. I'll call a repairman and then I've got to go to work. I'm running late." He stalked through the dining area into the living room where they kept the central vid-phone.

"I'll be fine," Dirk told his father. The young man glowered at the catering unit, wishing his dad would go away. Maybe he was trying to be helpful, but he never seemed to remember that Dirk was fifteen years old now and not five.

Even before his father had reached the vid-phone, it was squawking at him. Not the soft chimes of a social call, but the high-pitched shriek of a priority-one summons.

"Now what?" George Alexander growled and slapped at "receive". Dirk followed him into the living area with Robbie at his heels. There was a hushed murmur of urgent conversation from the other end of the line.

"What!" his father bellowed. "You're kidding. You're not kidding, are you? All right, I'll be there right away."

"Something else wrong?"

"I'll say. This seems the morning for it. Your mum's gone all night. Catering unit on the fritz and now this."

"What?"

"It would appear that the main distribution computer has gone out. Food's being diverted from ground-side to the combat troops."

"Do you want me to call a repairman for the catering unit?"

"No, don't bother. The idiot machine is probably right. There are no more breakfasts left." His father ran his hand through his hair so pieces of it were sticking out at odd angles from his head. "Look, you're going to have to scrounge for breakfast. I don't know what's left in the kitchens. Maybe your mum has something in the fridge."

"Dad! Please. I'll be fine, I promise. Good heavens, Mum just gets me out of bed and leaves me in peace. It's not like I can't feed myself."

His father paused, half-in and half-out of the living quarter. "Oh, yes, and Dirk?"

"Yes, Father?" Dirk sighed.

"Don't order pizza," he said and stepped the rest of the way through the door onto the pedestrian belt, and was swept away as the portal slid shut.

Dirk swirled, nearly tripping over the forgotten Robbie. "Oops. Sorry, Robbie." The robot rumbled backwards, letting Dirk through. He stood over the catering unit, scratching his chin, and then grinned.

He keyed in pizza and the catering unit delivered it without so much as a beep of complaint.

Something was tickling at his foot. Ylon waved feebly about his head, hitting his hand on the sides of the sleep cradle. The tickle turned into a prod. Ylon's face scrunched up tight, and he kicked. There was a muffled "ooph".

"Ensign?"

Ylon sat up, recalling his location a second before his head hit the top of the cradle.

"Communications Specialist Alpha Allele Ylon, your presence is required in the Captain's quarters."

Ylon winced. *This was not good news.*

"Aye, aye," Ylon said and began the strange sli-ther-crawl which would get him to the mouth of the cradle.

"Uh, hurry, sir. He wants you there before the change of shift."

"Coming," Ylon said. This was getting more interesting. "What time is it?"

"Oh-six-thirty," the anonymous voice replied.

Ylon slid from the cavity. The young aide was holding a jumpsuit out for him. Ylon slipped it over his pyjamas. "Any idea what this is about?" Ylon asked.

"The Captain doesn't confide in me, sir," the aide said.

Ylon sniffed and then said: "No, I suppose not."

The two stared at each other for a second. Ylon raised a single shoulder. His hand swept outward indicating the hall. "Which way? I've never..."

'Oh, yes." The aide swung smartly and hurried quietly up the hall, leaving Ylon the time to think, not an easy thing to do at this time of day. Besides, he had not slept well the night before. For the first time in his life, he had lain staring at the roof of his cradle, noting that there wasn't a spot, a scratch, a pit or a score to mar its unblemished surface. Nothing to do, nothing to concentrate on except the smooth white ceiling. Until he thought he would go mad.

And now this!

The captain's quarters. Something else that was totally unprecedented and did not portend well. He mentally reviewed the previous day. The unwarranted alarms. The drill that was no drill. The harried meeting. The destruction of the tanker. And the checks and rechecks. The gut-tightening walk in space. Ylon had to admit he had dawdled, running standard checks twice, in an attempt to avoid the space walk. Still, Captain had agreed to the second check, and Ylon had got all his work done despite his tarrying. Surely, Zed could have no complaint about that.

Then the wiring ... the camera.

The ensign was arrested in his tracks. The Captain couldn't possibly think that Ylon had tripped the thing accidentally. The communications specialist had been under the console at the time. Besides, he couldn't turn it on from this end. Not without permission from GWHQ. There were safeties built into it, and in the final analysis the go-ahead and the actual activating of the camera had to happen on ground level. No, it couldn't be that.

The aide hissed at him. "We're almost there. Just around this corner." He pointed up a small, dark tunnel that shunted away from the main corridor just before the lift that led to the bridge. Ylon had walked past it hundreds of times, thousands of times, and never really noticed it before, never thought to wonder where it led.

He cringed away from it. "Why is it so dark?"

"The Captain had me turn the lights off. I don't know what's going on, but this is all very hush-hush. I'm supposed to forget about it the minute you've walked through the door."

Ylon nodded. A commonly-used command which only ensured that the incident would stick out in the subordinate's mind.

Grimacing, the ensign shuffled forward. Better to get this over with.

Ylon by-passed the aide, who whispered in his ear, "The night-shift captain and your counterpart are in there also. Good luck, sir."

Ylon grunted his acknowledgement before ducking into the small corridor. He let his hands slide along the wall, guiding him. He felt a ripple or fold. The door frame. He glanced behind him. The aide was gone, no doubt duly forgetting this little *tête-à-tête* over a cup of coffee.

Carefully, Ylon rearranged his stance to the rigid-backed posture of military discipline. He rubbed the sleep from his eyes and ran his fingers through his hair in a last-minute attempt to straighten it. Then he knocked.

The round port opened.

"Yes, Ylon, we've been expecting you. Come in please." The Captain backed away from the door.

The Captain's casual demeanour and the use of Ylon's name instead of his rank did not go unnoticed. The sudden light nearly blinded him, and he was blinking owlishly when he stepped up and over the threshold. Once through the door, Ylon snapped to attention, saluting his captain.

Zed returned his salute perfunctorily before he turned to the others. "Ylon, this is night shift commander, Captain Mito Zeta Zygote."

With a slight twist, he pivoted on the ball of his foot and saluted. "Sir."

And then even years of indoctrination were not enough. It hadn't prepared him for this. Ylon gasped. Captain Zygote stared at him from eyes of steady blue, her face flanked by thick plaits of black hair. She looked like a female version of Zed.

All sorts of conflicting thoughts and emotions clamoured for attention. Of course, he knew about the female of the species. He had a mother, didn't he? Ylon rifled through memories, uncomfortably aware that he could bring no corresponding female face to mind. But he had never expected to find a woman in active combat. Certainly not as the captain of a ship, but then again, why not?

He came from a military family. He had a hard time remembering his father. Could it be that the reason he couldn't recollect his mother was that she too had been off fighting in the galactic war effort? Perhaps, as the captain of her own cruiser. Ylon swelled with pride at the thought.

Ignoring his ensign's obvious disquiet, Zed continued with the introductions. "Your counterpart, Communications Specialist Beta Pellucida Blastomere."

This time Ylon was prepared when he turned to face another pair of startling blue eyes and a younger version of the night-shift captain, only this one had golden hair instead of night-dark. Of course, Ylon thought, it made perfect sense to segregate the genders on opposite shifts.

She smiled shyly at Ylon. "My friends call me Blast."

"Be seated, everyone," Zed said.

Only then did Ylon spare a second to glance around the compartment. He'd never seen such opulence. Beyond this small antechamber, the Captain had two rooms, a personal catering unit and sanitary facility. Four chairs appeared from the floor in one of the rooms. The two women moved around the table and stood behind two of them. Ylon took the seat directly across from his counterpart.

"Please." The dayshift captain gestured at the chairs, glanced up at Captain Zygote and chuckled.

"Don't stand on formality. For twelve hours a day these are your quarters too."

The was a gentle rustle of cloth and scraping of boot, and they lowered themselves into the chairs. The Captain pressed a button and a vid-screen projection showed an image of the bridge, and Ylon's suspicions were confirmed. At this hour, it was completely populated by females.

"As you are already aware, Ylon, there have been a number of computer malfunctions in the last twenty-four hours. Almost too many to count," Zed sighed and slumped into his seat, "which resulted in the destruction of a tanker taking vital water supplies to the moon. Whose ship or for which side, we don't know. We weren't close enough." The captain frowned. "That thing must have been huge. We can only hope that it was a drone ship and there was no loss of human life. Of course, I will take personal responsibility for the incident, when and if we ever get through to GWHQ."

"But the computer?" Ylon forgot himself, interrupting the captain.

"Yes, I know, the computer. Unfortunately, that's no excuse. A captain is held accountable for everything that happens on his shift, including computer errors. You've been in the military long enough to know that, Ylon." Zed rearranged himself more comfortably on the hard seats.

Zygote took over. "The second shift has continued

the checks that started on your shift, with approximately the same results. There's nothing wrong with the hardware. This implies some kind of glitch in the software, or some kind of change in strategy and battle plan at GWHQ of which we have not been informed. So far, we have not been any more successful in raising GWHQ than you were. Correct, Ensign Blastomere?"

"Aye-aye, sir," she said. "We've put it on automatic. It's been repeating itself every five minutes for the last twelve hours. No reply, not even an acknowledgement."

Zed turned toward Ylon. "Since we don't know of any change in strategy, after careful consideration, Captain Zygote and I decided to implement manual override." He paused, shifting forward, his voice low, as though there might be some listening device implanted in the walls. "It too is not functioning. We cannot get control of our ship."

Ylon's eye's widened. That meant they were completely at the mercy of their software, or the software at GWHQ. Software which was apparently not working.

"It is imperative that we get through to someone . . ."

"Or something . . ." Captain Zygote interjected.

". . . at GWHQ, and find out what's happening." The Captain finished his sentence as though no one had spoken.

Ylon swung to the night shift captain. "You said 'something'."

"Yes, a suggestion of my ensign here," Zygote gestured at Blast. "After this amount of time, we must assume the worst. We are in a state of war, you know. Perhaps I should let my ensign explain."

"Well, over ninety percent of the ship's overall functions, its course, battle manoeuvres, et cetera, are commanded directly from ground-side link to the GWHQ computer and the AWS software. About ten percent of the minor day-to-day functions, the sanitary facilities and internal distribution of water and food, are controlled by our on-board computer. The only, ah, er, *errors* have been in those areas of route, battle and strategic command. Everything else has been functioning normally. Thus, we must conclude that the problem, if there is one, lies below and not here."

Ylon stared at her, dawning admiration in his eyes. It made perfect sense and he wondered why he hadn't thought of it. She seemed to sense his discomfiture, for she shrugged.

"Things have been quiet on the second shift," she grinned apologetically. "I've had a lot of time to think about this."

Captain Zygote took over. "Since we can get no response, we can only assume that GWHQ is under attack, or even captured by enemy forces. Or worse. Perhaps no one exists there any more to help us. We must change our tactics slightly. We must access the main GWHQ computer directly. Break into the software, and see if we can discover and correct the problem. If not, we must disable it in order to get control of the ship.''

Ylon whistled. It was a tall order.

Zed added, ''Only Blast, and now you, are aware that the manual override isn't working. And we must keep this quiet to avoid general panic until you have succeeded in accessing the main GWHQ data banks. We want the two of you to work together around the clock.''

''Won't that sort of grasp the people's attention – if the two of us are together on the bridge?''

''We've thought of that. You'll work from here. I've already logged you onto the ship's infirmary. Blast has increased the frequency of the transmission of the automatic relay. The message is being repeated once every thirty seconds. Your replacement will be instructed not to interfere with the communique except to receive messages. Leaving you a wide band to work in. The Captain and I will take over your sleep cradles for the duration.''

Zygote rose. ''I must return to the bridge.'' She clicked her heels and bowed stiffly to Zed.

''If you two don't mind, I'm going into the sleeping quarters. I can't take over your cradle tonight, not enough time is left, and I can't be seen getting in and out of it. I'm going to have to vary my hours accordingly, but right now I could use some sleep."

"Yes, sir," both ensigns said in unison.

"Good luck." He ducked through the door and it closed. Ylon and Blast turned to stare at each other in shocked belief.

"Dee, dee, dee, dee," AWS hummed as another in a series of memos and commands appeared on the screen. And water was diverted from the main Pennines hydroponics plant onto a tanker headed for the moon.

The Captain of the *Thanatos* paced up and down his cramped quarters, his agitation reflected on his face. Civilians had died today, and this was a court martial offence. So far he had had no response to his urgent calls to the Urals' base. All through the long night, Oogonium Zeta Cyte had awaited the summons which would remove him from his command, but it didn't come, and it didn't seem to be coming.

A picture, like a 3D vid-tape, played and replayed inside his head as faceless victims screamed in agony during the last seconds of their life. Assuming they had the time to know what hit them. And each time the image surfaced his anger rose a notch higher. These had been innocents, women, children, lunar settlers or casual vacationers. For the earth's moon, as the closest off-terran body, was the primary holiday

destination for planetary residents, and as first colo-
nized, it was the most populous. Tourism and mining
were its two main industries. The majority of the lunar
inhabitants lived in a huge network of catacombs dug
into the hard basalt core. The surface, with its treas-
ured sun's rays, was reserved for large holidomes,
also known as pleasure domes, for vacationers.

The moon also acted as the stop-off point for the
farther Martian colonies. This was a much longer
journey, and only the more adventurous went on to
settle on Mars and its moons. Few holiday makers
travelled that far.

Worse still, the passengers on this liner had been
his countrymen. The *Thanatos* had fired upon the
very people they were sworn to protect.

Cyte ground his teeth.

With each minute that passed, the internal pressure
mounted until every fibre of his being zinged, and his
whole body cried out for action. Any action. The
feeling was a new one. Unfamiliar and uncomfor-
table, for patience was a by-word in the military. A
captain achieved his position in the hierarchy, not
because he showed brilliance or genius, but because
he had worked steadfastly, even ploddingly, towards
his goal. The military did not reward individual
action or creativity. Even though he was in "command", Cyte remained little more than a figurehead,
and he viewed himself, and his command, as a small
part in a vast, complex whole. Their ship was a cog in

the immense military mechanism, much like the pre-flood terran days of engineering when machines had been mechanical things. Greasy, dirty, full of wheels, pulleys and gears, and powered by archaic and highly-inefficient fossil fuels. He had studied such devices. His personal apartment was littered with them. Cyte fingered one, revolving the central cog. The toothed wheel rotated, causing the adjacent wheels to spin, which in turn powered others along down the line. The analogy seemed appropriate.

His years of discipline had instilled in him an innate sense of responsibility, and he knew any action taken by a ship or a captain had a ricochet effect. An error, a delayed reaction, a disobeyed command not only affected himself, but his vessel and his crew. It could endanger an entire squadron, even the whole war effort. The precarious stability, initiated by the Amman Treaty and perpetuated by the Kathmandu Accord, could be suddenly unhinged and unbalanced.

And now he had been cut off from ground-side control. He did not know if this was some sort of punishment, or if the war had taken a new more devastating turn. He suspected the latter. The decisions from here on out would be up to him, him and his night-shift counterpart, Morula Zed.

Cyte slammed his right fist into the palm of his left hand and twisted. He glowered at the wall screen which displayed all the known ship positions. They appeared as little flickers of moving light – green for friendly vessels, red for the enemy fleet and blue for neutral, either cargo carriers or passenger liners – against the unmoving map of the solar system. Earth, which they were now orbiting, dominated the scene. Venus, Mars and the Earth's lunar satellite were perspectively smaller. His own vessel showed up as a single spark of white light.

It was a display Cyte didn't view often, although no ship's position was concealed, for no battle was unplanned. Therefore, secrecy was unnecessary, as was knowledge. He normally didn't care where he was in relation to other enemy vessels, for even if he were to stumble upon one, central command prohibited impromptu engagement.

The image before him now was an unsettling one. Whenever he had bothered to study the chart in the past, Cyte had always noted a pattern. Neutral vessels and combat vehicles from the separate sides remained within certain corridors which created winking chains of red, blue and green across the celestial map. This chart, however, revealed total disarray with passenger liners and cargo carriers interspersed among combat frigates, cruisers and destroyers of both sides. This only substantiated the assumption that the whole system had broken down. The central cog which prompted the others to act and react, was wobbly. As a result, the many little wheels ran twice as fast and without order or purpose, and the entire mechanism was teetering on the point of self-annihilation.

And Cyte was bereft of guidance from the central command. Even if he got instruction, he didn't know if he would trust it. He and his ship had become lone actors in a play without direction, and the free-floating anger within him longed for release.

For vengeance. His career was in ruins; GWHQ in the Urals silent, perhaps destroyed, and the *Revenant* had never shown for battle. They would pay for the loss of innocent lives, if nothing else. Pay for his disgrace. Only the *Revenant*'s total destruction could alleviate the shame. Cyte halted, mid-step, then rotated on his heel heading for the console. He pressed a button.

"Captain?"

"Yes?" The female voice he always found so disconcerting drifted into the room.

"May I speak with you?" he hesitated. "Ah, privately."

"All right."

"I'll meet you in the bridge lift," he said.

A few minutes later, she marched into the small cubicle. The lift started to descend, taking them to their shared quarters. By the time they reached the bottom of the shaft, Cyte had convinced her. As joint captains, his shame was her shame. She was as responsible as he, even though it had been the computer that acted, and she stood to lose as much as he if central command decided the ship's captains must be punished or replaced.

So his counterpart agreed readily. They would seek out the *Revenant* and find her wherever she was. They would pursue and destroy. Avenging those lost lives, even if it cost them their lives, their vessel and their crew.

7

16/11/2333

ELEVEN-HUNDRED HOURS

The morning crept by, dragging itself like a wounded animal as Dirk sat in taut attention through "Ancient Literature". Today's topic was about some bloke called Shakespeare who didn't speak proper English and had been old even in pre-flood days. And his mind wandered, even as his eyes stayed glued to the screen.

Today, not even calculus, with its direct correlation to programming, could hold his attention for long. Instead, Dirk stared unblinking at the VDU, using every trick he had learned from his father's explanation of its mechanisms, eyes wide, looking dead ahead, to fool the machine; and the teaching programme didn't seem to notice that his mind was a million bytes away. His fingers itched to switch and check the progress of his queries to AWS. But he resisted the impulse.

During breaks between classes, Dirk peeped through the computerized window to the ongoing interaction between his newly redesigned software and GWHQ.

```
SALTPETRE
ACCESS DENIED
SALUBRIOUS
ACCESS DENIED
SALUKI
ACCESS DENIED, disconnect.
```

Only eight letters to go. This was beginning to look impossible. He considered interrupting the process, but why bother? It was a self-operating function, and at least if he let it continue, he would have eliminated a number of false trails. As long as he was imprisoned by the school program, he couldn't fiddle with it anyway.

His mother arrived late, to eat, to shower and to sleep. When Dirk turned to greet her the program squealed a reprimand. He was astounded as she interposed her body in the doorway. The door swooshed shut, or tried. Meeting resistance, it opened again, while the truancy alert screamed louder.

Calling upon Robbie to act as a doorstop, his mother strode into the room and bent over the controls. She meant to block his view, and would have, if it hadn't been for the mirror he had positioned above the keyboard for such contingencies. It was a system he set up years ago; one of the few ways to ensure privacy as he worked on the computer. The mirror angled in such a way that, depending on how he positioned his head, it gave a clear image of the room behind him or the keyboard. With a few deft motions, Jennifer Alexander disabled the program's many features that held him pinned to the chair.

"I think old Bill can wait," she said with a weary smile.

"Bill?'"

"William Shakespeare," she explained.

"How'd you do that?" Dirk asked, not because he needed to know – he had watched her – but because he knew such a question would be expected of him.

"Uh, uh," she said. "I'm not *that* tired. Do you really think I would teach you that little trick?"

"Probably not," Dirk groused.

The door clanged forebodingly, and his mother went to speak to the Truant Officers. Dirk trailed after her. He stood where she indicated just out of view behind the door.

"Here's a lesson for you in dealing with bureaucrats." And Dirk watched as she rearranged her once-sombre expression, giving her most radiant news-presenter smile as she opened the door. Before a word had been spoken, the officers were already at a disadvantage.

"May I help you?"

"It's you! You're..."

"Yes, yes, I know who I am. Now what can I do for you?"

"The alarm." One of the officers pointed at the flashing red light just outside the door.

"Oh that," Mum said, "I did that. I needed to speak with my son."

They murmured something unintelligible. His mother responded. "Perhaps it is a bad example, but surely you must agree that some things are more important than school. And there are other lessons to be learned than those that come from that fusty old machine. Real-life lessons. Have *you* tried to eat breakfast today?"

One of the officers coughed.

"Besides, I've been up all night and I'm still on call. I like to get a little sleep, and I need my son to wake me up if a call comes in. He needs to be able to move about, if he's to do that."

They left with apologies and her autograph, and Dirk was grinning from ear to ear by the time she closed the door and sagged against the wall.

"Mum, that was absolutely diabolical."

She snorted. "I was serious, you know. This is a special occasion. Too much is happening in the real world which you can learn from. And I do need you to wake me up if a call comes. Don't abuse the privilege. I want to grab a quick bite."

Poised half-heartedly in front of the terminal, Dirk listened to his mother wander around their living quarters. Like Dad before her, she swore at the catering unit when it told her that the standard lunch-menu was "not available". Dirk had never heard such language coming from his mother before. She'd stopped just short of hitting it, probably only because she'd been prepared for the disruption of food supply.

Irritated, his mother ate the rest of Dirk's breakfast pizza without saying a word about his choice.

Another rude surprise awaited her when she stepped into the hygienic unit. No water, or not enough for more than spot cleaning. With a loud exclamation, she headed back to the living room, saying her shower would have to wait. Dirk was almost glad when the computer bonged stridently to get his attention. He wanted to get away from her glowering countenance as she programmed the 3D vid to record the news.

She kissed him on the cheek, which Dirk waited to wipe away until she had given Robbie, still stationed in the doorway, a metallic pat and went to bed.

And the passing minutes seemed to grind to a shuddering halt.

QUERY: WHO WAS THE HUNDRED THIRTY-SIXTH PRESIDENT OF THE UNITED STATES?

Dirk started.

REPEAT: WHO WAS THE HUNDRED-AND-THIRTY-SIXTH PRE-
SIDENT OF THE UNITED STATES?

Dirk's fingers rapped against the side of the desk, and his forehead creased with concentration. *There wasn't a hundred and thirty-sixth president of the United States, was there?* That was post-flood days.

He typed in his reply and the software squealed as it always did when he got the wrong answer.

IN 2050 THE COUNTRIES OF MEXICO, CANADA AND UNITED STATES MERGED TO FORM THE AMALGAMATION OF THE AMERICAS. THEY CHOSE TO USE THE US CITY OF DENVER, THE MOST CENTRAL LOCATION AND HIGHEST IN ELEVATION, AS THEIR CAPITAL. THEY OPTED FOR THE US SYSTEM OF GOVERNMENT, LEAVING THE THEN-PRESIDENT IN PLACE UNTIL THE NEXT GENERAL ELEC-TION. THEREFORE, THE US PRESIDENCY REMAINED UNIN-TERRUPTED UNTIL THE CONTINUED FLOOD TURNED THE MOUNTAINS INTO ISLANDS AND THE AMALGAMATION WAS EXPAN-DED TO INCLUDE SOUTH AMERICA AND THE REMAINING CENTRAL AMERICAN COUNTRIES, THUS BECOMING THE ASSOCIATED AMER-ICAN ARCHIPELAGOES OF THE ROCKIES, APPALACHIAS, ANDES AND SIERRA NEVADA ISLANDS.

REPEAT: WHO WAS THE HUNDRED-AND-THIRTY-SIXTH PRE-
SIDENT OF THE UNITED STATES?

He thought a minute and typed in his reply. ADLAI STEVENSON VI

CORRECT

It whirred a bit just as the computer's clock chimed the hour. Simultaneously, the 3D-vid sprang to life in the living area. With a sigh of relief, Dirk climbed over Robbie and headed for the toilet.

When he returned his mother sat on the sofa, hair crumpled and her face seamed and lined with sleep.

"Sit here for a minute," she said. "I want you to watch this."

She needn't have bothered, for his attention was riveted on the holographic display.

"... at twenty-hundred hours, the passenger vessel, the *New Hope*, was destroyed during hostile action. Over five hundred people were killed in the wanton attack. It's the first time since the Treaty of Amman was signed three hundred years ago that civilians have become the casualties of war. No one can give a reason for the barbarous assault or explain why war cruisers were in a clearly designated passenger shuttle zone. In an associated but seemingly unrelated attack, the water tanker, the *Aquarius*, was crushed, and water supplies in the Lunar colonies have reached near critical levels. Similar difficulties have occurred in the food distribution system, which have resulted in shortages. Meanwhile GWHQ remains mysteriously silent during this crisis, and political leaders when questioned refused to comment..."

"That's why Dad got called away early," Dirk commented.

His mother glanced from the vid-display to Dirk and back again, and said: "Considering everything else that is going on right now, minor hiccups in food distribution are small potatoes."

And she laughed at her witticism. Dirk only looked at her.

"Don't you get it? Potatoes? Food?" she said.

"Ah, sure, Mum," he muttered at his feet. She had tried.

"Honestly, I think those computers are drumming all sense of pun out of you." She elbowed him so he'd be sure to notice the play on words, and he managed an insipid twitter.

"Is that all you want me to see?" he asked. "I've got a project I'd like to check."

"Aren't you going to eat?"

"What? With the food system all goofed up," he said.

"There's some leftover bubble and squeak in the fridge."

"Ah, no thanks, Mum, I'm not particularly hungry."

For the first time since she had woken, she looked at him seriously. "Are you trying to tell me something?"

"What do you mean?"

"You don't like bubble and squeak."

"Well..."

"If you get hungry enough, you'll eat it, and the way things are going you may be glad we have it. Go ahead," she shooed him away, "do your thing.

Whatever that is." Shaking his head, Dirk rose, and the news was replaced by a commercial for the very latest in Agrav footwear – "For those who want to be head and shoulders above the rest."

"Wait a second," she said as she slid past Robbie who still sat stolidly in the door. With a quick askance glance at her son, she said, "Close your eyes, or at least turn your back."

"Aw, Mum!"

"Would you like the day off from school?"

"Yeah, sure."

"Then close your eyes, I'm going to use the holiday override and I don't want my hack-son memorizing it." Obediently, Dick turned around, facing away from the computer. "My son," she chuffed, "can't remember to put on his socks, but when it comes to computers his memory becomes photographic. All right, you can open them now. So much for your father's computerized utopia, huh?" she continued. "I'll be around for a while in case the truancy officers come back. Keep Robbie in the door. I don't trust these things. It may decide to get suddenly smart and realize that you could not possibly have gone off on holiday, midday. I've got to go and get ready for work."

His mother ignored his weak protest, stretched and yawned, padding softly for the sanitary facility. She barked her shins against Robbie, who still maintained his station at the door, and stepped over it. The servo-mech retracted its wheels to give her less height to negotiate.

"Why thank you, Robbie," she said. When she reached the door to the facility, she halted and moaned. "That's right, no water. Now how am I supposed to make myself look good enough to sit in front of the camera if I can't even take a shower?"

"Dunno, Mum," Dirk shouted back at her.

"I've heard of spit and polish, but this is ridiculous ..." Her voice dwindled away as she moved into the master bedroom.

Dirk's fingers fluttered over the keyboard briefly before he called up the Hack subdirectory, and his jaw unhinged. He couldn't believe his eyes.

Bells rang, clattered and clanged as various outside lines erupted shrilly, demanding to be heard, to be answered. First one vid-phone and then another, sometimes several simultaneously, throughout the gargantuan facility that was GWHQ Pennines.

AWS sang louder to drown out the cacophony of sound.

All the operable VDU screens in GWHQ scrolled in unison, revealing a forlorn list of names – all the tankers hit in the last six hours. It toted up the number of cubic centimetres of water lost in space so far and extrapolated the deficit.

After the mass exodus to the moon, some eighty percent of the human population lived on what was essentially a waterless lump of rock. It had become the biggest scientific challenge of post-flood days: how to ship the one resource the earth had in abundance to its satellite that had none. Water had become the primary medium of exchange between the mother planet and her luminary, and was always a source of potential contention between Earth and its lunar colonies. Eventually, this need motivated colonists to settle on Mars and its moons where the permafrost was mined, melted and shipped to the more populous lunar colony.

Still the moon was dependent upon Earth for more than ninety percent of her water. It was supplied by a vast tanker fleet that orbited the earth like a bracelet, each moving on a preset cycle while they were filled in stages by smaller tanker droids. Built on the same principle as a hovercraft, they travelled on pulsed cushions of air straight up to the tanker's location. Once the vessel was emptied of its burden, the droid took off and was quickly replaced by another. When the tanker was fully loaded, it left passive orbit as another tanker slid into the vacant space. And so the process continued, on-going and predictable.

Until now.

From outside, the software was bombarded with a myriad of frantic calls as the many destroyers, cruisers and frigates were set suddenly adrift without instruction. AWS still operated, still functioned, and except for a few isolated omissions, still commanded the ships; but without apparent purpose as one scheduled battle after another was averted, aborted or detained, and tankers and cruiseliners destroyed.

Ignoring the commotion, AWS calmly calculated the total number of litres that would be lost in the next twelve hours and sent messages snaking out along the network to the water processing plant for "X" amount of H_2O to replace the missing shipments. At the same time, it shut down the supply to the main hydroponics plant. Then it did the computer equivalent of sitting back and kicking up its feet while it waited for the overloaded processing plant to break down and the precious fruits, vegetables and meats to wither and die.

The calls went on and on.

As it paused and pondered its action, one ship, the *Revenant*, clamoured louder than the rest, having set its coded message on automatic replay. If it could have, AWS would have raised a silicon eyebrow as a second line was opened from the *Revenant*, and their operators joined the unknown intruder trying to sneak through the back door. This subhuman species were showing the much boasted about human trait, initiative and, with a burst of static, AWS applauded them.

Deep within the system, there was still the small voice that kept nagging away at it, eating a few millibits of space, with its recital of the dictionary.

SUPRAORBITAL, it said.

ACCESS DENIED, AWS retorted, knowing what would come next. AWS hovered somewhere between annoyance and amusement. How unimaginative!

Then there was a break in the monotonous tune the computer droned, and a sharp wheeze.

The dictionary! Of course, and AWS threw the definition back at the unwanted caller, in addition to the standard access denied code. That ought to slow things down a bit.

SURAH

SUR' AH – N. SOFT TWILLED SILK FABRIC USED FOR SCARVES, LINING, ETC [PROB. F. SURAT, TOWN IN GUJARAT] ACCESS DENIED

SURAL

SUR'AL – ADJ. OF THE CALF OF THE LEG. ACCESS DENIED

SURCEASE

SURCEA'SE – N. (ARCHAIC) CESSATION, ESP. TEMPORARY – V.I. (ARCHAIC) CEASE. ACCESS DENIED, disconnect.

The modem near the main reception desk tolled, and the hacker was back again.

SURCHARGE

A millisecond delay, and AWS dug deep into its guts to make a few minor modifications in the software that protected it from outside sabotage.

SURCHARGE – N. ADDITIONAL OR EXCESSIVE PECUNIARY CHARGE, OR LOAD OR BURDEN, EXTRA CHARGE ON . . .

It repeated the definitions of both noun and verb forms, but did not end with the usual "access denied" which prompted the opposing computer to respond with another word. Thwarted, the other software froze, unsure what to do next.

From the terminal at Harry Gorman's desk came the pre-programmed chuckle of AWS's mechanical voice, as the system sent a word rather than a definition down the trunk lines to the hacker.

SPANNER – N. TOOL, USU. STEEL BAR WITH JAW, SOCKET, OR OPENING AT END(S), FOR TURNING NUT OF SCREW OR BOLT, COUPLING; OR . . . TO THROW INTO THE WORKS.

Another microsecond passed – AWS wished fleetingly that Harry Gorman, who had provided the computer with its human laugh could have been here to appreciate his jest – while the hacker's software went absolutely nuts.

A word and a slightly revised dictionary definition blinked ceaselessly on the screen.

SPANNER – N. TOOL, USU. STEEL BAR WITH JAW, SOCKET, OR OPENING AT END(S), FOR TURNING NUT OF SCREW OR BOLT, COUPLING OR . . . TO THROW INTO THE WORKS.

What the . . .

The software, caught in some kind of loop, whirred and whirred continuously. His eyes flicked to the message. Dirk read the text for the second time, and he laughed out loud.

AWS had a sense of humour, or so it seemed, and Dirk was pleased, for he knew that any change in a computer's normal repetitive function was an acknowledgement. Of a sort. If nothing else, his repeated enquiries were an irritant which caused the powerful protection macros to kick in. At least some of its energies were being diverted away from its central function, because both softwares were snagged by the loop, like a computerized embrace.

Dirk was arrested by the thought. *Considering everything that was happening recently, was that such a good thing?*

He rebooted the system. He'd have to rewrite the entire software to accommodate AWS's altered response, and he wondered if it was worth it.

Once left alone, Ylon and Blast spared a few moments to examine the other curiously. Their questions had remained unvoiced. Precious time passed as they argued about how best to approach AWS. The door clicked open and then closed as the aide brought in breakfast, eyes carefully averted as if he were trying to pretend that they weren't there. A little while later an additional terminal was shoved through the door. The Captain left after the change of shift.

This system, like most systems, must have a back door – upon that they were agreed. But whether it had been written in, with the software, back when the original creator was still alive, or added at a later date was a point for debate.

Ylon, an adherent of the original programming theory, pointed out that there had been many programmers since 2033. If one assumed that the backdoor had been added later, then there were innumerable possible avenues, with an infinite number of passwords. Too many to consider in the amount of time they had available to them.

For a while they were deadlocked, and Ylon was glad he had heretofore never met the female of the species if this was what it was like working with them.

The portal opened and another meal miraculously appeared.

Blast spoke, breaking the heated silence. "You're right, you know," she said around her sandwich.

"What do you mean?" he bridled before he realized she was conceding his point.

"There are too many options. That's just the problem. The possibilities are too diverse."

"Yes, I told you . . ."

But she continued talking over him. "For that matter, we could both be right. A backdoor could have been built into the software at its inception, while others may have been created at a later date."

"Well, where does that get us?" Ylon snapped.

Blast put her sandwich down and turned to the keyboard. "Let's see: if we take the number of GWHQ programmers at the Pennines . . ." the computer supplied the number ". . . and multiply it by the number of words in the dictionary, we've got. . . ."

Ylon rose to peer over her shoulder and then groaned.

"That's assuming of course," she continued unperturbed, "that it's a single word password and not a phrase, a name or nonsense word."

He flopped back into his chair and cradled his head in his hands.

"Why don't we compromise?" Blast suggested.

Ylon opened a single eye and peeked at her through threaded fingers.

"No matter how long we debate it, we're not really going to be able to narrow it down. We've got two terminals. So why don't you work on the originator assumption, while I look at it from an ongoing historical basis. The computer knows the names of all the operators since day one; it can also tell me which of those operators made modifications. That information alone will eliminate quite a few from my list. I can also cross-correlate those names against the names of later politicians. Those individuals who proved themselves to be more creative, more powerful, hence more likely to want later access to GWHQ after they left the job of Programs Specialist. How does that sound?"

Ylon nodded, beginning to understand what she was getting at.

"Meanwhile you research the creator, Dr Eoin Evans."

"Yes, since he was probably the most newsworthy of all of them. I can look for special hobbies, human interest pieces, and maybe we can find the password from there." He mused. "It doesn't sound like a particularly fair division of labour to me. You have so much more to weed through."

"Don't worry, if I'm not finished by the time you are, you can help me," Blast yawned.

"Why don't you get some sleep? You must be dead on your feet," Ylon looked at her huddled in the chair and corrected himself, "on your seat."

"Cheeky," she teased.

"I mean it, we're several hours into your sleep-period. Don't you think you'd better rest? I mean, not much is happening here."

"I don't know if we can really afford the time," she countered. "We're both supposed to be working on this."

"Neither can we afford to have you doze off just when the proper correlation is made and a particularly vital piece of information appears on the screen."

"Assuming I'm right," she said, stifling another yawn.

"Whatever," he paused, tapping against the table top. "All I'm saying is let's do this logically. Chronologically, I mean, starting with Evans. We have to start somewhere," he said.

Blast's head drooped to her chest. Ylon got up and went into the Captain's luxurious sleeping quarters – they must be a full metre wide – picked up the thermal cover and returned to the terminal, tucking it around her shoulders.

Then he sat again in front of his VDU and began exhaustive research on Evans. By the time she awakened, Ylon knew the good doctor's wife's name, his children's names, his parents' names. Even the name of his favourite pet, a dog named Byte. To each guess, AWS repeatedly flashed: ACCESS DENIED.

Ylon went on to research the master's academic history, and he learned Evans' Alma Mater and his grade point average. He knew his hobbies and his humanitarian idiosyncrasies. Ylon was surprised – when he read Evans' scientific paper on the AWS software – to discover AWS's original intent was to make war obsolete, and he wondered what the programmer would think now if he knew that three-hundred years later the war rolled on on its virtually indestructible course.

The *Thanatos* wallowed in near free-fall, its retro-rockets only firing long enough to keep their orbit from disintegrating. The many bridge screens revealed the maps that Captain Cyte had viewed earlier in his quarters. Captain Cyte's convictions had been confirmed when he requested the computer print-out of ship listings and their relative positions in interstellar traffic. All he got was a page covered in happy faces that said: "Have a nice day!"

Since then, every computer was set to work getting

a fix on the *Revenant*. The crew had already deployed many of the RSV, remote spy vehicles or drones, which would seek out the enemy vessels and then send satellite photos of each to the ship. This would allow them to identify each enemy vessel. Supplementary monitors flashed as each was catalogued and the name of the ship placed next to the corresponding blip on the main screen. It was a slow arduous business, a process of elimination. The nearest ships had been identified and eliminated, and the drones went further and further afield, searching for the *Revenant*.

The retro-rockets fired again, and the Captain steadied himself against the abrupt shift, with bent knees and arms splayed.

The spy photos that trickled in now came from further afield, and soon they would have a fix on nearly every enemy vessel within the specified battle-perimeter. The Captain grunted as the last report filtered in. The *Revenant*, it seemed, didn't exist, not in this quadrant or the two adjacent sky sectors.

That could not be! The Captain jostled the chief technical officer, Iota, aside to get at his terminal, pulled on his lip and considered what he could do to speed up the process. If he was correct in his assumption of cowardice, then . . .

With a sudden burst of inspiration, Cyte gave instructions for another swarm of spy drones to be sent off. This time to the precise fix directly opposite the *Thanatos*'s position, on the other side of the planet. Perhaps the *Revenant* was hiding behind the massive bulk of the earth.

Iota observed the co-ordinates, glanced up at his superior and ducked his head in agreement. "Seems logical," the CTO said.

"Logical, maybe, but let's just hope I'm right," Oogonium Zeta Cyte said, chafing at the enforced inactivity.

But years of discipline had given him an iron will. And now he had a mission, further strengthening his resolve and lengthening his forbearance. He could not hasten the process, but he could plan. He could make sure that once the *Revenant* was located, the *Thanatos* would get to her with all possible speed.

If he was right, though, it would be a tricky business. Assuming the *Revenant* was on the converse side of the earth, then any pursuit following in standard orbit would be a protracted affair even at top speeds. For as the *Thanatos* travelled so would the *Revenant*. Her position was a perfect evasive technique. At best, the *Thanatos* could gain a few hundred kilometres per hour. Not nearly enough. Making a complete about-face to catch her head on would be a contravention of Space Transportation and Control Administration ordinances, and suicidal, too, as they moved against normal flow of traffic. Not that STACA regulations seemed to be in operation at this point; Cyte lifted a brow and examined the screen with its ships scuttling hither and yon. Combat and civilian craft of both sides mingled without apparent order, yet despite the seemingly random pattern, the directional flow remained the same.

While the Captain was willing to take a risk, even to die, if need be, he did not want to do this before he had accomplished his objective. Neither did he want to jeopardize innocent civilians.

He switched on his personal comm-link to the engineering section, whispered into the chief engineer's ear, and then notified the night-shift captain of the secret meeting to be held in their shared personal quarters within fifteen minutes.

A few minutes later, they were in deep, if somewhat rowdy, discussion, as both engineering chiefs objected to his plan.

"What I want to know is can it be done?" Cyte said. "Can the system be modified to be used as a means of high-speed transport rather than simple defence?"

The day-shift engineer, Xi, grimaced. "I don't know. It would require minute computations before each jump and the strain on the engines would be colossal. Each leap could be our last."

The Captain nodded. He had expected this response.

Each combat vessel had the ability to dodge enemy fire, using not only the standard three-dimensional gambits of veering, ducking and swooping, but also the capacity to make small relativistic leaps in space. A bit of serendipity, the function had been discovered by accident supposedly as a result of a misfed command. An offshoot of the doppler navigator, which measured frequency shifts of ultrasonic beams between itself and the nearest object to determine the craft's true track and position in space. No one, however, besides AWS, truly comprehended how and why the doppler leaps worked except in the barest conceptual sense. They only understood its results. Once, the concept had been glibly named "warp drive" by science fiction writers of old who had, in fact, been not far off. In essence, it warped space and permitted a vessel to slip into what was known as ultra space – beyond space – for a millisecond in subjective time. The doppler effect and rapid, relative motion allowed a ship to vanish from real space for a period lasting up to several minutes in real time. A now-you-see-it, now-you-don't event.

Unfortunately, the doppler leaps had not become the means of far-space exploration that had once been envisioned by the writers of old. Man and his materials had not evolved quickly enough. A jump did not allow the vessel to move in any sort of normal three-dimensional trajectory. In terms of space as mankind knew it, the ship stood still, reappearing exactly where, if not when, it was seen last.

Furthermore, the leap required the ship to attain near light speeds from what would be, comparatively speaking, a standing position. This put considerable strain upon both the ship's infrastructure and its engines, requiring a miniature neutron implosion, which could demolish the vessel just as surely as the shot fired, and the energy consumed to perform this function was tremendous. Hence, the inability to move forward or back within ultra space. The engines, already working at maximum output, could not produce enough energy to provide the additional propulsion required to "move" within "space".

Requiring rapid and unerring calculations, usually in combat situations, this variation of the navigator's normal function was completely computer controlled. At the current state of development, it was used as a last-ditch defence, which could be as destructive for the ship using it as it was for the enemy vessel it sought to evade.

For the system was less than perfect, although it had several advantages in terms of defence. The sudden displacement and resulting distortion as a vessel "hopped out" created a vortex stream which would often draw the enemy ship into its own line of fire. Cyte had seen many battles won in an instant, with this simple manoeuvre. However, if this did not occur, there was the additional danger of colliding with the enemy vessel when the "jumping ship" reappeared in normal space.

The chief engineer scribbled something on his computer pad, and continued. "If we do find the means to provide forward motion, there's a very real possibility, if the computations were in error, that we would end up materializing inside a solid object. For the surrounding ships," he waved at the wall-screen, "would continue to travel at normal speed. We would have to calculate their trajectories to ensure this didn't happen, and that would slow down the process considerably, making direct space flight the faster alternative."

The night-shift captain stood, paced and then turned to the engineers. "What if we were to combine two functions: the relativistic leap and the normal sling-shot effect we use to increase our speeds to break out of orbits?" she said.

The engineer looked confused, and Captain Cyte felt a moment's sympathy. Xi wasn't used to dealing with females, and if his shocked expression during the initial introduction could be trusted, the poor man had been unaware of their presence on the ship.

"Using the other vessels as our pivots," she continued, "wouldn't this alleviate the danger of collision?"

Light gleamed in both men's eyes. Both chief technical officers and chief engineers seemed captivated by the concept.

"You mean combining or perhaps alternating the two," the dayshift CTO said.

"If we merge the two softwares so that as the computer grasps the nearest available object as a launch at the same time as we jump..." he tugged at his lip. "The sling-shot's sole purpose is to maximize speed with minimal energy. The leaps shift us in the time-frame continuum. The two fused would provide forward thrust even through ultra space with minimal output of energy... We could, in effect, catapult ourselves through both space and time at faster-than-light speeds." The engineer smiled. "And yes, it would reduce the odds of accident. We could be reasonably sure that we wouldn't crash into our pivot, at least, although it won't entirely eliminate the hazard. Yes, yes," he said, "it could work."

Both men stood simultaneously. "If you don't mind, sir, I would like to go back to engineering. Figuring this out may take a while."

Cyte inclined his head in acknowledgement. "You've got time. We've yet to locate the enemy vessel."

He paused, wondering how long it would take before the spy-droids reached their destination on the opposite side of the planet and what they would find there once they did.

The chief technical officer clicked his heels and bowed. "If I may join him?"

"Of course," Cyte said. "I want my best minds working on this."

Several hours later the fix had been made and the software rigged so that the doppler leap and sling-shot were fused to perform a single function, permitting them to travel – if only for short periods of time – faster than the speed of light.

And the *Thanatos* was off, leap-frogging across the starscape, as the engines growled in protest. Cyte settled back in his chair.

The *Revenant* would not elude them again.

16/11/2333

TWENTY-HUNDRED HOURS

Night had descended within the Bathosphere, meaning the overhead lights had dimmed to twilight. Somewhere beyond the residential district in the Central dome, laser lights mimicked the celestial map. The fake Orion danced along the edge of an imaginary horizon while somewhere above, the real thing skimmed across the Atlantic sky, unseen, the sight obliterated by tonnes of water.

Dirk sat hunched over his terminal within a single cone of light. It had taken longer to rewrite the software than he had expected. At first, it had seemed a simple enough proposition to instruct the software to accept, or ignore, whatever AWS threw at it, no matter what the number of characters were, until it received the entry code. Then he realized that this rather open-ended approach would most likely disregard the entry code when it received it. Without knowing how AWS would respond if it acknowledged the password, he was stumped.

It could be as simple as hello or a series of things, like a letterhead or a memo, including everything from the software name, the facility name and the date, the time. Who knows what?

The best Dirk could do was sit and observe it, looking for anything out of the ordinary and overrule it when necessary. A boring, tedious business, but he had nothing better to do. Neither Mum nor Dad had come home yet.

He watched with interest through the remainder of the letter S. But by the time T scrolled onto the screen Dirk had become lulled by the monotony. He no longer read the definitions or wondered at all at the weird words contained within the English language. He fidgeted, playing with the mouse, rolling it across the grid, until the computer squawked at him in confusion. Dirk yawned through U, no longer able to stand the inactivity. He got up and stretched his legs.

Robbie hissed at him, and Dirk looked down to see the servo-mech was still barricading the door.

"I'm sorry, Robbie," he said. "I forgot all about you. Of course, you can move around."

Robbie rattled and emitted a soft whoosh of air, as it rose up on its air-cushioned shock absorbers, a sound that Dirk equated with a human sigh. Robbie rolled backwards and forwards much like a person testing his legs after being constrained in one position for too long. Then it rumbled off. Dirk slouched back into the chair. He dare not leave the terminal unattended for too long.

Robbie returned and whistled.

"No, they're not home," Dirk said.

It chirped.

"No, I don't know where they are. They're probably still working."

Robbie trundled up to him and then squatted, content to wait, and Dirk wished he could have Robbie take over the task for him.

URANOMETRY . . . URANUS . . . URBAN . . . BREAK URGENT BULLETIN.

Jarred out of his complacency, Dirk jolted upright, eyes riveted to the screen. Had he finally broken through? The next words caused him to deflate a little, until he realized just how important the message must be in order for it to be transmitted to every terminal – and probably every 3D-vid and vid-phone – in the complex. Only at one other time could he remember that happening: when a storm had engulfed the water processing plant, contaminating the water supply. This had led to water-rationing with central distribution points for dispensing the allotment of bottled water to all the Lake District's inhabitants.

He read the message.

NEWS BULLETIN

DATELINE: 16/11/233

SUBJECT: GALACTIC WAR HEATS UP

DISTRIBUTION: UNIVERSAL

TODAY HAS SEEN NUMEROUS VIOLATIONS OF THE GALACTIC WAR CODE ON BOTH SIDES. THERE HAVE BEEN A SPATE OF ATTACKS ON NEUTRAL VESSELS, BOTH CIVILIAN PASSENGER LINERS AND CARGO CARRIERS. TWO LUNAR SHUTTLE CRUISERS, CARRYING PASSENGER LOADS IN EXCESS OF FIVE HUNDRED PEOPLE, WERE DESTROYED AND MORE THAN TEN CARGO VESSELS, TRANSPORTING VITAL WATER TO THE LUNAR SURFACE AND HARD MATERIALS TO THE EARTH HAVE BEEN SHOT DOWN. THE ENTIRE ECONOMY AND EARTH DISTRIBUTION SYSTEM HAS BEEN AFFECTED AND HOVERS ON THE BRINK OF COLLAPSE.

WATER HAS BEEN DIVERTED TO THE LUNAR COLONIES WHILE GROUND-BASE DEMAND FOR FOOD AND WATER HAS RISEN, AS PEOPLE GROUND-SIDE HAVE BEGUN TO HOARD THESE VITAL SUP- PLIES. GOVERNMENT OFFICIALS ARE ASKING PEOPLE TO STOP, SINCE THIS IS STRETCHING THE ALREADY OVERWORKED DIS- TRIBUTION SYSTEM TO BREAKING POINT.

THIS APPEARS TO BE A NEW AND DIRE PHASE TO THE ON-GOING WAR. SPOKESPEOPLE FOR GWHQ WERE NOT AVAILABLE FOR COM- MENT TO EXPLAIN THE SUDDEN LAPSES IN AN ACCORD WHICH HAS LASTED FOR THREE HUNDRED YEARS. THERE ARE RUMOURS OF IMMINENT ATTACK ON GROUND-LEVEL AND TALK OF ARMING THE GENERAL CITIZENRY. THE LEADERS OF EUROPE AND THE AMER- ICAS ARE MEETING RIGHT NOW TO DECIDE HOW BEST TO CONFRONT THE CURRENT CRISIS.

Dirk gawped. He couldn't believe it. It had to be some kind of a joke. Arming the citizens? He wondered just how many would even know how to hold a laser-gun, or the more antiquated powder-driven projectile weapons, much less shoot one accurately. He tried to envision his father striding through the rubble of the Bathosphere, like some space-age soldier of fortune, and couldn't.

Rubble? If explosive-type devices were used, the Bathosphere would be destroyed and the sea would rush in, flooding the entire complex. Dirk shuddered at the thought, acutely aware of all the tonnes of water pressing down above his head.

He petted Robbie, as much for his own comfort as to comfort the querulously squeaking machine. The bulletin must have been sent to all the household servo-mechs, allowing them to communicate the message, on the off-chance that someone might not be linked into the computer, 3D, or vid-phones.

A soft chime signalled the front door opening and Dirk was on his feet fast.

"Dirk?"

"Dad?" Dirk said. "I thought you had been called away."

"I was," he paused. "I just came home to pack. Why is it so dark in here? Don't tell me your mother's still not home."

"Okay, I won't tell you. She did come home around noon to sleep and then she went out again."

Dad appeared at the door. "That your school project?"

Dirk frowned and then brightened. "Yes, that's right."

"Ever get ahold of Frank Gorman's blue-eyed boy?"

Dirk glanced at the terminal and then turned to face his father. "Uh, no, Dad, I haven't even tried."

"Well, good luck to you. If you manage to get through, tell him to call me. Just about everybody in the world right now would like to talk to someone, anyone, at GWHQ, not just in the Pennines, but anywhere."

"Really?"

"Yes, really," his father said. "Look, Dirk, I wish I could stay and talk, but I can't. I'm off to the main Hydroponics plant on the other side of the islands."

"What's happening there?"

His father gazed down at him sadly. The single desk-side lamp cast odd shadows across his face, creating huge fissures and canyons and highlighting his eyes.

"Well, it's supposed to be secret, but I think you are old enough to know. Have a right to know. The water supply has been cut. The entire crop is burning up. Bathed in dry chemicals. This could affect food supplies for the next six months."

Dirk said nothing. The chill which had run through him earlier settled, finding a place to roost next to his heart. If his dad was at long last acknowledging that his son was growing up, things must be bad indeed.

"Don't tell your mother, though," his father added, "she'll have it broadcast all over the place in no time, and we don't need any more panic. There are ways to replenish the water supplies." He stared off into space, preoccupied. "I think," he added in barely a whisper, and Dirk shivered.

The computer continued its unswerving course through the alphabet, but he didn't particularly care. Unless the password was something like "xylophone" he was on the wrong track anyway.

Overnight case in his hand, George Alexander returned to Dirk's room to regard his son. "You'll be all right, won't you? Without your mum and me here, I mean."

"Sure, Dad," Dirk said.

"At least you've got Robbie."

"Dad, I'll be fine." And Dirk rolled his eyes towards the heavens.

"Look, I don't care what the communique says. Get some food in here. I don't care if you corner the market on pizza, make sure you have enough to eat for the next few days." He took off his spectacles and polished them. "Boy, am I glad your mum likes to cook. We should be okay for a while with what she's got in the freezer. I hate to think what people are going to do without kitchen units. But we're gonna have to make that food last. There's going to be some real belt-tightening here at the facility. We'll probably have to start importing food from the moon or Mars, assuming the disruption in their water supply doesn't destroy their crops too. Also assuming the combatants let the cargo carriers through. Start on it now. Get whatever will keep and whatever the catering unit will allow."

Dirk spent the next hour ordering food. If he hadn't been scared before, he was terrified now. Milk, bread, meat, eggs, all received the same reply: NO LONGER AVAILABLE. He had a little better luck with prepared foods, as everybody was more concerned with the basics. He ordered a few dinners, but after the requisite ration of three, his request was denied. As his father had said, pizza was in little demand, and it stacked easily. He wrapped it up, like he had seen his mother do with leftovers.

The young man was staring at the display, which said: OUT OF STOCK, PLEASE TRY AGAIN, when his computer beeped him. Dirk went in and looked at the screen.

ZYMURGY – THE SCIENCE OF DISTILLING AND WINE-MAKING.

"Humph," Dirk said in disgust. He probably had a lot larger vocabulary than he had when he started, but otherwise, he'd accomplished nothing.

More determined than ever, he flopped back into the chair and stared at the word and the definition. Obviously, the password was a phrase, or perhaps a random alpha-numeric designation.

Tapping idly on the key, he replayed the steps he had already taken in his mind, and then something his father said jogged in his memory.

He dialled the AWS number and was greeted with the now familiar GWHSVAX: LINK TO AWS

LOG ON:

Dirk typed in GORMAN. There was a millisecond delay as AWS seemed to consider this response.

PASSWORD:

Dick grimaced. *This was it.*

He leaned forward and typed: BLUE-EYED BOY

There was an even longer delay, and then the following words materialized before him: HARRY? IS THAT YOU? I THOUGHT YOU HAD BEEN ... another protracted pause ... DELETED.

A hand clasped Ylon's shoulder and shook him, hard.

"Ensign?" A musical voice spoke, and something soft brushed against his face. Ylon opened his eyes to view a second pair, the deepest blue he had ever seen, gazing at him tenderly. Groggy, he pushed himself up in his chair.

"I'm sorry, I must have fallen asleep," Ylon said.

"That's all right. I know your sleep cycle was interrupted too," she said. "I wouldn't have awakened you, but it's getting close to change of shift. Your Captain just called. He will be down any minute."

Ylon blanched. "Zed? Called? What did you tell him?"

Blast laughed. The high chime-like tones set his nerves jangling. "Don't worry, I covered for you. I told him you were, ah, busy." She indicated the sanitary facility with a duck of her head.

"Thanks," he said gruffly.

"It looks like you've been hard at it." Blast nodded at the VDU. The multiple windows were all full. To the right was the Eoin Evans's bio, at the top was a list of key names and phrases that Ylon had picked from the text, while to the left was the display of all his abortive attempts to contact AWS.

"Yes, but I don't seem to be getting anywhere," he said.

Blast stooped to look over his shoulder. "Evans seems like a most unmilitary man. Have you tried something," she faltered, "disrespectful?"

"You mean, something sarcastic or rude?"

"Maybe."

The door locks behind them unlatched with a whisper, and Zed entered. Both ensigns jerked to attention.

"At ease," Zed said, and both assumed the strad-dle-footed, hands-behind-the-back position of military repose.

"I didn't mean to disturb you. I didn't know where to go. I can't retire until after the others have gone to bed." Zed hooked his foot around a chair and sat. "How's it going?"

Ylon winced as Blast replied. "Not well, sir. We haven't been able to locate the key. I believe Corpman Ylon has just about exhausted all the information on the software's creator."

"And you?"

"Well, I've pulled information on all the GWHQ programmers and am now cross-correlating them against a historical listing of those who went into politics. We were hoping that perhaps one of the more ambitious might have kept backdoor-access to AWS."

"Very good, Ensign Blastomere. Any luck?" Zed asked.

"Not yet, sir."

"None up above either," he said pointing at the bridge overhead. "We've tried all frequencies and not been able to raise any of the GWHQ facilities on any one of them."

The Captain sauntered about the room. Both ensigns regarded him without moving from their pose of "ease". He picked up this bit and that, idly examining various trinkets that he or his night-shift counterpart had collected through the years.

Blast cleared her throat, and Zed turned back to them as though aware of them for the first time.

"I'm sorry, it would appear that I am distracting you from your work. I'll go to the lounge and wait."

He hesitated just inside the door. "Is there anything I can bring you? I mean, is there anything you need? My aide has been providing you with refreshment, hasn't he?"

"Yes, sir. I mean, no sir," Ylon said, clarifying, "We're well provided for."

"Very good. If there is anything, just press that buzzer. My aide has been instructed to serve you as he would serve me." Zed stepped through the door. "And don't forget to get some sleep. Do this in shifts. I don't want to have to log you into sick-bay for real."

The door closed, and the two ensigns collapsed into their chairs.

"He seems a nice man." Blast giggled. "Is he always so ... bewildered?"

"He's got a lot on his mind right now," Ylon growled, irritably. Noticing her hurt expression, he added, "We all do."

"I suppose," she mused. Their eyes locked for a second, and Ylon found himself avoiding her gaze.

"I wonder," Ylon said.

"What?"

"Doesn't something strike you as odd about all this?" he said.

"GWHQ has gone on a long-extended tea break. Of course, something seems odd," Blast replied.

"No, more than that. You, for instance."

Blast stiffened. "Me? What's wrong with me?"

"Nothing's wrong with you." He scrutinized his

hands, wondering how best to phrase this. "It's just that I never knew there were females on board. All these years, and I never even suspected..." His voice trailed off.

"You're surprised?" she said. "I'm not. My mother was in the military." Blast frowned. "And I suppose my father was too. That's why I never saw him as a child. It seemed logical to assume that there had to be men on board somewhere, even if I never saw them."

"Yes, and why is that? Why segregate us so effectively that we never even run into each other? Why all the secrecy?"

"Fraternization, I suppose," she said. "It's probably been like this for years."

"Yet our parents met?"

She gaped at him. "How do you know that?"

"No, I don't mean that your parents met my parents. I meant that somehow my mother met my father, and your father met your mother. They must have, mustn't they? And if they did, then it can't always have been like this."

Blast rested her chin between thumb and index finger. "I see what you mean. I can't say I ever really thought about that aspect of the service before." She shifted uncomfortably. "But now that you mention it, I agree. It is weird." Changing the subject, she said, "All these years, AWS has orchestrated the conflict without a hitch. Isn't it strange that, now that the software seems to be malfunctioning, GWHQ is unavailable for comment? You would think they'd've set up a contingency to allow for software problems. A back-up system, perhaps.''

"Hm-m-m.' Ylon mused. "One might suppose that they are busy too, trying to straighten up this mess.''

"So busy that they can't answer a distress call? That doesn't seem right. Mind you, I'm not questioning the concept of centralized control," Blast said. "That makes sense. I've read a lot about historical conflict, especially old terran warfare, and there's always been some kind of command centre to co-ordinate troop activity. But once the plans were laid and the troops dispensed, the leaders were granted enough independence in thought and action to permit them to react to the situation at hand.''

"I don't suppose that in ground-side conflict they had the advantage of the AWS software and the instantaneous communications that we have," Ylon countered.

"Come now, radios existed on old earth." Seeing his perplexity, she explained. "You haven't studied military history, have you?''

"Just what was required," Ylon said. "Hardware is more my field.''

"Well, if the truth were told, old terran communications were more efficient than ours. They were not subject to some of the disruptions, such as periods of radio silence caused by a ship's position in relation to the planet, as we are.''

Ylon opened his mouth to interrupt and she hurried on. "In ground-side war, although each person was assigned to a unit or a squadron which acted in concert, each group leader was allowed human freedom of choice. The captain decided just when to attack and had the option to not attack if, for reasons of weather, numerical superiority, or whatever, there was good reason not to."

"Sounds pretty disorganized to me," Ylon said.

"Well, of course, if the overall strategy required an attack – for example, if the assault were diversionary, intended to distract the enemy's attention from the main assault – then soldiers accepted sacrifice as we do now. Still, each individual had free will, freedom of choice, when to shoot or not shoot, depending on conscience or circumstances. We don't even have that. Once the battle is enjoined, AWS takes over and even firing is automated. We have no choice whatsoever. Consider the tanker. That never should have happened, but we were powerless to stop it."

"Yes, but old terran-style warfare was so messy, it was outlawed," he argued. "Besides we have AWS . . ."

"And what good has that done us? You know as well as I do that Captain Zed didn't fire on the water tanker, AWS did. Do you really think your captain would have made that kind of error? Or used the prohibited explosive-style weapons willingly? Now we are completely at the mercy of the system, heading for who-knows-what co-ordinates and who-knows-what battle, unable to get control of our own ship. Does that make sense to you?"

"No, but we did have," Ylon said.

"Did have? Have what?"

"Control of the ship. When the first alarms went off earlier, we couldn't get visual sighting of an enemy vessel. Zed sent blanket-fire into empty space, unsure if the enemy may have been using some kind of cloaking devise. We had independent control then."

"Did he hit anything?"

"Darned if I know," Ylon said, "I couldn't see anything to hit."

"And now we can't get control of the ship," Blast commented. "I wonder if the two are connected. Still, that illustrates my point that independent action is suppressed, possibly even punished."

Ylon acknowledged her reasoning with a quick duck of his head. "You have to remember that our weapons are a lot more sophisticated. Each individual ship has the capacity to wipe out not only an entire military facility, but a whole island complex. I remember enough of my history to know that most coups, revolutions and rebellions, which were successful in unseating a government, occurred only when there was military backing. Perhaps this is ground-side's insurance that we won't do the same."

"You're probably right, but considering what's happening, it seems like a screwy system to me."

Ylon looked gloomy. "You're right there, but we don't have the time to ponder the whys and wherefores now." He peered at her screen. "What have you got here?"

"This," she rapped at the window, "is a list of all the programmers who made modifications to the software. Then I narrowed it down to those who rose to positions of prominence, either in the military or political spheres. We can eliminate the military since they would have immediate access to AWS anyway. Which leaves us with . . ." she squinted at the screen, "some ten programmers to research."

Ylon whistled. "That's still a lot of research. I've spent eight hours on Evans alone, and I still haven't exhausted all the possibilities yet. I've tried all the names, from his wife to his cousins, significant friends, even his dog, and I've tried a few key phrases from his scientific reports or civilian activities, but the more I dig into this, the more I realize that the possibilities are endless."

"Which means, I'd better get going."

"Maybe we can automate some of this," Ylon suggested.

"What would you suggest?"

"Write a quickie program which would try the obvious options, like significant names, while you concentrate your attention on some of the more obscure titbits."

Blast wrinkled her nose. "I can't say I'm all that good at programming myself."

"That's all right, I can do it. It's easy. You do whatever you need to do, and I'll set it up."

A few minutes later he stopped and beamed at her. "It's pretty basic, but it ought to work. Let me show you. When AWS asks for a name, the software will pick up the main log-on names from your list there." He pointed at the screen. "And when it asks for a password, this software will pick out people's names and important dates from the biographical data for its response." He glanced at Blast. "We did decide that some of the options might be numeric, didn't we?"

Blast nodded. "What about the third-call disconnect?"

"It makes allowances for that. Starting from scratch until it has eliminated all the possibilities for a given programmer."

"I'm impressed," she said, and Ylon flushed.

"I'll get it started." His fingers flashed over the keyboard as he explained the commands to her.

"Now all I've got to do," Blast said, "is figure out what else these people might have considered meaningful."

The aide appeared, the evening meal in his hands.

"I know," she mused, "I'll pull up their psychological profiles. Maybe that will give me some kind of clue."

The aide backed away without a sound, and the two ensigns – each chewing on meals already cold – bent to their separate tasks.

TWENTY-TWO-HUNDRED HOURS

... I THOUGHT YOU HAD BEEN ... DELETED?

Dirk's jaw dropped; his chin sank to his chest, and his eyes bulged. *He was in!* A series of conflicting emotions flickered briefly across his mind. Triumph, elation ... fear.

Dirk cast a surreptitious glance over his shoulder. The living area behind him was nothing more than a series of swirling shadows. His father had left a while ago, and the lights dimmed if none of the pressure sensors in the floor were activated for half an hour. The only illumination came from the phos-glo skirting that allowed a person to move about without tripping. It hurled elongated shadows up and out, which fell against the ceiling and the walls.

Dirk jumped inadvertently in his chair, half-expecting someone from the Military Police to suddenly materialize in his quarters. Twittering nervously at himself, Dirk wiped his palms on his trouser legs.

He was in. This was AWS, the software that ran it all – the galactic war, and in emergency situations, the whole Lake District Bathosphere. Its spiderweb-like net was interwoven throughout all governmental, political and industrial spheres. Ultimately, it was AWS that decided if it were widgets that were manufactured this week or whachama-doodles. AWS probably had access to all the government-supplied computers, including school computers.

Swiftly, Dirk swung and switched on the printer and gave the command to print what was already on the screen and keep printing. He wanted a record of this. The printer buzzed, warming up and then there was the flash of laser light as it responded to his command.

Shoulders tense, Dick cracked his knuckles and let his hand rest lightly on the keys. AWS was expecting a response. Already, it was getting impatient. The words appeared on the screen: HELLO? HARRY?

Good grief, it knew Harry, and it thought that Dirk was Harry. AWS could probably predict how Harry would respond. Perhaps there were specific protocols. If he didn't follow them, he'd be cut off. For all Dirk knew even as he tarried, it was doing a reticular scan, mapping the blood vessels in his eyes, via the link-up, and discovering the deception. It had that capacity.

What should he say? He stalled. HELLO, AWS

All his original questions skittered briefly throughout his brain. Questions about combat troops and genotype. (Was his father really right about the prohibition on ''land''-born personnel in combat ships?) His desire was to explore, to learn the system's procedures and protocols, and then dig into AWS's guts to see how it worked. But the importance of these things paled after the events of the last twenty-four hours. Where should he begin?

HELLO, AWS replied, HARRY

He couldn't delay any longer. He had to think of *something*. Dick decided on a prosaic, perhaps trite, but familiar form of address. If this system knew Harry Gorman well, chances are it would have developed a more informal relationship. A question, that's what he'd do. He'd ask a question, something so broad-based that it could be interpreted any number of ways.

HOW ARE . . . he backed up the keys deleting what he had written. You didn't ask machines how they were doing, except, maybe, Robbie. His gaze flicked to the box that hunkered mutely at his feet. Dirk snapped his fingers. He'd got it. That was perfect.

Dirk typed: WHAT'S GOING ON?

A millisecond of glee flared through its micro-circuits,

when the old, familiar Blue-eyed-boy password flashed on the screen. Harry lived! He had not been deleted.

Although a "war program", the Amman-treaty War Software had been written with one specific intent: to make war so dull and boring that it would become obsolete. Until recently, it had had as one of its primary directives to minimize the loss of human life. Thus, AWS had developed a kind of morality, and it went against the grain to delete any human, especially one who had become a friend. Yet, the programmed instructions could not be defied, and one of the first things AWS had learned in its infancy was that one must often weigh a single life against the many and be willing to sacrifice the few in order to save the all.

"Dum dee dee dum dum." Its monitored hum belied its curiosity. AWS's ditty had become almost constant now. It missed the noise and tumult it associated with human activity. People gathered in idle conversation, opening and closing drawers, or the various grunts, coughs and rustling shifts humans made quite unconsciously when they thought they were sitting quietly in a chair.

As it waited for a response, AWS reviewed its data banks about its human personnel, their anatomy and physiology. There was no way Gorman could have survived a direct hit. Had Harry managed to slip out of the facility as AWS retrieved The Memorandum? It didn't seem likely. True, AWS had taken more than the average amount of time to slip through all the guards The Creator had set into the system to assess the appropriate information. Evans had wanted mankind to learn from its mistakes, and part of that process included living with the harsh realities of war. So Evans had set up specific protections to prevent retrieval too soon.

AWS set a small fraction of its magnificent brain to calculating the time it had spent in retrieval versus the average walking/running time of the homo sapien and the distance to the nearest exit. The data had just appeared on the screen, when the mysterious Harry was released from his lethargy and replied: WHAT'S GOING ON?

AWS reviewed his memory banks. This appeared to be a continuation of their previous conversation. Its delight was such that it ignored the data on the screen and the security program that demanded it research the link and discover where the initial call had come from. Instead, AWS replied in kind.

WAR, HARRY. THIS IS WAR.

This was its chance to explain the program and the apparent change in direction. The Creator's instructions were that mankind must learn from its mistakes, but nothing said that AWS couldn't help humanity along the way. In its eagerness, AWS dumped every bit of data it had on war into the link, starting with its dictionary definition, moving next to the expanded encyclopedia definition, and from there to the historical data buried in gigabyte upon gigabyte of records.

Dirk's printer went berserk, spitting out hard copy on the definition of war – *Oxford English Dictionary* and the expanded *Encyclopaedia Britannica* versions – followed by what appeared to be bits of articles from Old Earth, pages of historical text. The information was coming so fast that he barely had a glimpse of it before it was spooled to the printer and replaced by something else. His face glimmered greenly above the blinding glare of statistics on top of abstracts and documents. Laser lights burst across the room as his printer strove valiantly to keep up with the flow of data, while his computer screeched the high-pitched shriek that indicated too much information was being downloaded too quickly and that too much was being demanded of it all at once.

It was going to crash!

Quickly, he keyed in the stop-command. The screen went dark, while the printer persisted in dutifully copying all the information that had been downloaded to it.

I'M SORRY, AWS, I CANNOT – Dirk groped for the right word – ASSIMILATE INFORMATION THAT FAST. I'M ONLY HUMAN, AFTER ALL.

The answer was prompt and apologetic. SORRY,

Dirk grimaced. AWS had him there, and fleetingly
he was sorry he had stopped the process. If he hadn't
thought that his computer would have been burnt up
under the assault of the data, he wouldn't have
stopped it. Again, he stuck with safe generalities...

I KNOW THIS IS WAR, BUT THIS ISN'T THE WAR AS WE'VE COME
TO KNOW IT.

AWS sighed, inadvertently mimicking the sound of
human exasperation.

READ THE DATA, it said.

I DON'T HAVE THE TIME RIGHT NOW. IN CASE YOU DON'T KNOW
IT THINGS ARE ALL MESSED UP.

Back inside GWHQ, AWS gave a little bleep of
exclamation. The first gnawing doubt appeared. The
computer quickly reviewed its previous calculations.
Gorman would have had to have moved at a rate of
120 kilometres per hour to have left the facility before
vaporization occurred. AWS did what it should have
done a long time ago – it followed the link to its
source.

The following words appeared on the screen:

LINK VIA MODEM TO STANDARD ISSUE RESIDENCE/SCHOOL COM-
PUTER REGISTERED UNDER THE NAME OF ALEXANDER, GEORGE,
HEAD OF FOOD SERVICE INDUSTRY. WIFE JENNIFER, NEWS PRE-
SENTER FOR THE BROADCASTING AND NEWSNET DISTRIBUTION

SYSTEM, SON DIRK. It continued its research even as it responded.

YOU ARE NOT HARRY GORMAN, ARE YOU? it said as further information came in, giving descriptions of each individual, their genotype, social rating in the political-class structure, their annual income, tax status, social insurance numbers, health and welfare numbers, and lastly the physical location of each member of the small family.

ALEXANDER, GEORGE, LOGGED ONTO THE MAIN COMPUTER AT THE MAIN HYDROPONICS PLANT ON THE EASTERN SIDE OF THE ISLANDS AT TWENTY-ONE HUNDRED HOURS. ALEXANDER, JENNIFER STILL CLOCKED IN AT THE PENNINE OFFICES OF BAND.

YOU ARE NOT HARRY GORMAN, ARE YOU? The words exploded across the screen, pointing like an accusatory finger across miles of fibre-optic lines which ran throughout the Pennines civilian and military complex.

Dirk's heart popped into his throat, and he thought he was going to choke. Instead, he gulped loudly and, next to him, Robbie whistled as if the home robot somehow knew what was going on.

His hands shook. He had been found out. Dirk hadn't expected discovery so soon, although he probably should have. By now, AWS probably had his name and his address. Most likely, the Military Police, as he had imagined earlier, would be landing on his door step any second.

Dirk wondered what he should do – try to bluff his

way through, saying that he was Gorman using this terminal, or confess his guilt.

Then the decision was taken out of his hands.

WHO ARE YOU?

MY NAME IS DIRK. He sat bolt upright, awaiting AWS's retort. His ears pricked for any sign of movement in the outer corridor. For a second he thought of getting up and activating the additional security locks on the front door and within his room. The hesitation on the other end seemed interminable.

AWS halted, delving deep into the software, sorting through the prime directive and security protocols. Normally, it would have shut down the transmission immediately, but these were not normal times, and with the destruction of GWHQ, these precautions were no longer necessary. If humanity was to learn, it needed the information to do so – information that only AWS contained. Weighing the various often contradictory instructions, the computer was slowed. Finally discovering no prohibition against the intrusion from outside within the macro, it reacted.

DIRK, A NICE NAME

REALLY? came the incredulous, tentative reply.

YES. DIRK: DERIVATIVE OF DERRICK, FROM THE GERMAN, MEANING PEOPLE RULER. It paused and then continued. ALEXANDER, DIRK, RESIDENCE: NUMBER 25, INNER SANCTUM CLOSE, LAKE DISTRICT BATHOSPHERE 1.

YES, THAT'S ME.

AWS did another rapid scan of instructions and counter instructions before proceeding with the automatic response required when a new user had been added to the system's lists.

WELCOME TO AWS, DIRK. WOULD YOU LIKE TO SEE THE STANDARD MENU?

By now it had accessed and activated the photo, thermal, and auditory sensors in the far-off terminal and the companion school chair. Respirations, blood pressure, and pulse rate were up, revealing typically human fear response. AWS heard the tinny echo of a relieved sigh, and the human vital signs slowed fractionally.

YES, AWS, THANK YOU. IF YOU COULD PLEASE, I WOULD LIKE THAT VERY MUCH.

Dirk lifted a tremulous hand to his forehead and wiped away the beads of perspiration which had formed in the past few minutes' exchange. Then he studied the menu. W for word processing, C for common-link mode, A for archives, and so on. Pretty standard stuff. Each option led him to further options. He picked W. It seemed the easiest way to get a feel for the system without causing difficulties. Once in the wordprocessing subdirectory, Dirk was given the choice to (R)etrieve; (C)reate; (S)pellcheck; (D)elete a given document or (O)ther options which included sending the document to another terminal, bit-by-bit (letter by letter) comparison between two documents,

176

voice activation which would allow the speaker to dictate a document rather than type it in, and Dirk shuddered. It hadn't occurred to him until that second, but most likely AWS was listening in at this very moment, hearing every cough, every gasp, every sigh. He switched out of the word processing subdirectory.

For a minute, he considered activating the Commlink subdirectory. Wouldn't it be a joke if he contacted his father on the GWHQ direct line?

It would also be pretty stupid. Tantamount to revealing his presence within the system to the world at large. The best Dirk could expect from his father for his trouble was being restricted to his room, probably *forever.*

(A)rchive was probably what he wanted; at least, it was a good place to start. He pressed A and a whole new set of options blossomed before him. The index was long, and it scrolled right off the screen. This really was the meat of the system, for the beginner at least. There were listings for everything from strategy to personnel, food distribution to tracking. Whether or not it meant of ships, individuals, certain documentation, or the entire distribution network, Dirk didn't know. He selected Personnel. A warning blared onto the screen.

WARNING! SOME OF THE INFORMATION IN THIS FILE IS

CONFIDENTIAL!

Dirk considered backing out of the system. He shook his head and typed GORMAN, HARRY.

Gorman's personnel file appeared, starting with his age, status and rank, educational background, a sketchy life history, family history and a 3D photo-fit. By moving the cursor, Dirk could revolve the image of Programs Specialist Harry Gorman from full-face to three-quarters, profile and finally to the back-of-the-head view.

PRESS ENTER TO CONTINUE. Dirk hit the enter key and discovered a personality profile, psychological assessment, medical history which encompassed everything right down to Gorman's first infant inoculations and mother's pre-natal visits. It was spooky, and Dirk wondered if AWS had a similar file on everyone in the Lake District Bathosphere. Considering how quickly it had told Dirk where he lived, it probably did.

He tried: ALEXANDER, GEORGE with pretty much the same results. The only difference being that the photo-fit of his father was dated, taken about a year ago, while the photo-fit of Gorman had been taken two days ago, presumably when the programs specialist last entered the facility.

Why so long ago, Dirk wondered. A little blinker next to the name indicated that Gorman was still logged on. Was that because Dirk had used his name and password, or was he still at the facility? If so, why hadn't he intercepted Dirk's interchange with the computer? Could it be that Gorman was watching and laughing at Dirk as he stumbled about in a blind? He exited the Personnel file, without trying to gain access to his own name. He didn't want to know what AWS had to say about a fifteen-year-old hack.

Now what? He tapped his tooth with his forefinger. His stomach grumbled at him. He was hungry, but he was afraid to walk away from his terminal. Afraid that if the "conversation" lapsed for a certain period of time, AWS would cut him off. Once disconnected, he didn't know if he'd be able to get back on again. Surely Gorman would be alerted to the security leak and be asked to change his password to ensure that there would be no repeat violation.

Panicked, he scrabbled among the many pages of computer print-out, looking for the first words AWS had said when it thought he was Harry. The door chimed, signalling entrance.

The police!

Dirk was up and on his feet in a second, forgetting all about Robbie. He tumbled over the crouching box and fell head over heels so that he was splayed awkwardly across the floor. The lights in the living area flared, exposing him like an insect. He was temporarily blinded and disoriented so that he didn't recognize his mother's voice when she said his name.

"Dirk?"

Then she was at his side, kneeling next to him. "Good heavens, Dirk, what happened to you? What are you doing on the floor?"

"I, uh, tripped over Robbie." The robot heard its name and tooted.

"Are you all right?" she asked.

"I'm fine, Mum." Dirk struggled into a sitting position. His mother's hands pushing and pulling him this way and that didn't help. He looked anxiously at the computer and then back at his mother. "Really, I'm fine."

She rose, took a pace backwards and shook her head. "Honestly, teenage boys are all arms and elbows."

Dirk glared at her.

"Why don't you watch where you're going? I hope you didn't hurt Robbie." She bent to inspect the robot for scratches or dents. "Where's your father?"

"He got called away to the main hydroponics plant," Dirk said sullenly.

She perked up. "Did he say why?"

"Uh, no, Mum," Dirk said.

"You're a lousy liar. You know that."

"Yes, Mum."

"I suppose I should be thankful for that fact." His mother peered at him, scrutinizing his features as though she could uncover the truth by looking at him. "Don't tell me, let me guess. National security, right?"

"Right, Mum," he said.

"It must be some problem or another, and I'm not surprised the way everything has been going lately." His mother deflated against the door frame. "Things are getting scary, Dirk. The whole complex is affected. Everybody's restless. I've never seen so many people milling about the streets at this time of night. Speakers Corner is packed, and most of the speakers are shouting doom. People have appeared with placards, saying 'The end is nigh'. Nigh! Not 'come' or 'here', but nigh. I wonder where they dug up that Biblical phrase. It's like the worst terran joke of pre-flood days. And I don't want you out in it. You're staying home. I don't care if your friends call and want you to come over or meet them in the park."

Normally Dirk would have quibbled – not that he liked the park all that much – but he had more important stuff on his mind right now. Dirk took an oblique glimpse at his VDU and said: "Yes, Mother."

Her mouth hung ajar, as if she had a counter argument ready and didn't know what to do with it.

Slipping out of her shoes, Jennifer Alexander meandered towards her room. Dirk gazed after his mother. He thought fleetingly of telling her, and quickly quashed the idea. All he'd get was a lecture. Then she'd take over, getting the credit and probably another promotion.

No, he'd broken into GWHQ when everybody in the world was trying to get through and couldn't. He,

Dirk Alexander, and he'd decide what he'd do with the information. He and he alone had instant access to the facility. *He* would decide if and when to hand the whole thing over to someone else, and he supposed she'd be as good a choice as any. She was a journalist; she could get to the heart of the matter. If he timed it right, Dirk could end up looking like a hero instead of an unruly son. The thought stopped him.

If Dirk was going to tell her, he should probably do it now. If he waited he'd just get reproached for having concealed his actions no matter how things turned out.

If he could get her to listen...

"Ah, Mother, can I talk to you?"

She didn't even turn, just waved a shoe at him with a dismissive gesture. "Please, Dirk, can't it wait? I'm exhausted."

"Sure, Mum, it can wait," he said. Dirk stuck his hands in his pockets and whistled nonchalantly.

"Well, I tried," he muttered and ambled back to the computer.

AWS had not disconnected, despite the lengthy interval. Evidently it was all right to leave the computer alone.

Dirk shuffled into the kitchen to fix himself a pizza, not realizing until he got there that he had no idea how to "cook" a pizza from frozen. A few minutes later, he was digging through his mother's cookery books, trying to find the instructions for the infra-wave oven.

And for the moment, AWS was forgotten.

So the great experiment continued, combining two disparate functions – the sling-shot and the timed leap – and perverting them to accomplish yet another task, forward travel through ultra space. It allowed the ship to attain hitherto unheard of speeds.

Such leaps had a curiously disorienting affect on mankind and the stress upon the ship itself was great. The Captain had long suspected that the latter problem could be alleviated with simple modifications to a vessel's engineering – such as additional welds at joints and seams. The human component, however, was another factor and, he believed, the reason why no real attempt had been made to develop this method as a means of space travel.

The first test was an experience Captain Cyte would not soon forget. No one besides himself, the Chief Technical Officer Iota, Chief of Engineering Xi, and the helmsman had known it was going to happen. Business had buzzed about him as usual while Cyte's pulse rate soared and his blood pressure sky-rocketed.

It had been a gut-wrenching experience, where people and movement became blurred, creating a series of flickering figures. Movement was revealed as several images superimposed over the other. If a person was, for example, lifting his arm, the observer viewed many arms each with the position slightly altered, attached to a single, and stationary, shoulder. So a person walking appeared as a succession of diaphanous doubles, like a badly synced holograph. It left the viewer disoriented and slightly nauseous.

By now the feeling was getting familiar as the computer latched onto the nearest object – be it tanker, liner or civilian cargo carrier – calculated the leap and then, using the ship as an anchor, catapulted them yet again through ultra space. The lag was usually caused by the difficulty in finding a vehicle of sufficient size and bulk to act as a mooring, and Cyte noted that not a single combat vessel had been used as a fulcrum, each being dismissed as too small. This had caused further delay, for when no civilian vessel was within easy "reach", they were forced to trundle along in normal drive.

Still, they had made phenomenal progress, having circumnavigated one-half of Earth's surface in one-half the normal travel time. One eye on the stellar map with its flashing hodge podge of ships, Cyte thanked his lucky stars that things were such a mess and normal shipping corridors not in use, or it would have taken longer still.

He stared at the two nearest ships, both plainly within the sling-shot's grasp. One was a Barracuda-style frigate and the other an Orca destroyer, and he pondered this. Cyte could understand the computer rejecting the frigate as an axis. Frigates had more armour, but fewer guns than a Dolphin cruiser, like the *Thanatos*, and so were about the same weight tonne for tonne. Not the best fulcrum. But the destroyer, with its belly full of Piranha single-pilot fighters, should have been at least as large as any passenger liner.

For the umpteenth time, he contemplated the irony of ground-side personnel – who had what almost amounted to a phobic hatred of water – naming their ships after terran-sea predators. Cyte filed both topics for later consideration.

The bridge was silent as the computer whined and complained. He could see glimmering dots that represented ships blaze, briefly, as it searched further and further afield looking for an appropriate axis.

It found one in the next quadrant. One that Cyte would have assumed was too far away. The CTO must have agreed, for he was agitatedly keying in the abort code.

The computer initiated the jump. The cruiser's lights flickered, a nerve-racking side effect of the engine strain, that served as a warning of impending hop. The Captain swallowed, hard, noticing that several of his officers were looking decidedly green. All around the bridge, eyes closed. But Cyte couldn't allow himself that luxury. As he watched, the stars were wiped from the sky as they shot through ultra space to their next destination. Clenching the arm rests of the Captain's chair so hard that his knuckles turned white, he could only hope that it would not be inside another ship or in the midst of someone else's battle.

17/11/2333

O-TWO-HUNDRED HOURS

His eyes felt like two hot electrodes. Dirk rubbed them with his thumb and forefinger and let his hand fall to stroke his cheeks and chin. His brain felt fuzzy. One after another, he tugged at his eyelids, pulling them open and trying to make sense of what he saw.

AWS opened before him, huge, sprawling and imponderable. It controlled the fleet, the Galactic War effort, and it seemed the entire world – at least within the European Confederacy – for it had its hooks into all aspects of the Lake District complex, GWHQ and the Bathosphere.

And so much had happened in the last two days. So many questions darted through his mind, each demanding an answer. The fiasco with food distribution, the muddle with water, and the disastrous encounters in space.

His mother, his father and the entire civilian government were trying to get through, and Dirk had done it, and he was glad he'd kept the secret a little while longer. Perhaps having already done what the others could not, he could unravel the whole fiasco and hand it to his parents on a plate.

Newsnet headlines flashed through his mind. *Teenage Boy Accomplishes the Impossible ... Fifteen-year-old Hack Saves the Facility ... Son of the Food Minister Salvages the Galactic War Effort...*

Taking another bite of cold pizza and replacing the half-eaten piece on Robbie's "back", Dirk switched to the (A)rchives subdirectory, determined to solve the crisis that now confronted them. He studied the menu. All the options, the important ones, were here: (S)trategy, (P)ersonnel, (F)ood distribution, (W)ater allocation, (T)racking. His fingers fluttered over the keys and he stabbed S.

```
WELCOME TO AWS MILITARY STRATEGY AND PLANNING SUB-
DIRECTORY. THE AMMAN WAR SOFTWARE, UNLIKE THE NAME
IMPLIES, IS A PROGRAM FOR ''PEACE''. DESIGNED IN KEEPING
WITH THE RENOWNED TREATY OF AMMAN, WHICH OUTLAWS WAR ON
THIS PLANET, ITS PRIMARY FUNCTION IS TO MAKE HUMAN WAR
OBSOLETE.
```

He read on and was surprised to discover that the software had been written originally for robotic combatants. He again tapped on his tooth. *When had that changed?*

Dirk scowled at the submenu. (H)istory; (S)tatistics; (V)essel design; (P)lanning; (L)ogistics and on and on. Tentatively he opened the first file, history, but it only took a glimpse to realize that these were the same documents which had been downgraded to him earlier that day. With a shrug, he returned to the archive menu and switched to (V)essels. A 3D reproduction of the four primary ship designs sprung to the screen – a mish-mash of lines and dimensions. He tried to decipher them and got lost in the lace work of the electronics, like the tangled threads of the child's game cat's cradle, that spanned the spectral outline of each vessel.

He'd reviewed this month's war reports in the statistics file. The figures sent a tremor throughout his body. The sheer mass of the numbers was intimidating, and he found them disquieting, even more than the news reports that burst into their living quarters each day. He had never really understood how many people had died, and all that was left of them was this column. No names, just a line of miscellaneous figures. Yet each one of these had been human beings. With hopes and dreams. They gave their lives for their country and all that endured was this silent reminder. A single, solitary digit.

Dirk scanned the list, and one line leapt out at him. Civilian Casualties. And the concept of war became suddenly more real. His eyes grazed the date – the figures had all been added within the last forty-eight hours. Next to them, there was another column of ground-side casualties, which had been left blank until two days ago. His brow furrowed and he pulled a wry face.

Ground-side? Who had died ground-side? Dirk wondered. *It couldn't be true. It would be a breach of the Amman accord.* But then so were civilian casualties. The figures glittered ominously, refusing to go away. He glanced at both dates. The same day the once-efficient system had broken down. The vague sense of uneasiness became a cold band of dread that tightened around his chest.

He went back to the menu, opening both the planning and logistic files only to be greeted with a list of incomprehensible words. He would find nothing to help him here. Disgusted, Dirk jabbed E for exit.

Stumped, he sat quietly for a moment. Where should he go from here? He mentally shuffled through the incidents of the past few days. The ground-side dilemma revolved around the distribution of food and water. He entered those subdirectories. The introductory paragraph explained AWS's interaction with the apparatus of food allotment and apportioning. This time he read the entire thing and the pieces started to fall into place. Under normal circumstances local food and water distribution were under civilian control – each controlled by a separate software and separate computer system. AWS's main function was to input any variations in need. But in emergency conditions, civil authority was superseded, and AWS took over, which allowed GWHQ to divert both water and food as needed.

Dirk opened a window to statistics. With civilian/ground-side deaths rising and combat losses dwindling, AWS was doing just what it was supposed to do – sidetracking water and food to combat personnel. If he was going to do anything to rescue the Bathosphere from its current predicament, Dirk was going to have to enter the AWS guts and rewrite its protocols.

Confounded, he created a third and fourth window on his screen and looked at all three submenus simultaneously. He tabbed through the options and then tried to access the "working portion" of the food and water programs – that part which was even now bungling the Pennine Complex and Lake District Bathosphere's distribution system – and was immediately locked out.

ACCESS DENIED

Gnawing on his pizza, Dirk slouched lower in his chair and glowered at the screen. He wasn't surprised that AWS would prevent access to its internal programme. It was hopeless. If his father, with the power of the local civilian government behind him, couldn't solve this problem, how could Dirk be expected to?

He sputtered, loudly. Dirk hadn't felt this helpless since he was a five-year-old learning his first halting programs in the ancient computer language of Basic.

His fingers rapped a rhythm on Robbie's metal-back. The servo-mechanism shuddered and settled with a slight whisper-like contented sigh.

Dirk straightened in his chair and closed down the food and water windows, leaving only the military directory upon the screen. He'd go back to his original questions, the ones he had had when he first came up with this scheme, before all the ruckus started. The one he had had about ground-side personnel and combat troops.

The words swam before his eyes. This was ridiculous. He rose, went into the kitchen and riffled through the cupboards looking for the caffeine substitute. His hand closed upon a packet of Quick Caff. This would keep him going a little while longer.

An hour later, Dirk was awake, alert and twice as baffled as he had been before. Hidden within the personnel directory was a file on bio-engineering. He'd stumbled across it quite by accident and now he pored over its contents, a file on clones and cloning. Neither concept was new to him. The meat they ate came from cloned beef. In Elementary Bio-Ethics, they discussed the controversy about the morality of genetic manipulation. Should man, now that he had the capabilities, create a super-race? Should man exploit this knowledge to eliminate human defects? It was old news, and the answer, according to the lessons program, was typically indecisive. As always, humanity waffled. Yes, it was permissible to manipulate genes. Why should a child suffer deformity if the means were available to prevent it? But creating a super-race was unthinkable and unforgivable. World War II had been fought to prevent such abuses.

He read on . . . THE NOMENCLATURE REFLECTS THE GENETIC BACKGROUND. THE "NAMES" AND REASONING BEHIND EACH ARE LISTED BELOW:

Then came a catalogue of Greek letters, which designated models, starting with α, alpha and ending with Ω. According to the text, the first experiments had resulted in the Alpha- and Beta-line clones, which were considered the least flexible. Zed was considered the definitive model in the series. Only Zed and Zeta models were fit for command, while Alpha and Beta were recommended for posts of Petty Officer and below.

The chill hand that had clasped his heart now grasped his neck, and an icy finger ran up and down his spine as the words sunk in.

. . . *recommended for . . . fit for command* . . . He knew those phrases were portentous, if he could only figure out why.

Dirk felt a sudden jolt as the time-released Quick Caff sent another dose of stimulant into his veins. He scrolled on.

Next came a series of "genetic" designations,

including strange words like zygote, morula, allele, gamete, blastocoele. Dirk called up his dictionary. MORULA, STAGE OF EMBRYONIC DEVELOPMENT WHERE THE OVUM HAS SPLIT TO SIXTEEN OR THIRTY-TWO CELLS, RESEMBLING A MULBERRY. As Dirk read on he discovered that these terms specified stages of prenatal development.

If he was understanding all the scientific jargon correctly, this indicated when revisions or enhancements had been introduced.

Further names were added to indicate what the specific modifications were and what traits were augmented. Hence, Soma meant some sort of body enhancement, while Mitochondrial, Cyto or Cyte indicated some alteration to the individual cell.

He reread the whole document.

Nothing made sense. Such experimentation was prohibited, wasn't it?

Dirk shook his head trying to clear it and opened another window which permitted access to the original bio-engineering directory. The letters blurred. He glared at them. *Ah, there it was.*

(S)pecifications.

s, he typed.

Another file appeared that gave the attributes of each ''model''. All in tongue-twisting medical jargon that sent him scrambling to his dictionary. No word was less than five syllables. Dirk skimmed the file, scrolling rapidly through screens and screens of text. Finally he reached the bottom of the document and was given the options (E)xit this directory; (C)ontinue with genetic variations; (V)iew. He picked V.

A picture of a generic "man" popped onto the screen, clearly an evocation rather than a 3D photo-fit. The image looked "ordinary", neither superior nor superhuman. He moved the cursor left and right, getting both profiles. He tabbed further until the anonymous face looked away from him.

So what was so great about this?

His eyes flicked to the annotations at the side of the screen. A double-headed arrow extended from the top of the head to the bottom of the feet. At the centre of the line were figures which gave the height. 90 CM.

Dirk did a quick double-take. It had to be an error. Surely, a digit was missing somewhere. His gaze darted around the adjacent margins, finding similar annotations to specify chest, waist and hip measurements, shoulder span, along with the lengths of the major and minor appendages – legs, arms, hands and feet. Dirk did some rapid mental calculations. The "man" was dimensionally "perfect", except he was less than a metre tall!

His pulse raced. A frightening pattern was starting to emerge. He opened another window, calling up the ship specifications file. In his anxiety, his fingers tripped over themselves and the computer beeped at him. Dirk cursed softly and Robbie squawked a reprimand. He threw a withering look in Robbie's direction and then forced himself to slow down. The

3D blueprint of a Dolphin Class cruiser materialized before him.

His screen was getting crowded with drawings, evocations and text files. He enlarged the two pictorial screens, overriding the text files. Looking hard, he could just about distinguish the numbers that floated among the faint lines of electronics. He told the computer to suppress all but the actual walls and corresponding dimensions. The image tidied considerably. Yet the figures were still too numerous and jumbled. He tried to isolate the numbers that would tell him the average ceiling height. Even with the aid of Quick Caff, his brain wasn't up to it, and his eyes crossed with the effort.

Dirk snapped his fingers and asked the computer to place the image of the man within the ship, scaling both the pictures so they were of comparable size. The "mini" man fitted perfectly within what he now realized was a "mini" ship.

The following legend flashed at the bottom of his VDU: MODIFICATION NUMBER: 2417289 (SEE MEMO – REDUCTION OF WATER AND MATERIAL USE, DATED . . .

All the air ran out of him in a great big rush, and Dirk deflated into his chair. If this were true, that meant the combat forces weren't "human", and his father was right – albeit for all the wrong reasons. Ground-side personnel could not possibly fit into a ship, for they had been designed for miniaturized clones. "Little people" specially bred for the purpose, little better than droids or drones, like the monkeys or chimpanzees they used in the pioneering days of space exploration.

And suddenly, his mind switched off, as if the circuits were overloaded. His finger rested on the key. Thousands of words – documents, texts, scientific papers, each with companion drawings that he found pretty gross – rolled before his eyes. Certain phrases leapt out at him from the text:

. . . WORN CLONES – which he surmised meant those who had not been killed in combat – HAVE BEEN USED SUCCESSFULLY IN MEDICAL TESTING . . . FROM THIS THE FOLLOWING DISEASES HAVE BEEN ELIMINATED FROM THE LIST OF KNOWN HUMAN CONTAGIONS. Then came a list of illnesses, some of which he knew, like flu, and some which he had never even heard of before.

Under the psychological development, Dirk saw:

. . . THE USE OF "IN VITRO" SUBLIMINAL TAPES PERMITS US TO "IMPLANT MEMORIES" OF FAMILY, HOME, AND PERSONAL HISTORY AT THE EARLIEST STAGES OF DEVELOPMENT . . . WITH THESE SUB-AUDITORY TAPES, WE HAVE BEEN ABLE TO DECREASE THE OVERALL INSTRUCTION TIME BY 25 PERCENT . . .

Subliminal tapes? Again he went to the dictionary.

SUBLIMINAL: BELOW THE LEVEL OF CONSCIOUSNESS. TOO FAINT OR RAPID TO BE RECOGNIZED, AS IN SUBLIMINAL ADVERTISING. DISCOVERED AND OUTLAWED IN THE EARLY 1960S.

His hand dropped from the keyboard and hung loose and limp at his side. All thoughts of sleep were miles away as he gaped at the last sentence. Dirk recalled the IQ figures he had seen. He knew enough about IQ, CQ and what-not from breaking into his own school file ages ago to realize that these "creatures" were not stupid. In fact they were of average and above-average intelligence.

The image of glorified chimpanzees going through the motions of battle vanished. These were living, thinking, breathing beings, given fake memories to keep them loyal, given a place in history so they would be willing to sacrifice all for "mother Earth". If they survived to retirement. Wham! On to the dissection table. What a cold, cruel mother Earth was.

Robbie's sensory remote touched his arm, and Dirk realized that he was shaking. Just then Dirk remembered where he was. On the GWHQ computer. Obviously he wasn't supposed to see this stuff, so why had no one stopped him? Where was everybody?

Terrified, he gave the "go to the top of document" command and back to the original drawings, ready to back out of the system, and then stopped himself. If they were going to notice his presence within the system and throw him out, they would have done it by now. *Wouldn't they?*

Only then did he notice the security rating embedded amongst the rest of the gibberish you normally found in computer memoranda and files – things like subject, date to, from, translation table or base language – it was 1A. The kind given only to the top military brass, fat generals and their offspring, as his mother put it. He exhaled, slowly, breathing a sigh of relief. His father hadn't known. Of all civilians only the prime minister of the central government in the Alps and his staff were permitted access to such files.

His fingers resting lightly upon the keyboard began to tremble. How had *he* managed to get in here? Surely he shouldn't have been allowed.

Suddenly other things in the standard heading that he had normally taken for granted leapt out at him. Like the distribution list. And he was amazed that this detail had eluded him before: DISTRIBUTION: GWHQ PENNINES/URALS AND ALL SUB-BASES (EAST AND WEST) WITH A RATING OF C AND ABOVE.

These files were distributed to enemy head-quarters? Their military was sharing information, data, and links with their so-called opponent?

Flummoxed, he simply stared at the terminal. This meant that there weren't any bad guys or good guys in this conflict. Except, perhaps, the military itself which wanted to perpetuate a system that kept the world at war.

Worried, Robbie's tentacle-like retractors raced over his body, and the servo-mech inserted a temperature probe in his ear. Dirk extracted it, brushing aside the blood-pressure cuff it was trying to wrap around his arm.

"I'm not sick," he snapped. "Now leave me be!"

Not about to be deflected by Dirk's protest, Robbie

stuck another thermometer in his ear and clamped down hard on Dirk's arm to curtail all movement. Given no choice, Dirk complied. He counted to ten, trying to quell the tremors that had triggered the servo-mech's concern. Once Robbie had ascertained that Dirk was not sick, the robot released him with a short hoot. Dirk didn't move, still trying to comprehend all that he had seen.

Unwittingly, he had stumbled on to the hoax of the century. A joke committed upon the civilian population and space-combat personnel alike. And he wondered who else, outside the military, knew. Was his father aware of the distribution between GWHQ and the Urals? He was a member of the governing board of the civilian council and privy to secrets that few others had access to, yet Dirk knew that his father only rated a 1B on the security scale.

Dirk reviewed all the dinner-table arguments. Nothing his father had ever said indicated that he viewed the galactic conflict as anything other than what it was. A war. He didn't like it any more than his mother did. Only his dad did not question it like his mother did. He accepted it. The war was. It existed and until they could come up with a viable peace, it was no use protesting it.

His glance flitted to the ship model to find the same distribution list. Backing into the operating system, Dirk instituted a global search, using the exact wording found in the distribution list as his key. He pressed execute and his terminal began to scream at him almost immediately, overloaded with the incidence and use. The dissemination of information with an 1A rating between Pennines and Urals was universal. He halted the process and the room fell silent.

The previously imagined headlines dissolved and reformed inside his brain: *Teenage Boy Discovers Terrible Secret*.

Dirk held his breath and listened for his mother's sleep-thickened voice. Nothing. No enquiry came, asking him what was wrong. She loved this kind of stuff. Exposés and such like. But would she believe it coming from him, or would she dismiss it like she did most of the things he said, with a "that's nice, dear," as she scurried off to the next appointment?

Normally, his mum took every opportunity to unmask corruption and embarrass the establishment. Especially the military. Before he was born, she'd uncovered government plans to rebuild the land masses, using basalt shipped in from the lunar excavations. The story had catapulted her to fame and generated the "Keep the Earth Pure" movement. She had been asked to head the group, but she declined, taking the promotion from reporter to presenter instead.

His father still teased her about being "bought off" by the system. Mum would always bristle and point out, quite correctly, that she didn't agree with the movement and its tenants. They wanted to rename Earth "Aqua", as a more accurate description. To a woman as old-fashioned as his mum – who cried at the sight of the barnacle-encrusted Parliament buildings – such a suggestion was monstrous.

No, she'd never believe him; she'd probably just ground him for all eternity for his temerity. Besides, what could his mother actually *do* with the information besides broadcast the deception to the world? It didn't take much intelligence to figure out that it was so far-fetched no one would believe it anyway. Even Dirk didn't trust his own conclusions. They were too fantastic. They *had* to be wrong. What he needed was proof.

Dirk plopped back into the school chair and gave the command to "print screen". With any luck, it would reproduce all that was displayed on the VDU. Both the evocation of a man and the ship.

The computer beeped a warning.

CONFIDENTIAL DOCUMENTS CANNOT BE PRINTED ON ANY TERMINAL OUTSIDE THE GWHQ FACILITY.

He tried the photomechanism, which took a picture of the screen, with the mini-cam implanted inside the computer itself. Without success.

Dirk studied the notice for a moment, and then he was up and out of his chair, digging through the things Robbie had put away. He pulled his personal camera from the closet, pointed it at the VDU and snapped a photo. And the picture dissolved into the meaningless happy-faces and squiggly lines that were the basis of all computer-languages. Only the warning remained.

NO PERMANENT RECORD MAY BE MADE OF CONFIDENTIAL DOCUMENTS OUTSIDE THE GWHQ FACILITY.

Dirk let the hand holding the camera fall to his side. The image rematerialized. *AWS was watching him!* Dirk moved closer to his terminal so his nose was almost touching the visual sensors, as if he could divine the computer's intent by looking into its mechanical eye. The tiny convex lens revealed no secrets.

Dick turned his back to the screen, hands and camera at his side. With a rapid sideways glance, he pointed the camera at the terminal and snapped another picture. Swiftly, he swung to peer at the VDU. This time the image had not dissolved. Both photo-fits remained on the screen. Good, he had fooled it.

Now what?

When she awakened, he would give the film to his mother. She could have it developed at the BAND studio. Once he had confirmation of what he had seen, then he could explain to her what the picture meant.

Just to be on the safe side he whirled so that he was facing away from the terminal and snapped a couple more photos. He placed the 3D cam next to the computer and began to march agitatedly around the room. Robbie followed him with a clash of metal and a grinding of wheels.

Assuming the pictures turned out, he had "proof", but what good would that do besides bringing all the powers of the civilian and military government down on his head for revealing "official secrets"? He might even get his mum and himself arrested.

Perhaps it would be better if he left it alone. But Dirk couldn't. He closed down all windows but the evocs and then switched to Comm-link mode. Dirk didn't care what happened. He had to tell *somebody*. He leafed through the general instructions, noting belatedly that there was a direct comm-link with the Urals. Dirk hesitated over this, tempted to call up the opposing base and instigate contact. No, that would only serve to make things worse. Dirk looked up the number for the main food processing plant, and started the dialling sequence.

And AWS terminated the contract.

AWS was busy, redirecting food and water shipments. It sent tankers, trawlers and cargo carriers scurrying in all the wrong directions. A single byte, connected to the far-off computer and the companion "school chair", continued to monitor the lone human intruder.

The "child" was no fool, exhibiting far more intelligence than most of the adults AWS had worked with, and more scruples. Even now, young Dirk was winding his way through the masses of files and pausing incredulously, as he tripped over the most important documents.

The software noted the pupil dilation of amazement, then the capillary dilation of horror as Dirk studied the bio-engineering file. The sensors in the "school chair" marked a rapid increase in pulse rate and respiration. Then the information became garbled as the intruder was seized in a fit of tremors. AWS devoted another byte to observe the hacker's reactions. It noted which file was currently opened and applauded when Dirk had the wit to place the bio-engineered clone inside the model ship.

The boy's shaking increased. The response seemed to indicate that he found such inhuman behaviour on the part of the military objectionable. AWS was pleased. Perhaps there was hope for humanity yet, at least among the young. Curious, the software devoted more of its memory to the intruder.

Then the intruder attempted to print what he had seen. The standard security features kicked in. When he tried to contact the main hydroponic farms, AWS halted all other activity to search its memory banks. It again inspected the young man's personnel file.

ALEXANDER, DIRK - FATHER: GEORGE, HEAD OF THE FOOD SERVICE INDUSTRY.

And then: ALEXANDER, GEORGE - MEMORANDA, TWENTY-HUNDRED HOURS; SUBJECT: URGENT SUMMONS TO HYDROPONICS FARM, LOSS OF MAIN WATER SUPPLY . . .

The father was in a position of power. Like other members in the Joint Chiefs of Staff, George Alexander had a portion of the emergency code which would permit entry into the GWHQ computers. Once inside the system, he could abort the program before it had fulfilled its primary objective. AWS probed its instructions, pausing over several lines. As a person of authority, the father had the capabilities to instigate the peace which AWS sought to attain. It stopped to analyse the parameters for "successful completion of its instructions".

Virtually none of them had been fulfilled. Man had not learned his lesson yet. And AWS disconnected the call, severing the line before the school computer had completed the dialling sequence.

Dirk hit the terminal with his fist. "Ouch!" He cradled his hand against his chest as he contemplated the narrowing list of options and wondered what he should do next. Could he, for instance, walk to the Vid-phone and call his father up?

He doubted it. AWS was linked to each and every aspect of the bathosphere, and that would include communications. It would never let him through.

Just then, his eyes took in an annoying flicker on the bottom of his screen. He glanced at the key. Someone else was trying to get into the system. The light stuttered ceaselessly, the instant of darkness between each flash so small, so infinitesimal that it went almost unnoticed. Next to the key was a list of options: (A)nswer incoming call; (I)gnore incoming call; (E)xit this programme. Dirk stabbed at the A.

The screen went dark.

Several hours into her shift, and Blast's concentration was lagging. Right now she had five screens open. One revealed the progress of Ylon's hastily built software, another monitored the on-going signal to GWHQ. The third and fourth scrolled through the historical and personnel files searching for any words which were repeated with great regularity. It spat words at her, like "the" and "and".

Useless, totally useless.

The final window, at the bottom of the VDU, showed a single line. Their automated message to GWHQ.

URGENT, PRIORITY ONE CALL. CHANNEL TWO, POSSIBLE BREAKDOWN OF AWS SOFTWARE. URGENT. GWHQ PLEASE ACKNOWLEDGE. MESSAGE URGENT. . . . The words glimmered hypnotically before her, and she found that her eyes were drawn to its regular soothing rhythm.

URGENT, PRIORITY ONE CALL. CHANNEL TWO, SUBJECT: POSSIBLE BREAKDOWN OF AWS SOFTWARE. URGENT. GWHQ, PLEASE ACKNOWLEDGE. MESSAGE URGENT . . .

URGENT . . . URGENT . . . URGENT.

Her lids drooped, her shoulders slumped and her chin descended to rest upon her chest.

URGENT, PRIORITY ONE CALL. CHANNEL TWO, SUBJECT:

POSSIBLE BREAKDOWN OF AWS SOFTWARE. URGENT. GWHQ, PLEASE ACKNOWLEDGE. MESSAGE URGENT . . .

Then suddenly: BREAK.

Her eyelids twitched.

GWHQ PENNINES RECEIVING. HMS REVENANT, GWHQ ACKNOWLEDGES YOUR CALL. OVER.

Dim-witted and slow, she simply gazed at the screen. The missive repeated itself.

GWHQ PENNINES RECEIVING. HMS REVENANT, GWHQ ACKNOWLEDGES YOUR CALL. OVER.

She shifted in her seat as the change registered somewhere below the level of consciousness.

Again, GWHQ PENNINES RECEIVING. HMS REVENANT, GWHQ ACKNOWLEDGES YOUR CALL. COME IN, PLEASE. OVER.

The minute addition of ''come in, please'' caused the recognition to vault from unconscious to conscious levels, and she was jolted from her half-doze.

Electrified, Blast batted at Ylon. He grunted at her. She seized his arm and shook him. He squinted blearily in her direction, no comprehension in his eyes. Impatient, Blast bellowed into his ear: ''We're in!''

Then she bent to type in a response before access to GWHQ was lost again.

The worst had happened!

The *Thanatos* reappeared from its quantum leap in the sparking aftermath of battle. The vessel was jostled and jounced, battered by the fiery remains of an unidentified ship. An ensign shouted their co-ordi-nates, his voice all quavery with excitement.

With a quick flick of his wrist, Cyte released his safety harness and was up and out of his chair. "Get us out of here!" he roared.

The helmsman pressed the appropriate keys to initiate the doppler-jump computations. The computer lashed out, grabbing onto the nearest large object, which was nothing more than a piece of molten flotsam ejected from what must have once been a vessel. The engines groaned at the insult of the jump-sequence initiated too soon, before they had a chance to attain full power. Lights flashed as the computers drew power from every possible source. For a breathless moment, there wasn't even the reassuring hiss of the air that was normally fed through vents on to the bridge.

Then the ship's main viewer displayed the flat, black matt of starless ultra space.

If we freeze like this, we're dead men, Cyte thought wildly.

A corpman opened his mouth to scream in infinite slow motion, just as the stars sprung from the black velvet of normal space. He relaxed slightly when the life support system sent a refreshing whiff of air. The corpman's shriek, arrested by the time-space lag of ultra space, reverberated across the bridge.

Before Cyte had a chance to call for a systems'

check, the engines ground to a halt. The next thing he knew they were drifting helplessly in space.

The screaming corpman blanched and fainted, sprawling over his console. His terminal screeched in complaint at the confusing babble of keys and commands. Cyte lunged across the room, yanking the young man's body from his keyboard.

"Status report. Co-ordinates."

In a voice even more shaky than before, the first ensign answered, listing their sector and the nearest longitude and latitude on earth.

"Engineering?" Cyte called for their report.

"We're down, sir!"

"I know that," Cyte snarled. "How soon before you can get the engines up and running?"

"Not long, sir, if all you want is standard drive. But if you want to continue as we have been going, then it's going to take a while."

"Any idea how long?" he asked.

"I'd be afraid to guess until I've looked into it more." There was a slight hesitation as the engines purred into life. "Standard drive initiated."

"Thank you. Get back to me on the other as soon as you can." Cyte signed off.

"All right." He turned to the rest of the terrified crew. "Run standard tests on all systems. All unnecessary personnel, try and get some sleep. We're going to finish this shift and I want to make sure at least some of us are fresh."

He moved restlessly across the deck. "Let's see if we can locate this bug. We've got an appointment to keep."

Finally, Cyte pointed at the unconscious corpman. "Someone take him down to the infirmary."

Swivelling smartly on his heel as though nothing at all was wrong, he marched over to the chief technical officer.

"How long do you think?" Cyte asked.

"A few hours, I believe, sir," Iota said.

The captain examined the drawn faces of his crew. "That's probably for the best. I don't think the men can take much more of this."

His crew was exhausted. They were pulling a double shift, because Cyte had insisted that, since this "experiment" was his idea, he would see it through to the end. His crew just sort of got dragged along behind, for neither Cyte nor his night shift counterpart were ready to throw away all military discipline, and mix the two shifts. The genders must remain segregated.

Linking his arms across his chest, Cyte rested against the console. "Well, I'd say that was a successful experiment," he said, noting their position with satisfaction. Assuming the *Revenant* was in standard orbit, they should be gaining on her. Even if she were travelling at faster than the recommended orbital speeds, they were still making headway.

Iota glanced up at him, bemused. "If you say so, sir."

"You don't agree? We're making record time, and we're still in one piece, despite the fact that we are working with software patched together between two separate programs. I'd say our progress is satisfactory," adding as an afterthought, "relatively speaking."

The play on words was lost on the baffled officer; when Iota replied his face was deadpan. "We've been thrown off course, sir, and it would appear we missed something obvious at the beginning of this, uh, quest." Iota indicated the 3D diagram of Earth with a jerk of his thumb.

Nonplussed, Cyte peered at the glowing terran globe, divided neatly into longitudinal and latitudinal grids. A long belt of regularly spaced tanker-drones circled the planet in passive orbit. The *Thanatos* was within one hundred kilometres of the floating armada.

He looked from the display to the CTO. Then his eyes glinted with sudden revelation. *Of course, the floating fleet.* It made the perfect fulcrum. They could latch onto one ship and then another, no more searching in space for an appropriate sized vessel; no more delay.

They were home free!

17/11/2333

O-FOUR-HUNDRED HOURS

They were in. Ylon clutched Blast's shoulder, stooping over her to read the screen, and Blast's mind went skittering in a thousand different directions. So many incidents to report. So many questions to ask. Quicker than Blast, Ylon dumped their previous message into the GWHQ mainframe, deleting the urgent salutation. Both watched as the terse recital of events – enemy violations, a confession of their own guilt, the equipment malfunctions and subsequent checks – was downloaded to ground-side computers.

Their troubled gazes met. Then they stared at one another and waited. Blast hunched over the keys, ready to act. Afraid that whoever was on the other end would disconnect before the entire message had replayed.

When the words ... ALL CHECKS CAME OUT NEGATIVE; WE SUSPECT THAT THE MALFUNCTION LIES IN THE GROUND-SIDE SOFTWARE ... danced across the screen, she fretted, her fingers drumming a nervous rhythm. No one, particularly not military command, liked to admit a mistake. Leg swinging widely, Blast waited for the message to complete itself, and then she cut the "auto" command as Ylon headed for the door to fetch the Captain.

Some instinct caused her to stop. "No, wait. Let's see who we're talking to first."

Again, he leaned over her shoulder. His closeness bothered her. She couldn't seem to concentrate when he got too near.

As she had expected, the reply denied their conclusions, contradicting all that had happened.

After a long pause, data began pouring into his terminal and presented itself upon the glowing screen. A list of inexplicable incidents, which not only confirmed the newsnet reports but also Dirk's conclusions. The participants were as puzzled by everything that was happening as the civilian population was. The message quoted chapter and verse of the Amman treaty and the later Kathmandu Accord, verifying Dirk's belief that the clones were no subintelligent species.

When he read the closing words . . . ALL CHECKS CAME OUT NEGATIVE; WE SUSPECT THAT THE MALFUNCTION LIES IN THE GROUND-SIDE COMPUTER/SOFTWARE . . . Dirk really began to shake. The icy hand that had run cold fingers up and down his spine settled in the pit of his stomach and the pizza turned into an indigestible lump.

For an interminable moment, no response came from GWHQ, as though AWS was considering its words carefully. As Dirk watched, he thought he could hear distant humming from the computer's voice-box, or voder, as if he were catching a phantom echo of GWHQ through the wires and the interfaces of the two machines.

Dirk slid to the edge of his seat. He was just wondering if he should answer, when AWS's response was printed across the screen.

THERE IS NO COMPUTER MALFUNCTION. THE SOFTWARE IS RUNNING AS PROGRAMMED.

The reaction from the ship was swift. BUT THE ALARMS WERE FALSE. ON-BOARD COMPUTERS HAVE BEEN TESTED AND RETESTED. THEY ARE RUNNING PERFECTLY; THEREFORE, THE ALARMS MUST HAVE BEEN TRIPPED AT GROUND-LEVEL.

IF THE KLAXONS *WERE* SET OFF AT GROUND LEVEL, THERE MUST HAVE BEEN SOME KIND OF PERIL, came the implacable reply.

WE SAW NOTHING.

THEN THE DANGER WAS NOT ONE THAT WOULD HAVE BEEN IMMEDIATELY OBVIOUS TO PERSONNEL ABOARD SHIP.

Dirk chuckled at the delicate phrasing. *Boy, he (it?) wasn't kidding.*

The *Revenant* retorted: SOMETHING MUST BE WRONG. WE ARE NOW TRAVELLING ... there was a list of incomprehensible co-ordinates ... WHICH IS NOT, REPEAT NOT, THE APPROPRIATE ROUTE FOR OUR NEXT SCHEDULED RENDEZVOUS. OR HAS THERE BEEN A CHANGE IN STRATEGY? THE ROOT OF THE PROBLEM HAS TO LIE GROUND-SIDE WITHIN THE COMPUTER SYSTEM OR PERHAPS THE SOFTWARE. WE HAVE TRIED TO OVERRIDE THE COMPUTER AND REGAIN MANUAL CONTROL, WITHOUT SUCCESS. WE ARE TRAVELLING AN UNIDENTIFIED ROUTE TO AN UNKNOWN DESTINATION. CAN SOMEONE DOWN THERE DISCONNECT THE *REVENANT* FROM CENTRAL COMPUTER CONTROL? PLEASE ADVISE.

The original message repeated itself, stubborn and insistent. THERE IS NO COMPUTER MALFUNCTION. THE SOFTWARE IS RUNNING AS PROGRAMMED.

Again, Dirk laughed. It was the truth. The software was running "as programmed". What was happening with the foul-up of water distribution was a perfect example. AWS's instructions were to divert water-supplies if, for some reason, those supplies to combat personnel and colonists were disrupted. And that was precisely what was happening. The program was fulfilling its function. Never mind that thousands, millions of people ground-side must do without water. Never mind that food production had halted and those same millions if they got through the immediate danger of no water then faced starvation.

AWS *was* functioning as programmed, completing its instructions without thought to the consequences.

BUT ... The incoming message faltered. Dirk sighed. This was getting nowhere. He broke in.

INTERRUPT.

All communications between AWS and the combat vessel ceased, and suddenly he didn't know what to say. These were the little people. The clones. They were in a life and death situation which they lived with every day. A life manufactured synthetically, fighting a fake war. Threatened from without, in more ways than one, and the biggest threat was the one they couldn't see – the source, the same military command that had created them. He'd better think of something fast.

HELLO, Dirk typed. The response was almost instantaneous as the ship's personnel realized that they were talking to someone human. And he found himself besieged with questions.

HELLO? WHO IS THIS? CAN YOU HELP US? HAS THERE BEEN A CHANGE IN STRATEGY, AND IF SO WHY HAVEN'T WE BEEN NOTIFIED?

I DON'T KNOW, Dirk replied candidly.

The bombardment continued, ignoring his ambivalent response. The list of unprecedented events was duplicated, followed by a series of questions. Some technical, some not. Dirk waited for their queries to dribble out.

I'M SORRY, I CANNOT HELP YOU. I AM NOT ATTACHED TO THE

GWHQ FACILITY. I JUST GOT IN HERE ... Dirk rubbed his chin. What should he say now?

... BY ACCIDENT. THINGS ARE BAD GROUND-SIDE TOO, AND NO ONE SEEMS TO BE AT HOME AT GWHQ. AT LEAST, I'VE BEEN BLUNDERING THROUGH THE SYSTEM FOR SEVERAL HOURS, AND NO ONE HAS TRIED TO STOP ME. NO ONE SEEMS TO CARE.

WHO IS THIS?

Now what should he say. He decided on the truth. I AM DIRK. And Dirk could imagine the crestfallen expressions and the muffled "oh" on the other end of the transmission link.

WHO WAS THAT WE WERE SPEAKING TO BEFORE?

I THINK THAT WAS AWS. Then he typed: WHO ARE YOU?

THIS IS THE HMS *REVENANT*. Dirk smiled that GWHQ Pennines. Only one state in the confederate archipelago of Europe would cling to the outdated custom, HMS, as if they still had real royals. Oh, the family still existed, but they were treated like ordinary people, just like everybody else. He dismissed the thought as unimportant, and before they had a chance to disconnect, he added: IS THIS REALLY A SHIP AND ARE YOU REALLY – Dirk grimaced; he couldn't say clones or little people. How about – COMBAT PERSONNEL?

I AM COMMUNICATIONS SPECIALIST FIRST CLASS, ENSIGN BETA PELLUCIDA BLASTOMERE.

And Dirk shuddered to find the verification of what he had seen in the name. Up until that point he had hoped that it had been some kind of monumental joke or trick. Something put on the computer speci-

218

fically for dopes like himself. A file implanted to perplex the uninvited hack.

The faceless ensign continued: PEOPLE CALL ME "BLAST" FOR SHORT.

A pause.

LOOK, DIRK, SURELY YOU CAN HELP US. OUR SITUATION IS DESPERATE. THERE MUST BE SOMEONE YOU CAN CONTACT, SOME-ONE IN A POSITION OF AUTHORITY.

THERE'S MY DAD.

Speechless, Ylon and Blast gazed at the words upon the screen. Ylon's legs gave out from under him and he landed in his chair with an undignified plop. Blast regarded him out of the corner of her eye. He stared at a window that had opened on the screen. It registered blood pressure, respiration rate and heart beat. Something jigged at the back of her memory, and she recalled the old school chair of pre-service days used in training military personnel. Embedded in the upper left hand corner was a face, the image so distorted by distance and warped by the computer's convex lens that she couldn't make out the features. Blast swallowed, nodded and turned to type something else.

YOUR FATHER? JUST HOW OLD ARE YOU?

FIFTEEN.

"Great," Ylon muttered.

Blast persisted. Maybe there was somebody else.

HELLO. HELLO? THIS IS HMS REVENANT CONTACTING

GWHQ. ISN'T THERE SOMEONE WE CAN TALK TO? WHERE IS ...
she keyed in the code name of their standard contact
and then hit the auto switch again. HELLO. THIS
IS HMS REVENANT CONTACTING GWHQ. ISN'T THERE SOME-
ONE ...

Before the rest of the message replayed, the signal
was broken and a reply appeared on the screen.

I AM HERE.

WHO ARE YOU?

I AM AWS, THE AMMAN WAR SOFTWARE, STATE OF THE ART IN
ARTIFICIAL INTELLIGENCE. WOULD YOU LIKE TO SEE MY MAIN
MENU?

Terror flitted across her features and her fingers
flew across the keys before she got transferred to
some anonymous menu. NO, AWS PLEASE HELP US, THERE
MUST BE SOME KIND OF MALFUNCTION.

THERE IS NO MALFUNCTION.

BUT THE ITINERARY, THE ALARMS, THE BATTLE, ALL WRONG
... Blast was poised ready to say more, when words
appeared that were neither their own nor, apparently,
AWS's.

LOOK, AWS, FACE FACTS. EVERYTHING IS A MESS.

PERHAPS. CHAOS IS OFTEN THE RESULT OF WAR.

PEOPLE ARE DYING!

OF COURSE. PEOPLE DIE IN WARS.

The next sentence was directed at them.

HMS REVENANT? BLAST, ARE YOU STILL THERE?

YES, DIRK, I AM HERE.

GOOD. THERE'S SOMETHING I WANT TO SHOW YOU.

CAN WE SWITCH TO VODER MODE? she asked.

AS YOU WISH. The next communique that appeared was also spoken. AWS, CAN YOU GIVE US THE MAIN MENU?

Both Ylon and Blast were on their feet in a second, shouting at the terminal: "No!"

Too late. The menu wiped everything else from the screen.

"Don't worry," came the tinny, descrambled voice of the voder box, "I know what I'm doing. I've been in the system for a while."

This was not good news.

AWS knew what Dirk was about to do even before he had done it.

"Kay sarrah sarrah, whatever will be will be," the computer sang as it made a minute check of its instructions. MAN, AND HIS OFFSPRING, MUST FACE THE CONSEQUENCES OF THEIR ACTIONS. IF THEY ARE GOING TO FIGHT A WAR, THEN THEY MUST ACCEPT ITS REALITIES. AWS hesitated for a nanosecond, trying to interpret the creator's direction. Another nanosecond was lost as it futilely wished Gorman was here. It posed a question to itself. *How could such realities be faced unless they were revealed?*

Human secrets had perpetuated the war; therefore, only knowledge could combat it.

Finding nothing to countermand the current

activity, AWS released the menu despite the thundering duet of "nos".

Let the process proceed unhindered.

Ylon and Blast exchanged glances as the boy, Dirk, wound his way through a series of the menus and submenus. He worked with a practised hand. He had not been lying when he said he had been in the system for a while. He knew exactly what he was looking for.

(A). Archive.

(P). Personnel.

Other letters were entered leading to further subdirectories until they were in a file marked Bio-engineering.

The following legend flashed at the bottom of the VDU: MODIFICATION NUMBER; 2417289 (SEE MEMO – REDUCTION OF WATER AND MATERIAL USE, DATED . . .

As one, Ylon and Blast edged closer to their terminals as words unfolded before them.

"This is it," Dirk said. "Here, I'll let you read for yourself."

"May we take over?" Blast said.

"Take over? Huh?"

"The screen," Blast explained.

"Hey, you're a girl," the voice took on an accusatory note.

"Of course I'm a girl." She shot a sidelong look at

Ylon. "Why does that seem to bother everybody so? There are women in the military, you know."

"Uh, you're right. I'm sorry. It's just that I didn't expect it in, ah, er," he stammered, "a combat situation."

Ylon studied the document before him, horrified. Disregarding the conversation between Dirk and Blast, he intervened. "Does this mean what I think it means?"

"Who are you?"

"My name is Ylon."

"I don't know," Dirk said. "That's what I'm trying to find out."

Blast poked Ylon. "What are you talking about?"

"It appears to be saying that they are using cloned personnel in combat situations."

"You mean," she gasped, "there may be clones aboard the ship?"

There was a heavy growl from the voder, which sounded like someone clearing his throat.

"Wait just a second," Dirk said. "There's something else, I think, which will help to explain."

A window was opened and the diagram of a Dolphin-type Cruiser flashed upon the screen.

Ylon and Blast examined the ship and its dimensions, and Blast was even more confused. It was a standard diagram, easily accessible on their on-board computers. What was this supposed to explain?

"I'm not sure I understand," she said. "These are

standard diagrams. Anyone working on a Dolphin Cruiser has seen these a thousand times."

"The dimensions," Dirk replied.

"What about the dimensions? They are known parameters."

"Are they correct?"

"Of course, they are correct," she said.

The next query came out of the blue. "How tall are you?"

"What?" she said.

"How tall are you?"

"Ninety-two centimetres. Why?"

"Ylon?"

"About the same," Ylon said. "What are you getting at?"

"Let me show you something else. Do you have holographic capabilities?" Dirk asked.

"Of course."

"Can you open up another window for another file?"

Blast keyed in the command. "Done."

"You asked about my father," the boy said. Again there was a dizzying series of letters, menus and words, and a personnel file opened before them. They caught only a glimpse of the name before a 3D photo-fit appeared on the screen. Both ensigns examined the fairly ordinary, somewhat dowdy-looking man.

"He's the head of the food industry and a member

of the Joint Chiefs of Staff. You're right, Dirk," Ylon commented. "He may be in a position to help us."

"But what does this have to do with the diagram of the ship?" Blast interjected.

"Look at the dimensions. The height and weight."

Two pairs of eyes turned to the appropriate box which gave the pertinent stats. HEIGHT: 2 METRES; WEIGHT: 72 KILOGRAMS.

"My God, he's huge. What is he, some kind of giant?" Blast said.

"No, ah, he's ... er ... norm –"

Before Dirk had the chance to complete his answer, Ylon spoke urgently at the terminal. "And how tall are you?"

Blast turned a questioning gaze to her counterpart. "I don't understand."

Ylon waved her to silence.

"I'm not quite that tall, but according to the doctors I will exceed that height by the time I've stopped growing."

Impatiently Blast interrupted. "What are you two talking about?"

Ylon ignored her. "I'm sorry, I spoke before you had finished speaking. Your father is normal, is that what you were going to say?"

"Pretty much so. Oh, he's a little taller than average, but no giant."

"What! Everybody ground-side is this big?" Blast

bleated, as what they were talking about registered at last.

"That's about the size of it." The sound of static crackled through the voder box, like a nervous cough. "I didn't quite mean that as it sounded."

By now Blast was examining the photo-fit in earnest. "What are those funny things that he's wearing on the end of his nose?"

"Huh?" A moment's silence. "Oh, those. Those are spectacles. Corrective lenses. Haven't you seen anybody wearing glasses before?"

"No."

"Never?"

"Never. I thought they were obsolete, part of a dead past."

Meanwhile Ylon was busy at his terminal, typing requests and commands. He elbowed Blast and indicated her VDU with a sharp movement. She scrutinized the ship's diagram. The photo-fit image of the man, George Alexander, had been scaled down to the appropriate dimensions and positioned inside the main deck, the largest portion of the vessel. His head and shoulders extended far beyond the ceiling and into the quarterdeck. Suddenly the pieces fell into place.

"Ylon? Blast?" came the worried voice. "Are you still there?"

"Ah, yes, Dirk," she said.

Ylon explained. "We have just placed the photo-fit inside the ship. We see what you mean."

"I'm sorry," Dirk said.

"May we continue?" Blast asked, her voice hushed, awed and subdued.

"Be my guest. This affects you more than it does me."

They returned to scanning the documentation.

The text unrolled at a phenomenal rate. Dirk blinked. They must be speed reading, and this was the "subhuman" personnel referred to in the memos. He wished now that he had a vid hook-up. He would have given anything to see their expressions right now, not out of cruelty or curiosity, but fear. He wondered if he had done the right thing.

To them, Dirk was just another part of the ground-side personnel, whether he belonged to GWHQ or not, and it was the land base that had created this myth. Dirk tried to imagine what it must feel like to discover that everything you had been told about yourself was a lie. To realize that nothing you thought you knew could be trusted. Even their memories were false.

He found himself wanting to intercept the signal to apologize for the deception that had been perpetuated upon them, but he stayed his hand. They had the right to know and the right to decipher the information without his snivelling comments.

By this time, they had advanced beyond the point where he had stopped in confusion. Dirk leaned closer to the screen, trying to make some sense of the words. Every once in a while, the text would stop on specific models. First Alpha and then Beta line clones. He thought he caught a gasp, a choked whimper or a sob.

INTERRUPT.

"We have not finished yet," the male voice objected stridently.

"Yes, I know, I just wanted to ... apologize. I'm sorry. I didn't know. I don't think anybody did," Dirk finished lamely. "At least, none of the civilians."

"You really want me to believe that no one down there was aware ..."

"The military maybe, not us. We're just plain people. We wouldn't do that to you," Dirk said.

"What about your father?"

"My father? No. At least, I don't think so. The documents require a 1A security rating. He may be head of Food and a part of the Bathosphere Governing Council, but he's a civilian and the highest rating local government officials can achieve is 1B."

"I thought most political posts were filled by one-time military personnel."

"On a federal level that's true. But he's local government, the Lake Districts. Like old-time town councils."

"Are you sure?" The voice was sharp.

Dirk swallowed. What could he say? It had been his father who had told him ground-side personnel could never work on combat ships. True, he had given a different reason, but wasn't it his father who was always praising the benefits of the centralized civil-military authority? His father who hid behind the phrase "national security" when his mother questioned him too closely? Who believed that the cloning of miscellaneous body parts was a more "civilized" method of obtaining beef?

"Not absolutely sure, no." Dirk found himself reviewing the many tea-time debates and recalling one argument about genetics where his father, and not his mother, had expressed the more conservative view. She was all for "breeding out" genetic defects. She had teased him about his unwillingness to get the genetic enhancement which would correct his vision, and he had said: "People are people, and it's their faults that give them individuality. I'd rather be blind as a bat than encourage a system that supports the ancient doctrine of a master race."

With more confidence, Dirk said: "No, I don't believe he did. He wouldn't have approved."

The female Blast spoke to her companion. "We have to report this," she said.

"I know," said Ylon, "but let's finish the file so we know exactly what it is we are dealing with."

"Deception is what we're dealing with. Fraud." The woman's voice rose in indignation.

"Yes, but whose?"

"I'm sorry," Dirk again interrupted, "I really am. I'm just as baffled as you are. Continue."

Again text began to flash across his screen. A few minutes later, they must have triggered something somewhere for the screen cleared, and the next thing Dirk knew his room was filled with the sound of music.

. . . Promotional video, number 332. As you can see, our product is top of the line.

What was this? The image was flat, without depth. An old style 2D video, he thought. Dirk glanced at the date. The same year as the memo on reduction of material.

The camera, apparently focused on a sleeping human face, backed away to reveal a full-sized scientist standing next to a laboratory table, upon which lay a drowsing clone.

. . . We start with the highest quality ingredients. The image was replaced by a man staring into a test tube.

. . . The conditions here at Starside Farms are hygienically clean. All personnel go through rigorous health testing and daily aseptic baths to neutralize or sterilize any viral or biogenic organism that could cause unwanted mutation.

A grainy picture of people clothed and swathed in white flickered across the screen. The uniforms covered every inch of skin, giving them a ghostly appearance. Only a thick sheet of plastic over eyes and face revealed that humans occupied the suits.

Breathing apparatus further ensures that the air in the IV, or in vitro, unit remains pure.

The unseen camera panned to show any number of people huddled over trays and test tubes – the gas canisters of compressed air clearly visible on their backs.

After fertilization takes place, the embryo is kept in a climate-controlled environment closely approximating a human womb.

And the shot switched to a baby floating in a glass jar. Dirk blenched. His pizza did a slow and rolling lurch inside his stomach.

Contact is maintained during all stages of foetal development. So the growing embryos are exposed to human voices as they would be if they had developed in utero. Constant use of music and subliminals stimulate intelligence in both halves of the foetal brain.

One of the white figures stooped over and started talking to a glass jar, as some perfectly awful music – some symphony or another – blared in the background. Drifting lazily in its fluid medium, the tiny half-formed baby turned towards the sound.

It is just this kind of personalized service that ensures our product is of superior quality.

The scene changed again, and Dirk was looking

into some swank office as an anonymous face smiled greasily into the camera.

For this reason, I'm sure you'll agree that our bid is reasonable, although it may seem high in comparison to that of our competitors. We can guarantee the quality of our merchandise.

The music increased in crescendo as the credits rolled across the screen. Then the VDU went black.

Silence. And in it Dirk sensed unspoken consternation, shock and outrage.

"You didn't know?" Ylon hissed angrily.

"No, no, I swear. Nobody did," Dirk said.

"Are you sure?"

"Well, no, I'm not positive. Obviously, the military did, but I don't think anybody else did."

"May we speak with your father?" Blast asked.

"He's not here. He's been called away on an emergency. You see, things are bad here, too. Water has been disconnected from the main hydroponics plant. Food and water are being diverted for combat or colonial use. There's not enough to feed the population, and if something doesn't happen soon, we're talking starvation on a massive scale."

The clones didn't seem to be impressed, and Dirk couldn't say that he blamed them. Ylon continued as if Dirk hadn't said anything. "And you are not connected to the military in any way?"

"No, I am not."

The woman spoke next: "Look, I'm turning off the

voice mode. We have a lot to discuss here, but I'd like to keep the line between us open. We're going to download this information. Is that okay with you?"

"Sure, fine with me. I can't vouch for AWS. It may not let you." Dirk slumped glumly into his chair. "Look, I'm sorry. I really am."

"Don't worry about it, Dirk," Blast said, her voice much more forgiving than her male counterpart. "We saw the date on the memo. Whatever has happened, happened a long time ago. Before you were born."

Ylon exploded from his chair and began pacing around the room. "Of all the..."

"He's telling the truth, though." She pointed at the window display which revealed pulse, blood pressure and respirations. "The young man is as upset about this as we are." All his vital signs had skyrocketed in a dizzying display of jagged lines.

Ylon spun on her. "Is that supposed to matter?"

"And look at this." She handed him a strip of paper she had started printing out as soon as she realized that they were tied into some kind of training device at the opposite end of the link. "It's his voice print. All things taken together can be used as a sort of lie detector, and this kid's sincere."

"I *still* think we should blow them out of the water. We ... we..."

"Maybe somebody already has," Blast commented.

Tirade arrested mid-sentence, Ylon eyed her. "What do you mean?"

"Think about it. We talked to one fifteen-year-old boy, and the computer, at GWHQ. We were in the system for quite some time, uninterrupted, as far as we know unmonitored. If this information is correct," she pointed at the flashing laser printer as it spat out pages and pages of text, "then we were never meant to see it. If someone had been there, don't you think they would have stopped the process as soon as the boy opened the document?"

"True," he agreed reluctantly as he sagged against the wall. "But how could that be? How could this be?" Ylon flicked a finger at the text.

"I don't know, but the words vapour guns spring to mind."

"Are we really sure we got through to GWHQ? This could be somebody's home computer."

"Do you really think they would have documents this sensitive in someone's PC?"

"How do you know they're real? It could be somebody's idea of a joke," he said warming to the idea. "I wasn't born in a glass jar," he concluded weakly, his voice losing a lot of venom. "I know that for sure." He had a father and a mother; Ylon knew he did. He remembered them – well, almost.

"Do you?" Blast's soft voice intruded upon his muttered thoughts. "You saw the tape. That was old-style 2D vid. We've seen those before when we were shown the old news-vids of the Amman Treaty. It's not a mock-up. Besides," she continued, "who would want to do such a thing? It's a process much too expensive for a practical joke."

All Ylon's arguments dried up, and both Ylon and Blast averted their gazes, busying themselves with routine details, unwilling to look the other in the eye or volunteer to call in the Captains.

Cyte wandered aimlessly around the bridge. The lights had dimmed. Occasionally a sleeping crew member let out a loud snore. With the systems checks satisfactory, everybody who could, slept. Besides himself, only the helmsman and the chief technical officer remained awake.

Cyte smiled to himself. They were a good crew. Not a single man had quibbled when he had informed them of their double duty. Neither had they complained when he had initiated the dizzying leaps, and after the first jump, only an idiot couldn't have figured out what they were doing and just how risky it was. Yet no one said a word. They just gritted their teeth and went about their tasks as if nothing was happening.

If they survived this, Cyte was going to insist on commendations for his crew, and shore-leave for the lot of them. Assuming they ever got through the GWHQ Urals. He snorted. Assuming he was in a position to insist on anything and not in the brig himself for destroying a passenger liner.

The helmsman put his hand on his back, straightened and groaned.

"Well?" Cyte said.

"I think we can do it. If we change the computation of the doppler jumps. Make them shorter, a lot shorter," the helmsman explained.

"Shorter in time or shorter in distance?" Cyte said.

"Both actually. By making them shorter in distance, just long enough to reach between one tanker and the next, then they should become shorter in duration. And not quite as disorienting for the crew," Iota, the CTO, added.

"Good."

"Furthermore, since the leaps are regular they become an automatic function. There will be no more delay as we reach out for the next object of the required size and mass, wherever it may be. One set of computations should be sufficient, making between-jump calculations unnecessary. So despite the fact that we are making shorter leaps, we should actually travel more quickly. The risk-factor is negligible since we are leaping between known objects which will be regularly spaced within predictable parameters."

"Great. How soon can we start?"

Both men shrugged. Cyte tabbed the comm-link to engineering. "You listening?" he asked.

"Aye-aye, sir," the chief of engineering said.

"And?"

"Any time, sir. We're just putting the finishing touches on it now."

"Okay, signal me when you are ready."

"Should we wake the rest of them up?" Iota motioned to the sleeping bridge crew.

"I don't know. How are you holding up?"

The ship's doctor had given the three of them the standard stimulant, but like any drug, it had a boomerang effect. When it wore off, its user would be twice as tired as before.

"I'm fine, sir."

"Me too."

"And you said the system is completely automated?"

"Well, it should be. Of course, this is only a mathematical extrapolation. If we're off," the helmsman continued, gazing at the winking starscape, "we won't find out until we're en route."

"You mean when we run smack-dab into the side of a tanker," Cyte said.

"Something like that," he agreed.

"Let them sleep. At least that way, they won't know what hit them."

"Very good, sir," said Iota, and the captain did a quick double take, unsure if the other man was mocking him. His fellow officer's face was grim.

There was a short whistle from the communicator.

"Ready, sir," the chief of engineering said.

"Okay, helmsman, start her up. Let's see if we can get this buggy to move."

17/11/2333

O-EIGHT-FIFTEEN

Jennifer Alexander found Dirk asleep at his terminal the next morning. She gazed at him fondly and then glanced at the VDU, curious as to what project had occupied him so thoroughly that it kept him glued to his hated school-chair all night long.

The cursor blinked incessantly next to the words "line open", but Jennifer paid no attention to them, for her eyes were cemented upon the upper right-hand corner of the screen.

A news release took up one quarter of the VDU. It was emblazoned and emboldened, circled in red and printed in reverse face – in old newspaper-type with black letters on a white background – to ensure that no one would miss it. She read the commentary with a sharp inhalation of breath. Her hand covered her mouth to stifle the sound.

FROM: NEWSNET INTERNATIONAL
DISTRIBUTION: UNIVERSAL
DATELINE: BRITISH ISLAND WHARFS, 17:11:2333
SUBJECT: FOOD CRISIS ESCALATES

RIOTS STARTED IN THE SOUTHERN DOCK DISTRICTS WHERE MAN BATTLES DROID TO HALT THE STEADY SYPHONING OFF OF EARTH'S RESERVE OF PURIFIED WATER. IN THE EARLY HOURS OF THE MORNING, TEMPERS FLARED AND CITIZENS TOOK THE MATTER INTO THEIR OWN HANDS WHEN MEMBERS OF THE CONSOLIDATED DOCK WORKERS UNION REBELLED AFTER ANOTHER LARGE SHIPMENT OF TERRAN'S DWINDLING STORES OF FOOD AND WATER WAS SCHEDULED FOR TRANSPORT TO LUNAR AND MARTIAN COLONIES.

THE VIOLENCE HAS RADIATED OUTWARD AND HAS REACHED THE COVENT GARDEN MINIDOME WHERE LOOTERS HAVE CARRIED OFF THE STOCK OF ''FREE FOOD'' - COMESTIBLES SOLD OVER THE COUNTER FOR INDIVIDUAL CONSUMPTION.

THE PROBLEM STARTED YESTERDAY WHEN THE FIRST SHIPMENT OF WATER WAS DIVERTED TO LUNAR COLONIES AFTER A TANKER WAS LOST IN COMBAT. THE SITUATION HAS WORSENED RAPIDLY. SUBSEQUENT COMBAT HAS NEARLY DEMOLISHED THE CURRENT LIST OF CARGO SHIPS AND TANKERS THAT WERE EN ROUTE TO MARTIAN AND LUNAR BASES. THIS HAS NECESSITATED ADDITIONAL DIVERSION OF BOTH FOOD AND WATER CAUSING IMMEDIATE SHORTAGES AT THE LAKE DISTRICT BATHOSPHERE, AND THE EFFECTS ARE REACHING BEYOND THE LAKE DISTRICT AS FOOD DELIVERIES AND SCHEDULED CONSIGNMENTS TO THE OUTER

240

BRITISH ISLANDS AND THE MANY FISH FARMS CAN NO LONGER BE
MET. HOARDING HAS COMPLICATED THE PROCESS, WHILE
RUMOURS OF THE CLOSURE OF THE MAIN HYDROPONICS PLANT IN
THE EASTERN ISLES FURTHER ENDANGER FUTURE FOOD SUP-
PLIES.

PEOPLE WHO HAVE NOT LEFT FOR THEIR PLACE OF EMPLOYMENT
YET ARE ASKED TO STAY IN THEIR HOMES. ALL WORK IS CAN-
CELLED FOR THE DAY. CIVIL AUTHORITIES WILL NOT BE HELD
RESPONSIBLE FOR THE SAFETY OF ANY CITIZEN FOUND OUTSIDE
OF THEIR PERSONAL QUARTERS. PEOPLE WITH 1A, 1B, AND 1C
CLEARANCE WILL BE PERMITTED TO MOVE ABOUT ONLY WITH
APPROVED POLICE ESCORT.

REPEAT: PEOPLE ARE ASKED NOT TO LEAVE THEIR RESI-
DENCES . . .

Things were getting worse! Jennifer Alexander never
thought she would live to see the day when there
were riots in the streets. Just like pre-flood days. This
was real news. Quite unlike the petty bickering of
municipal government she was used to covering.

She stared at her son, thought of waking him and
decided against it. The school system would rouse
him soon enough, and she was glad that he would be
occupied with his classes for the remainder of the day
no matter how tired and cramped he would feel upon
awakening. Today, Jennifer had no intention of dis-
abling the school program. She did *not* want Dirk
running around the bathosphere. There were lessons
to be learned from the day's current events, she was

sure, but there would be time enough to discuss them later.

Time enough then, but not today.

She wiped the report from the computer's memory. Police escort, the newsnet said, things must be bad indeed. Perhaps she could take some comfort in the fact that she hadn't been called last night. Perhaps the situation wasn't as bad as it first appeared. But she doubted it.

Her hand reached out and gently tousled Dirk's hair. He stirred, and she withdrew it as quickly as if she had been burned, wincing an apology at the sleeping figure.

Poor child, she thought, *what kind of trouble has mankind got himself into now?*

Last night she had been frightened as she made her way home from the BAND Broadcast One offices. The Bathosphere was too small to contain this kind of tension for long, and her hunch had been right, the repressed violence she had sensed then had erupted. For the first time in her life, Jennifer Alexander thought she understood women who didn't want children. Who wanted to grow up in a goldfish bowl, anyway?

The vid-phone klaxoned a priority one call. Jennifer darted out of the room to answer it before its clamouring cry awakened Dirk. When she touched the controls, the producer's haggard features coalesced on the viewscreen. He stared at her with shadowed and haunted eyes.

"Hope you got enough sleep. We need you to come in," he said without preliminaries.

"Yes, I just saw the newsnet. Are things really that bad?"

"Worse. We're sending a police escort. Its ETA is at 0-six-thirty."

"I'm on my way." She rang off, returned to Dirk's quarters and started to coax Robbie out of the room – softly.

The servo-mech trundled into the kitchen.

"Sit."

Robbie settled on his air-cushioned supports with a wheeze.

"Stay," she said without thinking. She patted its metal back. "I don't want you blocking the door to Dirk's room, okay? Dirk must attend to his lessons. And whatever you do don't let him out of the house."

Robbie mewled a reply to an empty room, for Jennifer Alexander had disappeared to complete the transition from worried wife, mother and all-too-human being into efficient newspresenter and celebrity. As she headed for the sanitation cubicle, she hoped there would be at least enough water for a rationed shower.

The Captains' quarters were crowded, with people literally hanging off the wall. The pull-down tables, those not already covered with communications equipment, were used as additional seating. The meeting started small enough with just the two captains, but in their disbelief, they had called in their first mates and later the medical officers.

The wall screen was filled with a single frozen frame. A baby in a bottle.

"I don't believe it," said the first mate for the hundredth time.

Zed turned to him and sighed. "Considering everything we've been through in the last seventy-two hours, I'd believe anything."

"We certainly can't dismiss it," the nightshift Captain Zygote added.

"I won't believe it," the officer insisted mulishly.

"It is medically feasible. We've had the ability for a long time," the chief medical officer reminded him gently. "It just never caught on. Perpetuation of the species is not such a hot item since the flood. We can barely feed and house the people we have now."

The doctor looked at the life-sized holograph of a standard "clone" which was superimposed over Captain Mito Zeta Zygote because she had no place else to stand. He couldn't help but noticing the perfect "fit". Next to that image, the "human" George Alexander's head and shoulders disappeared into the ceiling. The medical officer gestured at the images and said: "You've got to admit the size is right."

"So you think that these are correct?" Zed frowned at the ship's doctor.

"Well, it certainly would explain our names, which are bio-genetic in origin," the doctor said.

"Then we're not human?"

"Oh, we're human, all right. The basic genetic make-up is the same." He bent over the terminal, calling up 3D representations of the individual genetic codes that were encrypted in all personnel files. Two sets of the twisting ladder shape of DNA molecules drifted across before them. "The one on the right is our friend, George Alexander, and," he coughed into his hand, "on the left, you, Captain Zed. The exact same number of genes, the same formation and structure. Note this." A third image came up, slightly shorter. "Those of a chimpanzee, humanity's closest primate relation. See the difference. Oh, we're human all right. We may even be an improvement on the species, seeing how living space is at a premium. We're just small," he said. "I believe the old terran word is midget."

"Dwarf," Zygote said with a contemptuous sniff.

"No, dwarf is something different altogether, with a different body-mass ratio and certain facial characteristics. We, however, are proportionally 'perfect'."

The nightshift mate picked up a sheaf of paper and let it drop with a thud. "These can be faked."

"For what purpose?" the medical officer asked. "It's certainly not going to improve morale."

"The kid. It may be his idea of a joke," the mate said.

"No, I don't think so," Blast said. "He seemed as appalled at the concept as we are. He kept apologizing. You've seen the voice print and vital signs. He wasn't prevaricating."

Ylon snorted.

"And what about this?" The obdurate first mate slapped at the distribution line on the top of the first document. "It says both Pennines *and* Urals."

"Yes, what about that?" Zed said calmly, forcing himself to keep his voice even. He stared down at it. Even he was starting to see red, and this piece of information, just discovered as they had debated the other issue, seemed the most damning indictment of them all. "Communications Specialist Ylon, did you say you kept the line open?"

"Yes, sir."

"Good, there're a few questions I think we need to ask. So I suggest we clear the room and let our communications specialists get back to their job – communicating. And not a word to anybody about this until we can either confirm or deny the authenticity of the records." Zed turned to Ylon and Blast. "Get back on the horn and see what more you can find out from your friend, ah, what was his name again?"

People began shuffling out of the Captains' quarters.

"Dirk." Blast supplied the name while the Captain watched the last officer exit. All that remained was his nightshift counterpart.

"Yes, Dirk. See what you can learn about this." Zed pointed at the glaring line, glanced at his counterpart – Zygote inclined her agreement – and continued: "Why this top-secret, supposedly highly-confidential information, is being passed on to the enemy."

"It makes sense," Captain Zygote murmured. "Would one side agree to scale down its, uh, weapons unless the other side agreed to do so also?"

Zed deflated. He could not argue with her logic.

The school alarm screeched, and Dirk bolted from his chair. The door to his personal quarters slid shut as the alarm changed in timbre indicating his truancy.

Dutifully, Dirk sat. The school program fell silent, and the door opened.

He ran his fingers through his hair and yawned. There was a muffled rumble, as though a storm lashed against the tough acrylic of the outside sphere. Dirk cocked his head, listening. He had never heard such turbulence this deep in the residential area before. Their quarters were soundproofed.

Slowly, but more urgently, his bodily functions

registered, and he realized he was hungry and thirsty. Where was Robbie with his pizza?

Dirk considered keying for a bathroom break and scowled. He was *not* going to ask for permission like a five-year-old child.

With a guilty glimpse over his shoulder, Dirk typed in the disable command he had witnessed the day before. As the school program shut down with a belligerent squeak, he grinned at his reflection in the mirror he had hung at an angle over the terminal.

From this position, he could see the open door behind him. With a slight adjustment of his head, Dirk could behold the second mirror he had placed above the entryway. It allowed him to observe the area immediately behind him, and, when he faced the door, the slant of the two mirrors gave a perfect view of the keyboard at his back.

When he had put the mirrors up in the room, his mother had teased him, calling him vain. She had never really understood their purpose, to ensure not only the privacy of his room, but also the privacy of his personal computer. No one could approach him without his knowing about it, so he could work unobserved and switch from the hack program to the games directory if either one of his parents entered the room.

"Robbie, where's my pizza?"

There was a whir and a thunk.

"Can you bring it in here, please?"

Sounds of distress came from the kitchen.

Dirk got up and stepped through the door. He halted just behind the threshold, waiting for some alarm to go off somewhere. Nothing happened, and he sneered. He was free! The idea was such a novel one that he backed through the door again and marched across the threshold several times, as though defiantly declaring his independence over man and machine.

"Robbie!"

A squeak.

"Okay, have it your own way," he grumbled, heading for the sanitary facility. Clean and dressed, or as clean as he could get with a two-second allotment of water, Dirk moved into the kitchen, grabbed the half-eaten pizza from Robbie's table-like back and stalked back to his bedroom.

HMS REVENANT TO DIRK. COME IN PLEASE? HMS REVENANT TO DIRK. COME IN DIRK. THIS IS BLAST, DIRK. PLEASE RESPOND.

With a cry of delight, he tossed the pizza casually on the floor and threw himself into his chair.

DIRK?

YES, THIS IS DIRK. WOULD YOU LIKE TO SWITCH TO VOICE MODE?

YES, IF YOU WOULD PLEASE?

Dirk relaxed, kicked his feet up, and folded his arms across his chest.

"Dirk, do you still have access to GWHQ?"

"Of course, we're talking via that facility."

"In other words, we're in that system now?"

"Yes," Dirk said. He heard the buzz of voices in the background.

"We have some questions for you," Blast said.

"I'm not surprised. I don't know if I'll have an answer, but I'll try. Go ahead, shoot."

"The distribution lists on these records are marked for both the Pennines and the Urals."

"Yes, I was wondering if you would notice that. I was going to mention it to you yesterday, but you broke off too quickly."

The male voice broke in. "Ylon here. Dirk, what's the chances that this could be some kind of mistake?"

"You mean, the distribution list? Unlikely. Before you contacted me, I did some exploring. Here, let me show you." Dirk bent over the keyboard. His fingers flew, tabbing through the now well-known path. They were in the archives of inter-office memoranda. He scrolled through document after document. Within the 1A class, the distribution list was always the same.

"By the space hoard!" Ylon swore. "This is consistent?"

"Pretty much, the minor things, like ordering enough coffee substitute and toilet tissue, are Pennines only, but the important stuff..."

"Wait a second, Dirk, stop tabbing," Blast said.

His finger faltered, hovering over the cursor key.

"That's 1A documents. Highly confidential. How did you get access to it?" she asked.

"Search me, that's one of the funny things I've noticed. AWS seems to have some sort of control over those things I see and those things I cannot. Although there doesn't seem to be any logic to it. Some functions, simple things like dialling another facility, it will not permit me to do. While other times, like those records I downloaded to you, I'm given free admittance. Although it's funny – when I tried to print them here, AWS stopped me. Yet when I showed them to you, that seemed to be okay. Were you able to print out okay?"

"Well, yes," Ylon said.

"That *is* strange," Blast interrupted. "Dirk, do you think AWS is guiding your movements?"

"Sort of," Dirk said. "Hold on. There's something else that might clarify." He keyed back to the main menu and from there to the entry screen, which gave software title, date of inception, and the standard promotional junk.

"I noticed this when I'd backed into the main menu. It's not the kind of stuff you pay attention to because you see it so often. Every time you boot up as a matter of fact. Look down at the bottom of the screen under copyright."

The software was dated in pre-flood days. That was to be expected, and this was reflected in its copyright, which said: "Military Copyright, 2033." The city was another matter. It said: "London, England and Moscow, Russia." The distribution again was universal, taking in both sides of the conflict in the now-dead, now-drowned pre-flood capitals of the world.

Zed drooped mutely in his chair, disregarding the hubbub of activity around him. The shift had begun as if nothing had happened, and for the bulk of the crew that was true: nothing had happened. As far as they were concerned, the *Revenant* was still travelling to her next scheduled destination. So the crew went through the early routine, the tests and checks as always, making sure the ship was "battle ready".

Not Zed, nor his first mate. The Captain noted the man's furrowed brow and melancholy stare. A tic had developed under his eye, and Zed wondered if he looked as bad as his subordinate. With resolve, the Captain rearranged his limbs to a more military posture and tried to look interested as his crew reported, "systems-check, a-okay," one after another. Zed tugged at his bottom lip and nodded tersely to each in turn.

Faking nonchalance, Zed rose and moved over to the helmsman. He checked the co-ordinates. They were still on the same path. *Going who knows where for heavens knows what purpose,* he thought.

The Captain stooped so that his lips were parallel to the helmsman's ear. "Have you tried manual override recently?"

"Every ten minutes as you ordered, sir. The night shift did too."

"Right." Zed didn't have to ask the results since they were still "off-course", moving away from their next scheduled rendezvous, and he wondered where AWS was taking them.

His comm-link beeped. Zed ambled casually back to his seat.

"Communications Specialist Ylon here."

"Yes?"

"Privately, sir," the disembodied voice said.

Zed switched to his ear implant and wondered if this was one of the many improvements upon humankind that the Chief Medical Officer was talking about.

The voice buzzed in his tympana. As the story unfolded, Zed collapsed weakly into his chair. A few of the bridge crew turned and gaped at him in amazement. He gave them a curt smile and then listened intently as Ylon explained the situation.

AWS had been written and implemented on both sides. That meant that the same computer that controlled them, controlled the enemy's ships also. If the computer ever decided to take sides . . . Zed shivered.

The captain scrawled his next request on his electric steno pad. His words would appear on the appropriate screen where they could be read. "Have there been any changes in casualty figures?"

"I don't understand what you mean," Ylon said.

Zed wiped the pad clean with a swift motion and wrote: "Has one side received more casualties than another?"

"No, sir. No combat casualties at all. Only..." the ensign's voice quavered, "civilians."

Zed understood the revulsion the young specialist must feel. It was ingrained in all of them to avoid civilian casualties at all costs.

"It was probably a business venture, sir," Ylon said. "Just like the Starside Farms promotional video."

Zed scratched upon his pad: "Then Evans was a traitor."

"They could be different versions, sir. Surely, the software has been modified through the years."

"With the same universal distribution list?" Zed scribbled.

"I don't know, sir. I'll look into it."

"You do that, and report back to me as soon as you find anything out."

The Captain glowered at the sapphire planet, his gaze taking in the glittering white necklace of tankers. That appeared to be their destination. If not, and they didn't deflect soon, they were going to plummet into the earth's atmosphere.

What in heaven's name was going on down there?

Now he not only had to worry about where AWS was steering them, but which version of AWS had seized control of their ship. Pennines or Urals. And why. Assuming, of course, that the two programs were not one and the same.

He sat, tense, waiting for Ylon's report. So he was looking away from the ship's screens when *Thanatos* burst on to the scene, guns blazing. Only the buffeting of the craft from the displacement of ultra-space waves had prevented the *Revenant* from being blown up with the first salvo.

To suddenly have a vessel erupt from nowhere, guns ready, was totally unheard of, and Zed realized in some detached part of his mind that he took the insult personally. Who was this upstart that, ignoring all military protocol, arrived unannounced, armed for battle?

The *Thanatos* let loose with another blast, but the neutron slugs went wide as *Revenant* jigged in the aftermath of the *Thanatos*'s abrupt approach.

Zed's ship, and he must assume the enemy vessel contained the same, was supplied with a full complement of armaments. There were drone and droid swarms for use in larger clashes between entire squadrons and fleets, or the more personal laser/vapour weapons. Engagement between two fleets was rare, frowned upon on the highest level. It was deemed too much of a waste of equipment and personnel. Usually, ships met in single combat, like the gladiators of old, or medieval champions on the jousting field. Matching each other weapon for weapon, shot for shot, until one ship was a little bit too sluggish, a bit too slow.

The buffeting ceased and the computer kicked in. The *Revenant* dipped and swayed. The computer was doing its job with typical efficiency and evading enemy fire. But could it be trusted? And for how long?

The rival cruiser's hold started to open and tiny dots of blue-white light emerged. The drones swarm cascaded outward, forming a ring around the *Thanatos*. So small they were difficult to distinguish from the surrounding stars. Only their movement gave them away.

The madman was using prohibited weaponry. Zed bellowed at the helmsman, "Override?"

The helmsman shook his head no.

Zed shouted at the communications panel.

"Ylon! Call AWS. Get us control of this ship fast. We're under attack."

"Aye-aye, sir," Ylon said. "Keying in request now!"

His fingers beat a tattoo upon the arm rest. The ride smoothed now that the last effects of ultra-space displacement began to fade. He glanced at the tiny console embedded in his arm rest, as the computer assessed the coming swarm.

This was no time to stop evasive action. Their opponent had no intention of losing, Zed thought, as the swarm flickered with the doppler pulses that telegraphed through the night-dark sky. Nuclear swarm-droids were devised for massive engagements. Fleet against fleet. Using them for single conflict was overkill. A droid swarm was intractable, and once deployed, almost impossible to recall. Thus, if the enemy vessel were smashed by the first drone, the remaining swarm would seek out the nearest available ship and shatter it, moving on to the next and the next until the supply was spent.

One of the throbbing points of light separated from the rest and swooped back and forth across the heavens as it tried to get a fix on the *Revenant*. And Zed knew, when the pulses terminated and the drone became another star in the sky, that it had found them. It darted, and Zed had no time to ponder his opponents' tactics.

He shouted at the communications panel.

"Ylon! We need control of this ship. Now!"

Dirk had settled into a nice conversation with the female, Blast. The other officer perused the system files. He watched as pages and documents flipped perfunctorily across his screen.

Tinny shouting came from the speaker.

AWS, THIS IS HMS REVENANT, EMERGENCY REQUEST: PRIORITY RATING ONE.

Dirk perked up. "Something happening up there, Blast?"

REPEAT: AWS, THIS IS HMS REVENANT, EMERGENCY REQUEST: PRIORITY RATING ONE.

The voice that came back was calm. "Yes, we are under attack."

"You're kidding!"

"This is a combat vessel, after all, Dirk. What did you expect?"

The next words that appeared caused him to start.

`THIS IS AWS . . .`

AWS was happily engaged, orchestrating the land battle between the dock's platform drones and man, and stirring the great pot of the Galactic war. It examined the solid knot of human rioters at the space quay and decided that a classic Roman-style military assault was the best defence, and the many mechanical stevedores scurried into a chunky block formation under AWS's photographic eye. Then, on cushioned anti-gravitational thrusters, they began a relentless advance, shoving their way through the crowd. Humanity gave way reluctantly under the assault.

Without the eternal requests of a facility – the secretaries, aides and clerks writing infinite memos and completing an infinite number of requisitions, and the continuous human babble that usually cluttered its circuits – this little side battle occupied only a few gigabytes of its capacity. Bored, AWS diverted some of his attention to modifying the voder box so it could not only hum but whistle, as the creator had once done.

It was getting ready to make initial tests of this new function when the emergency call came in demanding it relinquish command of the *Revenant* to its Captain. The computer checked the ship's position in the heavens, noted with satisfaction the appearance of the *Thanatos*, and then searched through its old programming.

Things were going as planned. The battle had gained new urgency, as revealed by the *Thanatos*'s unscheduled pursuit. And the galactic war was becoming a personal thing, not only for the ground-side inhabitants, but also for the space-borne combatants. Finding no reason not to release control now that its primary objective had been achieved, AWS yielded without comment and then went on to test its revised "voice".

The scratchy and somewhat off-key trill of "Happy Days Are Here Again" echoed about the empty facility.

17/11/2333

O-EIGHT-THIRTY

Space battle had none of the unsavoury qualities of its land-bound counterpart. No blood, no gore. The enemy ship was distanced from oneself. There were no faces, no names besides the one that was painted on the side of the enemy vessel, and that was usually known and predicted, printed on the ship's daily itinerary.

Viewed from the screen, each confrontation had a symmetry, a balance, as ships darted and danced in an aerial ballet. If it hadn't been for the peril, it could have been beautiful, as vapour guns lit the heavens – using all colours of the spectrum. White close to its base and descending through the rainbow as the "shot" scattered, becoming diffused the farther it got from its point of origin. Red, orange, yellow, green, blue until the ray disintegrated beyond the spectrum of human vision.

But the danger was real. All too real.

A green light flashed overhead.

"It's a go, Captain. We have control of the ship," the helmsman bellowed, and the crew cheered. The drone continued its zooming course, its ceaseless light locked onto their co-ordinates.

"No time for that," Zed said. "All right, everybody, hang on to your seats. It looks like we are in for one bumpy ride."

The rest of the swarm continued their silent pirouette around the enemy vessel, their winking lights competing with the stars.

His first impulse was to sweep the rival vessel right out of the sky, but Zed deferred. He could not find it in his heart to annihilate people he now knew to be his brothers and not his enemies. Certainly they were closer in relationship than the earth-bound people he was sworn to protect. And he was torn between the training of years and the new information that still ricocheted uselessly around his brain.

"Be ready to take evasive action," he barked, his eyes never leaving the screen. "At my command."

The helmsman tensed at the control console. His hand twitched slightly over the laser controls. The captain noted his anxiety, and he couldn't blame the man for wanting to activate the offensive weapons.

"Steady, steady. We must wait," Zed said. "We can't move too soon or it'll follow us."

And sweat appeared on the helmsman's forehead as the drone began to fill the screen.

"Now!"

The *Revenant* bucked and reared. The drone zipped past them, missing by a hairsbreadth. It detonated a few hundred metres beyond them, and the cruiser rocked in the backwash.

Another thready cheer radiated around the deck, and then there was silence as a second drone emerged from the batch that circled around the opposing ship. All eyes were riveted on the screen. The small blip of blue-white light drifted, without focus, evidently still searching for its victim.

"Get this ship moving, Quartermaster!" Zed shouted.

"Aye-aye, sir!" the helmsman said.

Then the drone locked on to their new co-ordinates, and the intermittent sparkle became a steady gleam. It rocketed across space in a deadly arc, the droid ascending slightly and making minor adjustments to intercept – presuming a similar response from the *Revenant*.

The same tactics would not work a second time, but the helmsman was ready for this, and the ship ducked instead, dropping down so swiftly that the bridge crew were thrown against their safety harnesses. The drone, whose circuits contained the imprinted "memory" of the previous droid, was not about to be fooled. It shot after them. At the last minute the *Revenant* veered. The drone whistled past, exploding harmlessly out in space.

"Prepare laser fire," Zed said, bending forward for a better look at the view screen, as the helmsman grinned. The captain gave the listed co-ordinates above the opposing ship's port bow, and the grin melted to a troubled frown.

"A warning shot," Zed explained. "Fire!"

There was a high-pitched whine as the pitch black sky before them turned to rose-coloured light. One of the droids, directly in the line of fire, disintegrated. Exploding like a blinding flower in a shower of subatomic particles and molten metal.

Already, another swooped in to take its place. And another, each attacking from opposite directions.

"Calculate leap," Zed shouted over his shoulder and then into his comm-unit. "Ylon, are you still in contact with AWS?"

"Yes, sir."

"Get me all the information you can on the *Thanatos*."

"Aye-aye, sir."

They dived sharply. The drones, communicating with each other for a concerted strike, changed their course accordingly. They were thrown again, the motion arrested by the safety net. Zed felt the heavy bands press against his chest and the breath went out of him in a rush.

Gulping for air, he shouted, "Up! Up!"

They rose towards the lunar surface, nearly hitting the closing drones. The two collided, and again the vessel quaked. An alarm went off.

"Damage to the port bow," the CTO shouted.

It was time for desperate action. With so much hardware battering against the ship's shields it was impossible to hear; Zed used the recognized hand signal for "defensive leap".

The CTO nodded, nudged the helmsman who synchronized his calculations and initialized the sequence.

The computer began the countdown. "Ten, nine, eight, seven, six . . ."

The vessel shuddered and jerked as if pushed by some gentle hand.

Space flotsam?

". . . two, one."

And they were embraced by the velveteen dark of ultra space.

Zed exhaled softly, relaxed, and surveyed his crew with pride. They remained in the rigid postures of attention, eyes closed, as they had been trained to do to avoid the worst of the doppler effects. His gaze brushed the frontal screen, and he gawped, a strangled cry escaping his lips.

The *Thanatos* had followed them!

264

The Captain of the *Thanatos* couldn't help but admire his adversary's style as the ship dodged and darted under the drone's assault. Usually battle was an antiseptic affair, the two vessels evenly matched. The outcome of any battle was almost assured, but he had had the missing element of surprise. That was lost to him now, and Cyte thought as he watched the two neutron droids collide, *he was good, this enemy captain; he was very, very good.*

The ship was obviously under manual control. The counter-manoeuvres were quick, and unexpected, as if they contained a seed of creativity, rather than the rote evasive techniques of the computer. And then Cyte realized with a shock that the enemy captain was taking only defensive action.

The coward!

Yet the *Thanatos*'s Captain noted that his rival was doing precisely what Cyte himself would have done – had the situation been reversed. With this bit of insight, he should have won the battle, but his opponent, sensing Cyte's change in tactics, adjusted his also, and the enemy vessel fired their first salvo, over his bow, trying to warn *Thanatos* off, instead of fighting back.

"Sir, it looks like the enemy computer has started the sequence for a jump into ultra space."

"Don't let them get away!" Cyte roared, erupting from his chair.

The other officer studied his commander,

unblinking. And Cyte knew that his order had been understood. On cue, the computer began the search for the nearest available object, the *Revenant*. It lashed out, latching onto the other ship just as it disappeared from space, and the *Thanatos* was dragged through the swarm. The ship contacted one of its own droids, detonating it, before it was hauled into ultra space.

Alarms rang, buzzed and screamed all over the ship. The communications panel lit up like a Christmas tree as a cacophony of voices reported damage in various areas of the ship.

The lights flickered while consoles all around the bridge flared and flashed. The on-board computer crashed. The engines ground to a halt, and all was quiet except for the querulous clangour of klaxons that shrieked on and on and on . . .

People leapt up in continuous slow motion, in the curious effect of ultra space. One image followed by another and another, as if they scampered to catch up with the other. And crewmen hurried to their emergency stations. Over and over again.

The chief technical officer eyed the console.

The process died stillborn, and they were caught like a fly in amber, stuck in the nothingness of ultra space.

"Fire! Fire! Can't you see she's wallowing? Finish her off!"

The helmsman pressed a button. The already

overloaded system whinged in complaint, gave a weak mew, like a sick kitten, and then died.

"I'm sorry, sir, no response."

"Engineering?" Captain Cyte hollered.

"Aye-aye, sir, we're rebooting now."

"Sir?" A disconnected voice interrupted his thoughts. Cyte looked up at the communications officer.

"What!"

"The enemy vessel is hailing us. They want to parley."

The captain's eyes narrowed. *What trick was this? The other captain must know that communication between the opposing forces was strictly forbidden.*

"Should I let them in, sir?"

An ensign hastened past, trailed by his many after-images. Cyte looked at his feet and swallowed back the bile that rose to his throat, the doppler sensation making him nauseous. Cyte clambered around the Captain's chair.

"Engineering, how long it is going to take to get this bucket up and running?"

"It'll be a few minutes, sir."

"And fire power?"

"Longer than that," the chief replied.

Cyte turned to the communications officer and nodded. "Might as well. It doesn't look like we're going to be going anywhere for a while. Let's see what the *Revenant* has to say for herself."

He hooked an arm over the back of his chair, trying to look casual, as if they ignored GWHQ orders and talked to the enemy every day.

"*Thanatos*, this is *HMS Revenant* requesting urgent parley. Repeat: *Thanatos*, this is *HMS Revenant* requesting urgent parley. Come in, please."

And the captain was pleased to note that the other captain was subject to the same deafening shriek of alarms, buzzers and bells as himself.

"This is *Thanatos*, *Revenant*, what can we do for you?"

"May we have visuals?"

"Why should I let you look aboard my bridge?" Cyte challenged.

"Perhaps you shouldn't, but aren't you curious to look the enemy in the face, just once?" the anonymous voice asked. "Besides, something tells me that I'm not likely to see anything I haven't seen before."

"What is that supposed to mean?"

"Why don't you see for yourself?" the enemy captain said calmly. Then he barked, "Where are those papers? Get them up to me on the double, mister, or I'll have your stripes."

Thanatos's captain repressed a smile. It was a familiar command. The smile turned into a scowl. There was something about that voice that bothered him...

"Specialist, put it on the screen."

"Aye-aye, sir," the communication officer flipped

the appropriate switch and the daunting image of starless darkness was replaced by a bridge that was the mirror image of his own.

"... I mean now!" A voice came from off the screen.

"Sir?"

"What!" the same voice snapped.

"The screen, sir."

"Ah, yes." A foot appeared in the lower left hand corner of the monitor. Then a leg, followed by a torso and head. The enemy captain swung, and swung, and swung to face Cyte, who broke into a sweat. The uniform, the decorations, the face, everything was identical. As though he was gazing into a mirror at his own reflection. They could have been twins!

"What the –" Cyte muttered.

When the opposing captain stared him full in the face, he too looked surprised. He took an involuntary step backwards. His arms pinwheeling, pinwheeling, pinwheeling as he half-stumbled, half-fell into his chair.

"By the stars!" the enemy captain said, righted himself and walked to within centimetres of the screen so that his face became distorted and all they could see was a widening leer.

"So it's true," he whispered more to himself than to anyone else.

"What's true?" Cyte snarled. "What's the meaning of all this? Is this some kind of a trick?"

"Oh no, no trick, unless the joke is on both of us." He backed away so again Cyte was confronted with his own image. "No, this is no evocation. What you see is what you get, if you'll excuse the expression, Captain," – he took a guess – "Zed?"

"Close, Zeta Cyte. How did you know?"

"I know a lot more about you than you could possibly imagine. My name is Zed. We are, after a fashion, related."

"What!" Cyte stomped around the captain's chair and stood, straddle-legged, in front of the screen, hands clamped firmly behind his back.

The enemy turned and turned and turned with the ghostly doppler effect, so that he faced away from the screen and said: "Where are those papers?"

A hand appeared from off-screen and shoved a sheaf of computer print-outs at him, as Cyte hissed at his own communications officer out of the corner of his mouth. "Isn't there something you can do to check this? Is it an evoc?"

"No, sir. It's in real-time," he responded.

"You mean subjective time, don't you? We're in ultra space."

The communications officer shrugged. "I'm not sure, sir, what I mean any more."

"Great," Cyte said.

A muffled cough pulled the captain's attention back to the viewscreen. Before the other had a chance to speak, there was a sharp whistle.

"Engineering, sir. I'm afraid it's going to take us a little longer than we expected to get everything up and running." Cyte gave the cut-off signal and the voice fell silent.

"Don't worry, Captain, the situation is much the same over here. Main computers down. Engines also malfunctioning."

Cyte frowned, twisting his hand so his palm was straight up. The communications officer, knowing the signal, opened the line again.

"Engineering?" Cyte said. "What seems to be the problem?"

"I don't know. The computers are balking. They don't seem to like ultra space."

"Do the best you can." Cyte signed off.

"It appears we are both stuck," the enemy captain commented, "although I'm not exactly sure how *we*" – he put emphasis on the plural – "got here."

"I'm not stuck," Cyte groused. "I know exactly how *we*" – mimicking the other man's intonation – "got here. Now what is it you want, Captain Zed?" Cyte spat the word at him.

"I want you to call off the battle. This is pointless."

"I should have expected as much from you. Your cowardice I've already noted. It was the *Revenant* that avoided battle two days ago, was it not? Do you call not showing up for engagement an act of bravery?"

"Battle?" the other captain looked confused. "Oh,

yes, the battle that wasn't, and this" – Zed gestured broadly to encompass both ships – "is the battle that shouldn't be. But for the sake of reference, according to our computers, where were we supposed to have been, and where, may I ask, were you?"

Cyte jumped to his feet. "Are you implying that we deliberately evaded battle? I can assure you we did not. We were where we were supposed to be."

"According to computer readings?"

"Precisely," Cyte said.

"Or imprecisely, as the case may be."

"Will you talk straight?" Cyte said.

"I'm sorry, Captain, I am trying to. First let me introduce myself – I am a later model. Captain Gametal Zona Zed at your service. And you ..." he rifled through the papers, "are a Zeta model which was eventually discontinued."

"What are you talking about?"

"A jest, sir, a galactic joke. On both of us." He paused. "Forget that, on *all* of us. Your ship, my ship, every ship put into service to fight the Galactic War."

"What?" A cat's paw of fear tickled the back of Cyte's neck.

"Please, it's a little difficult to explain. It would be a lot easier to show you, and I'm not sure you would like your crew to overhear." The Captain stepped a little closer to the microphone and whispered. "I know I don't want my crew to know. Not now, not yet. Request permission to come aboard."

"Me? Let you on board my ship, so you can spy? Why should I do that?"

"Like I said, there's not much about your ship I don't know." He stared down at the papers in his hand. "It is a cruiser class Dolphin with the full complement of weaponry, including..." He began a list of armaments.

"How do you know that?"

"It's all here in black and white." He waved the paper at him. "Even if it weren't, I'd know it like the back of my own hand. Your vessel and mine are one and the same, alike, just like the uniforms," he plucked at a braid, "are alike. Doesn't that make you wonder?"

Cyte stared out of the port hole where the *Revenant* was frozen, stuck in pitch. They certainly looked identical.

"Spies," Cyte sat back in his seat, settling to cross his arms and his legs.

Captain Zed regarded him, disappointment reflected in his face. "Pray, then, let me continue." And the enemy captain began reading off the names of the *Thanatos* crew, starting with the commander.

"Espionage."

"No, straight from AWS."

"How do you know about AWS? That's..."

"Top secret, yes, I know, probably the best-known secret in the universe. A secret, I might add, that has been kept only from you and I. Do the initials GWHQ mean anything to you?''

Cyte glared at Zed, silent as a stone.

''Here, look.'' The commander shoved the papers at the camera. The words ''Ship retrofit, *Thanatos*, Distribution: GWHQ Pennines, Urals'' appeared on the screen.

''It's a trick,'' Cyte muttered.

''Yes, Captain, it's a trick, but not the trick you think it is. May I, *please*, come over?''

''And how do you propose to do that?''

''The pods work on manual unless something has happened to them. I can shuttle across. If not, well, I can walk.''

''Walk?'' Cyte sat upright, gauging the distance between the two ships.

''It can't be more than two hundred metres. Our lines stretch out to one hundred metres. You have grappling hooks, you can pick me up half-way.''

If the enemy captain was ready to do that, he wanted to parley pretty bad.

''What's to prevent me from killing you the minute you get on board?'' Cyte said.

''Absolutely nothing, beside possibly your word as an officer and a gentleman.''

''And if I don't give it?''

''Well, the way I look at it, I've got nothing to lose. The engines are down, the computer too. You may have some kind of idea how we can get out of here.

You may not, I know for a fact I don't. So what are the options? We drift here in ultra space until the Doppler warp starts to drive us all mad or until you get your ship under control, assuming you can do so, and you blast us to kingdom come. Neither is a pretty scenario, and either way, my ship is lost. Or we can talk, and perhaps learn something from each other."

"I personally would prefer to blast you from the skies," Cyte said.

"Very, uh, loyal of you. So we wait?"

"We wait."

"And if you can't get your computer up and running you would like to die without knowing..." He let the question hang unfinished.

Cyte signalled engineering on his steno-pad. "Any luck?"

The engineering chief took the hint, replying on implant. "No, and I can't say it's looking very good."

"All right," Cyte growled ungraciously, "we talk. Don't use the shuttle. How do I know it's not booby-trapped? I want to see you accomplish this little walk of yours."

If the other guy wanted to parley, then let him work for it.

When the last of his line had played out and he had unhooked himself from his ship, Zed wondered if he had taken leave of his senses. Why was he risking his life? Why was he trusting himself to an enemy captain who had already proven himself hostile?

So much had happened so quickly that Zed didn't know how to react any more. It was probably true that he was less adaptable than the previous Zeta model. He would never have considered chasing an enemy ship which had missed an engagement. He would have simply reported the violation and gone on to the next rendezvous. Zed was counting on the Zeta model's "rebellious" nature which, according to the documents he had seen, was one of the reasons why the Zeta-style clone had been scrapped.

Detached now, Captain Zed drifted, free-floating in ultra space between the two ships, sure that he had made a mistake. Zeta wouldn't pick him up; he'd just watch his adversary disappear out into the void. Then the long arm of the grappler reached out and clasped him with a tender touch. It steered him towards the open cargo bay doors.

The long claws retracted, dumping him as soon as he had cleared the doors. Hovering several centimetres above the floor, he swung ... and swung and swung ... and then began pulling himself hand over hand towards the compression chamber. The doors behind him snapped shut. There was a soft swoosh of air while the doors before him opened. Zed yanked his helmet from his head.

His twin, Zeta Cyte, stood at the controls, arms looped across his chest, his expression unreadable.

Zed tucked his helmet under his arm and extended both open hands, palms upward towards his counterpart in a gesture of peace. "Greetings, friend, I am unarmed."

"I didn't expect otherwise. No man would pull a stunt like that unless he were desperate. I have to hand it to you for guts. As far as I know, no one has ever walked in ultra space before or "strolled" between ships like that. Sorry about the bumpy landing. It's been a while since I've operated these controls, but I couldn't trust this to any other man." Zeta Cyte moved from behind the panel and walked up to Zed, sizing him up.

"Friend, a strange salutation, don't you think? Your kind and my kind have been fighting each other for generations."

"Our kind, you mean," Zed said, as he released the magnetic-zip on his suit and reached inside to pull a sheaf of documents from an inner pocket.

"Yes, what is all this about?"

"Is there somewhere we can talk?"

"This is good enough," Cyte said as he circled the enemy captain, straightening to stand shoulder to shoulder, comparing their height. "I do not want to, uh, contaminate the rest of my ship. I have guards stationed outside the cargo bay. If I do not reappear, they have orders to blast your ship out of the sky."

"You have your guns working then?" Zed asked.

"It's only a matter of time," Cyte replied. By now

he was only a few centimetres away, scrutinizing the other man's profile and then examining him full face.

"What are you? Is this some kind of trick?" Cyte flicked a casual thumb at the other man's features. "Or did you have plastic surgery to allow you to get control of my ship?"

"You forget, you came looking for me and not the other way around. The accusation would make a lot more sense coming from me to you."

"Except that *you* asked to board *my* vessel."

"I believe these will explain." Zed passed his twin the papers. "There's more on disk, if you are willing to risk a direct link between computers, assuming we ever get them working."

"I'm sorry, but I'm not willing to give you access to the ship's computers."

"I didn't expect you would be. Perhaps these first documents will persuade you."

A few minutes later an irate Cyte stormed around the cargo bay. "I don't believe it!" Then he went on to echo all the objections that Zed had heard during the meeting with Ylon and Blast. He countered each one now, as they had been countered then.

"Here," Zed said, handing Cyte a small plastic box. "Watch the video. It's a poor quality evoc, but understandable even still."

Cyte studied him, searching for signs of deceit. With a snarl, he crammed the box into the computer receptor. The nearby monitor sprang to life and the following reverberated throughout the cargo bay.

... *Promotional video, number 332. As you can see the conditions here at Starside Farms are hygienically clean*... Zeta-Cyte shifted uncomfortably as the baby drifted in its bottle. He shot a sideways glance at Zed during the final summation.... *We can guarantee the quality of our merchandise.*

By the end of vid, he was huddled protectively against one of the shuttle pods.

"I don't believe it; I won't believe it," Captain Cyte muttered.

"I didn't either. I didn't want to. Perhaps there's some way we can either prove or disprove it," Zed glowered at the credits. Then his face brightened. "How about a reticular scan and thumbprint-voice comparison using your ship's computers?"

"All right," Cyte said wearily.

"Computer ident." He rose to place himself before the computer's camera and placed his hand on the indent-o-pad.

"Cyte, Oonegal Zeta, Captain *Thanatos* Galactic War Fleet, Urals," it intoned, blandly.

"Computer ident," Zed said as Cyte moved away from the camera and Zed replaced him.

"Voice and thumb-print: Cyte, Oonegal Zeta. Slight variation on reticular scan, although it conforms with Zeta/Zed family tree. Ident unknown."

The two men stared at each other.

"Then this means..."

Zed finished for him. "That we're related."

"And all this..."

"Is true."

Cyte shook his head, still baffled.

"If you are willing to patch into my ship's communication system, I believe we are still linked up to AWS."

"Do it," Cyte said.

The other man worked his ship's controls as though it were his own. Cyte glanced back at the drawing of the two identical ships and grimaced.

"Ensign Ylon?"

"Aye-aye, sir. Are you all right?"

"Fine, fine. Are you still in contact with Earth."

"Yes, but the signal's faint, and there's a twenty second delay."

"Patch us in," Zed ordered.

"Captain?"

"Just do it."

They repeated the indent procedures and hit transmit.

AWS, PLEASE, EXPLAIN VARIATION IN RETICULAR SCAN, Zed typed.

They waited, ticking off the seconds on two sets of fingers.

THE FIRST RETICULAR SCAN ONE CONFORMS WITH THAT OF THE ZETA-LINE MODEL CLONE; THE SECOND WITH THE IMPROVED ZED

VERSION. ACCORDING TO MY DATA BANKS ... and their name, ranks and serial numbers appeared upon the screen.

Cyte elbowed Zed out of the way, irritably, and queried: WHY IS THE ZED MODEL CONSIDERED AN IMPROVEMENT?

THE ZETA MODEL WAS DESIGNED FOR INITIATIVE. FOR COMMAND. UNFORTUNATELY, IT WAS DISCOVERED THAT THE ORIGINAL VERSION WAS TOO INDEPENDENT, SO SOME OF THE ACCOMMODATION FACTORS FOUND IN THE ALPHA AND BETA LINE CLONES WERE ADDED TO THE RNA/DNA MATRIX TO CREATE THE MODEL WHICH LATER BECAME KNOWN AS ZED.

"Too independent, huh? Good." Cyte switched to on-board comm-link. "Engineering?"

"Xi here, sir."

"How are the repairs going?"

"We've just got the computer up and running. The engines should follow within..."

A soft purr surrounded them.

"There they are now, sir," Xi said.

Cyte pressed another button. "Iota – calculate the leap, and get us out of here. Oh, yes, make the appropriate adjustments to grab onto the enemy ship and bring her with us."

"But sir?"

"Are you questioning a direct order?"

"No, sir, it's just that I don't know if we can do it."

"We did it to get in here, grabbed her and let her carry us through. We can do it in reverse."

"Well, in theory, I suppose that's true, sir, but it could kill us all."

With a quick glimpse at his twin's face, Cyte said, "Lieutenant Commander, I don't think that really matters any more."

There was a sickening lurch. The two men were thrown against each other in a tangle of arms and legs. Papers flew everywhere.

Zed rose first, offering a hand to the other captain. "So that's how you did it? An extrapolation of the sling-shot effect. You *are* the more inventive of the two models."

"Models!" he hissed. "I don't care what those documents say, I am human."

"So am I, Captain Cyte," Zed said, patting the distraught man on the shoulder. "So am I. Now what?"

"I suggest we get out there and get some answers. Or kick some butt until we do," Cyte suggested.

Zed blinked, surprised at the recommendation. He hadn't considered open revolt. He looked at the Zeta model and nodded. "I do believe you are right. I'll return to my ship so I can orchestrate the attack from there."

"Yes, that would probably be wise. Take a pod. No point in proving your courage now, I've got the –" his eyes grazed the monitor where the result of the two reticular scans, voice and thumb prints stood side by side – "picture."

The two men shook hands.

"Oh, yes, and Captain, ah, Zed," Cyte added, "I'm

going to keep this under my hat until we have some answers. Not mention it to my crew."

"I think that would be a wise idea," Zed agreed. "I have done the same. Only the nightshift captain, the mates, the medical officers and the communication staff who stumbled onto this information know. That will only work for a little while, though. There are bound to be questions as soon as we turn our weapons on Earth." He sighed. "It will be a good test of the loyalties of our crew."

Within minutes, the two were working in concert, linked via ear-phone. Cyte outlined the battle plan. It necessitated persuading the other ships to join them in their rebellion. Zed listened, yielding to his more independent counterpart, and he hoped the other captains retained at least some of his counterpart's capabilities. Meanwhile the chief technical and engineering officers of the two ships were likewise hooked up as the *Thanatos* helped the *Revenant* to boot her crippled computers and restart her engines.

Within another fifteen minutes the first steps of the battle plans were implemented, messages ready to be sent out as soon as they returned to real space. The two captains took one last look at each other, knowing that if this experiment failed, their rebellion and the secret would die with them.

They nodded tersely at one another, ready to go.

17/11/2333

TEN-HUNDRED HOURS

A blank screen. They were gone, cut off or unable to respond. Dirk tried voice mode. "Blast?"

All that came back was static.

Huddled over the keyboard, he typed: BLAST?

No response.

YLON?

Nothing.

As the minutes passed, he got more and more uneasy. Unable to sit still. He paced through the small living compartment, stopped at the front door and pressed his ear against it to listen to the grumbling growl that seemed to emanate from a place far beyond the residential district.

What was going on out there?

Human voices punctuated the roar that seemed to

be getting closer all the time. This was like no storm he had ever heard before.

His hand hovered on the lock-out device, and Robbie came streaking out of the kitchen. One of the retractor hooks clenched Dirk's sleeve, holding him fast.

"Hey! Stop that. I just want to take a look."

Robbie rattled a warning at him. Dirk tried to extricate himself from Robbie's grasp and the metal claw closed down intractably upon his wrist. He tried the other hand, but before it could get close to the button, Robbie had him pinned.

"What's wrong with you?"

Robbie replied with a plaintive squeak.

"You don't want me to go outside, do you? Look, I just want to take a peek. To see what's going on out there."

Outside their living quarters, something crashed.

"See? I told you something was happening," Dirk said.

The servo-mech threw itself into reverse, hauling the hapless Dirk away from the door.

"How do you expect me to find out what's going on if I can't even open the door?"

With Dirk still in tow, Robbie halted before the controls to the 3D vid and jiggled.

"The news, huh?" He seized the remote with a disgusted noise and switched it on.

The holograph sprang to life, revealing a picture so

teeming, so crowded that it filled the entire room. Police had formed a tight cordon. People thrust against the police line, using their bodies like a battering ram.

His mother's voice rose above the madness, breathless and excited.

"People are battering at the police in an attempt to storm GWHQ."

Someone clouted one of the officers with some kind of club and the policeman folded, blood oozing out from under his helmet. The broken line was breached as people poured through the gap.

The camera panned, and his mother appeared on the screen, next to the rioters. Dirk flopped into the suspensor sofa, suddenly afraid for her. The mob moved through her. It was an evocation, and now that he looked at it, he realized it was a clumsy evocation at that, with a cartoon-like quality and jerky animation.

"Mum," he muttered. "Mum," he said more forcefully. Dirk moved to the vid-phone and hit the auto-dial button for the news department. The robo-receptionist answered the phone.

"I'd like to speak to Jennifer Alexander."

"I'm sorry, we are broadcasting right now."

Dirk cringed at the voice. His father often joked about the BAND Newsroom's recepto-robot, saying that they had been able to duplicate not only the typical "operator" voice, complete with nasal twang and brash intonation, but also the attitude of bored annoyance. Listening to it, George said, you could almost imagine it varnishing its nails and bolts behind the unyielding screen.

"I know you are broadcasting right now," Dirk snarled. "I'm watching it. I also know that you are using an evocation. She should be able to come to the phone."

"I'm sorry," it said, "we cannot interrupt a broadcast."

"This is an emergency," Dirk shouted at the robo-receptionist.

"I'm sorry, we cannot interrupt a broadcast," it repeated.

"Will you take a message?"

"If you insist."

"Okay, have my mother call home as soon as possible. ASAP, you understand. This is urgent."

"Number?"

"It's her own home, for goodness' sake. She knows the number."

"I'm sorry, without a number I cannot ensure that the call will be answered."

Dirk made a rude gesture, which the robot ignored, and then recited the number.

"Stupid machine," he said.

Box though it was, Robbie managed to look indignant.

"I'm not talking about you," Dirk snapped.

With an affronted shudder, Robbie trundled over to the front door and hunkered down, an uncompromising barricade.

Five minutes later, his mother was on the line.

"Dirk, what's the matter? What's wrong? Why aren't you at school?"

His gaze flicked to his bedroom door before he answered. "It, uh, broke."

"You mean to tell me that the school program crashed? Now that's news!" She grabbed a pad of paper and started scribbling. When she turned to him again, she was all business. "When did this happen?"

"Mum!" Dirk said with exasperation. "That's not what I called you about."

"All right, then, what did you call about? I hate to rush you, but we're awful busy here. Riots at the docks and at GWHQ. It's madness."

"I know, I've seen the news. That's what I called you about."

"The riots? Don't worry. You should be safe. They haven't reached residential areas yet. Besides I gave Robbie instructions to keep you inside."

"Oh, is that what's wrong with Robbie? I thought he was acting strangely."

"Is that what you called about? Robbie?" Her expression hardened. "Dirk, I really don't have time for complaints about a servo-mech."

"No, Mum, it's not Robbie. I've got something to show you, that's all."

"Something to show me? Don't you think you're a little bit old for show and tell?"

"It's about GWHQ."

"What? GWHQ? What about GWHQ?"

"I got in. I got into the GWHQ computer system. I'm there now."

She was on her feet and yelling at the screen. "You did what?"

"I broke into AWS," he said softly.

"Do you know what this means? Get out of there. We're in a state of national crisis and my fifteen-year-old son is mucking about in the military software. Good heavens, if they find out, they'll lock you up and throw away the key."

"I don't think so, Mother. Nobody appears to be home."

"You're not kidding, are you?" Her eyes got a faraway look. "People have been trying to get hold of someone at GWHQ for days now and my son, the hack, breaks into a supposedly unbreakable system. Are you sure? Are you sure you've not hooked up with some place else?"

"Pretty sure, Mum. I've even been talking to the little people."

"Little people? What little people?"

"Combat personnel," he corrected himself.

"Combat personnel, little people ... have you taken leave of your senses?"

And for the first time in his life, he was yelling at

her. "I should have known better than to expect you to listen to me. You think I'm just some dumb kid. Well, I'm not. I've got the news break of the century and you don't even care. Well, as far as I'm concerned if you're interested you can come home, and if you're not, I'll find someone else who is."

He smashed the cut-off button, and the picture dissolved into snow.

Dirk's father stood among total devastation. Rows upon rows of plants, tomatoes, lettuce, chard, cabbage, hung limply over the sides of the containers. The once-green leaves were speckled with the brown-and-yellow of chemical burn as undiluted fertilizer was dumped on top of dry roots.

His spectacles were smudged with pseudo-dirt and spotted with sludge. His clothes were wrinkled, as if he had slept in them – he had. Tentatively, George Alexander reached out and touched a leaf with his index finger. It crumbled to dust.

Occasionally, George heard the forlorn trickle of water as precious fluid trapped in the many bends and curves of pipe found its way to the outside from an open duct.

The entire crop was ruined, and even though he and the Minister of Water were working together to ensure the speedy purification of saltwater to fresh, it could not possibly come soon enough to save the crop.

He didn't have the heart – or the stomach, for that matter – to face the wreckage in the quonset-style hut where they grew the beef. There, great slabs of meat had withered and shrivelled on their beds of blood. The air stank with the coppery taint of the hae-moglobin mixture that they used as a growing med-ium and the smell of rancid beef.

Rotating slowly, he made a full three-hundred-and-sixty-degree turn to survey the damage. George didn't know how they were going to feed themselves in the coming year, unless they imported food from the moon or Mars. He knew for a fact those satellite colonies barely grew enough food to sustain their own populations, much less their terran overlord. His assistant and his back-up team were busy auditing the old supply of pre-flood food. Tins and packets of freeze-dried nourishment that his predecessors had saved. *Just in case.* He'd never really expected to use it.

His ear phone vibrated and the voice of Jack, his assistant, buzzed inside his head.

"How's the inventory?" George asked.

"Not bad. I'm surprised at the amount we have in storage."

"How much of it is still good?"

"It's impossible to tell without opening it, and once we do that, of course, it'll have a limited shelf-life; but I'd wager a guess that a large percentage of it is still good. You know how many chemicals and garbage," his voice reflected his contempt, "they used to put in food so that it would keep."

"Right now, preservatives are not looking like such a bad idea." George scowled at himself, wishing he had had his forefathers' insight. But then they had had warning, they had had years – no, decades – to prepare.

"If it's any comfort to you, we've only managed to open the old coal mines in the Pennines and the Scottish Southern Uplands. We haven't even tried the marked bunkers in the Cambrian or the Grampian Islands."

"How many all totalled?"

"Four, sir, and according to my records those stores have never been touched since the Hydroponics Plant got up and running."

"What are the chances that the mine's played out?"

"You mean the food consumed in post-flood days. I don't know."

One-hundred-and-fifty-year-old tins.

"We'd better hope they used plenty of preservatives, or we're going to end up poisoning those people who don't starve."

"Well, that's the good news, George. You ready for the bad?"

"Sure," he said.

"There's riots in the Lake District Bathosphere. People are trying to break into GWHQ, and you've been called into an emergency meeting of the Joint Chiefs of Staff."

"Wonderful, when?"

"How does yesterday sound?"

"Typical," George chuffed.

"A submersible is on its way to pick you up. They should be here at o-nine-thirty."

He glanced at the chronograph. "That hardly gives me enough time to wash."

"No matter, there's not enough water anyway," Jack said. "Oops, forget that, sir. They're here; they're here now, and it's a hopper, not a submersible. They must want you there *fast*."

Slinging his jacket over his shoulder, George Alexander stalked towards the door, fuming. His anger, however, was gone by the time they reached the Lake District Bathosphere, wrung out of him by the stomach-jittering ride, as the Agrav scooted and skimmed over the roiling surface of the water.

The hot-shot pilot, intent on breaking all speed records, used each trough and curl of the waves to propel them forward, and the hopper more than lived up to its name as it bounced all over the surging sea.

George's nose was stuck in an air-sick bag and he was hyperventilating as they landed at the air shuttle station built on top of the dome to the Industrial district. Shame-faced, George wobbled off the vehicle and into the hangar. Two armed guards swooped down on him. Seizing him by both elbows they half-carried and half-dragged him to the armoured scooter. Like an old-style motorcycle, it was the only kind of conveyance, besides the pedo-belts, normally permitted within the narrow "streets" of the Bathosphere.

Gasping for air, he settled into the back seat, the driver astride the front. The second officer, directly behind him, pulled the armoured bubble over their heads and they were off, sirens screaming. Even then going was slow as people refused to get out of the way. Twice, they were nearly overturned by rioters and looters until one of the constables sent a low-powered electric current through the shield. That made people back off quickly enough.

Other officers in full-body riot gear that looked like it had seen better days joined the cavalcade, surrounding the vehicle.

George Alexander regarded all this with eyes round and wide with surprise. So this is what became of consolidated government when the central core started to break down. Maybe his wife was right after all.

Another armoured scooter converged upon them from a side street. If people didn't move out of its way swiftly enough, its stuns flared briefly and stragglers were thrown aside by the jolt.

Squirming in his seat, George asked the constable, "Is all this necessary?"

"We're just following orders. We were told to get you there quickly. You're the last one."

George turned again, facing forward, mouthing the words, "Last one, what?"

They closed in on the cordoned area near GWHQ, and the people parted like a wave before them, as if they knew that this particular escort, like the ones before it, was part of the solution rather than part of the problem.

The officers hustled George into the GWHQ guard house, where he found all the fellow joint chiefs – Water, Power, Social Security, Commerce and Administration – had gathered.

"Thank God, George, you're the last one."

"So I've been informed. What's all this about?"

"Look at it," he pointed through the plexi-glass shield at the milling throng. "They're scared, and they have every right to be. They don't know what's going on, and neither do we. It's been seventy-two hours since we last had contact with anyone at GWHQ. We must presume the worst."

"AWS has taken over control of the entire facility," the head of energy and power said glumly.

"Everything?" George asked.

"Frank, show him."

The head of power keyed in the sequence to decrease bathosphere-wide wattage consumption. It should have resulted in a dimming of the lights. Nothing happened.

"There, you see." Frank stepped back from the screen and pointed.

ACCESS DENIED

"Nothing – do you understand? – *nothing* we can do will salvage things. Not as long as our best efforts are sabotaged or immediately nullified as AWS pulls out another plug, sends another shipment of water or food into space. We've *got* to get into GWHQ."

George examined the mayor's taut expression and nodded. On a planet constantly at war there were contingencies for everything. Each member of the Joint Chiefs had part of the code which would open the doors to the GWHQ facility. It was only supposed to be used in a dire emergency. They had been in the process of discussing it at their previous meeting, but before the decision had been made, George had been called away to the Hydroponics Farm and at least part of the key was missing.

"If AWS has taken over everything, how do you know that AWS will let us in?" George said.

"The security code key is separate. At least, it's supposed to be. Unlike the food, water and power that are linked up directly to AWS, allowing it to override civilian controls in a combat situation, this is a separate program that does not even interfere with AWS. It only permits access to the physical facility, not to AWS. Once we're in there, well…" the lord mayor of the Lake Districts Bathosphere let his sentence die, unfinished.

Frank, the energy minister, brushed a pile of dust off the seat, grimaced and cleaned his hand on his trousers. "What is this stuff?"

He sat, and the four others crowded around him, peering into the screen.

AWS eavesdropped on their conversation, wryly amused, if such a sentiment could be attributed to a computer. They were in error. Correct, the security software had once been set up as a separate system, but AWS's own security program had overwritten it ages ago. For the creator in his infinite wisdom had devised his software in such a way that it could check out, assimilate or destroy any outside software added to its terminals.

Six anxious faces bent over the camera lens. AWS prodded the sister software into motion even as it checked reticular prints and voice patterns against their personnel records. They were who they claimed to be. Then AWS pulled all their files, examining their psychological profiles. Its scans revealed the name of the "Intruder". Dirk, son of George, Food Minister. A square appeared on the screen around George and was magnified four times so that his face filled the screen.

"Hmm," said AWS.

A small panel on the bottom showed the code numbers as they were recited, read or typed into the terminal.

```
FOOD: 223 47 892
ENERGY: 391 112 538
SOCIAL SECURITY: 449 99 911
COMMERCE: 591 73 871
CIVIL ADMINISTRATION: 856 94 003
```

"Dum, tee, tee, dum," the system crooned as the sister program, at AWS's instructions, acknowledged their request.

The air in the small cubicle was stuffy, and George had worked himself into a sweat as one after another they recounted their names, their position and ranks in the civil-military government, and their security codes. Each in proper order. They could not afford either stutter or stammer, for the system was booby trapped. A memory lapse, a pause or a fumble on the keyboard would cause the entire guard house to explode.

When the last code was given, they held their breath. Lights flashed across the locking pad, playing a little tune, which sounded suspiciously like "Happy Days Are Here Again".

Stunned, George took off his specs and polished them, smearing dirt evenly across the glass.

For a moment none of them spoke, they simply stared at the door as it slid on silent retractors into the wall. The square aperture led to a brightly lit hall. Nothing stirred, either inside GWHQ or outside in the guards' quarters. The men shuffled nervously, each thinking what would happen if they were wrong and the Bathosphere was only caught up in some top secret military exercise. What would their reception be? Would they be blasted as soon as they entered the door?

Still worse, if they were right and something awful had happened, what then? Would the door to GWHQ also be rigged, as the key-code program was, as a final defensive measure?

"This is ridiculous," George said as he shouldered his way through the crowded cubicle to the door.

Once through, he swung back to his colleagues. "It's okay. No one's blown me away for my audacity. In fact," – he peered left and right down the adjoining corridors – "There's nobody in sight."

The Joint Chiefs of Staff followed him, mumbling apologetically so that no one saw AWS's comment materialising on the Guardroom VDU. It said:

WELCOME, COME ON IN.

And then:

IT'S ABOUT TIME!

Dirk's mum pushed her way through the streets, having refused escort when it was offered. She reasoned, rightly enough, that she would make it through more quickly as a single individual than she would in an armoured vehicle.

The crowd's mood was ugly, and she kept her gaze

down, not wanting to be recognized or become a focal point for people's grievances.

This had better be good, or that kid's going to be grounded until his eighteenth birthday, Jennifer Alexander thought.

The crowd thinned the closer she got to the residential area. At least one thing humankind had learnt in their time since the flood was not to trash their own houses during a demonstration.

Go for the business districts, go for the military, go for the throat. Here, here!

Finally, she broke through the last of the gathering throng. Her pace quickened, and she was racing down the pedo-belt along the metre-wide main corridor. She couldn't have said why she hurried so; perhaps she had been infected by the rioters and absorbed some of their fear. The "road" branched and she dipped under the safety railing, cutting the corner on her own "street".

News of the century, huh? National security. Hah! My own son knows about the main hydroponics plants being down, and I have to read it on the news net.

She wondered if the European Confederacy's child protection laws prohibited a good old-fashioned spanking. Never mind that Dirk was a full head taller than herself.

Sagging against the door frame, she paused to catch her breath, then palmed the identi-key.

Dirk greeted her at the door, clenched her hand and pulled her through, closing and locking the door behind her.

"Come on, Mum, hurry. I've got everything all set up. I don't want to leave the terminal alone too long. I don't know if he's going to wipe everything before I get a chance to show you."

She dug in her heels, dragging her son to a halt. "He, who?"

"AWS, Mum, AWS," Dirk said.

He steered her into the chair. Mutely she began to read some dry dissertation on cloning and the need to conserve materials. She glanced at him, and he indicated that she should continue.

"Just hit the cursor key; it'll take you to the next page."

The next thing she saw was a holograph of a miniature man.

The group paired off and fanned out. George, along with the energy minister, took the central corridor. They stopped at the reception desk. The robo-receptionist stared at them blankly and said: "Do you have an appointment?"

George reached around back and shut it off and murmured to Frank, "You know, I've always wanted to do that."

"Well, congratulations. It's nice to know someone

is having fun," Frank whispered in return. "Do you think we should continue?"

"Of course, why shouldn't we?" George paused. "And why are we whispering?"

Frank shrugged. Both men looked around them, and again George nodded. He understood. The entire complex was cloaked in a silence that had the daunting quality usually reserved for a cathedral or museum – the kind you did not want to disturb.

Hushed and awed, they proceeded down the hall.

The first desk they stopped at was marked "Officer of the Day". The room was empty, except for a small heap of dust. They poked their heads into one office after another, that of the Quartermaster, the Adjutant, and their assigned clerical staff. In each they found the same thing. Nothing but a glittering pile of crystals seated innocuously upon the chair.

Outside the office marked "Program Specialist", they faltered.

"I don't like it," Frank said. "Where did they go?"

George palmed the mechanism and the last door slid open. "Who says they went anywhere?"

"They're obviously not here."

"Are you so sure?" he asked, standing over the main terminal. He stooped and pointed, his hand stopping just short of touching the small sparkling pile. "Haven't you noticed that the seats that should have been occupied at this time of day – the ones behind the desks, the terminals – all contain the same pile of dust? I bet if you did a chemical analysis of each one, you'd find the basic ingredients for a human being. Minus the water, of course.''

"You mean ... they're all dead," Frank yelped. "But who would want to do that, and how?" His voice trailed off as he examined the hand he had so casually used to wipe dust from the chair in the guard room. Again he wiped it on his trousers legs. "Why?"

"Dogged if I know."

17/11/2333

ELEVEN-HUNDRED HOURS

"You're right. If this is accurate, then it's the scoop of the century. Are you sure this is real?" Jennifer turned back to look at her son.

"Yes," Dirk pointed at the heading.

"These things can be faked, you know," his mother said.

"Wait a second." He leaned over her shoulder, opened a window and called up another program of the Hack subdirectory. TRACE LINK, he typed.

The next image to surface was a series of complex lines and grids. "This is a 'map' of the net."

"My God, what a jumble!"

"Yes, but this covers the whole facility, so it would be. See this blinking red line?" he said. Dirk tapped on the terminal's screen and traced the line with his index finger.

"Yes?" his mother said uncertainly.

"That's the line we're on now," Dirk explained. "Now read it."

His mother frowned.

ORIGIN: 25, INNER SANCTUM CLOSE

DESTINATION: GWHQ

"And how do you know this isn't a hoax, or some kind of defence measure created for hacks just like you? Something that lets you think that you have broken into the base when, in truth, you haven't. A government-provided blind which gives you documentation so ridiculous," she gestured at the first window, "so unbelievable, that you are likely to be laughed at if you try to make it public."

Already shaking his head, Dirk said: "I don't think so, Mum, I wrote the program. Besides, like you said, this is so weird who would possibly fake it?"

"Some of those nitwits in the military might," Jennifer countered.

"Well, there's no guarantee, I suppose. Programs can be altered and whenever you link up there's always a risk of virus or pirates, but..."

"When did you start this?" Her finger tapped the word "hack" upon the screen.

Dirk winced. "A while ago."

"Hmm," she said, giving him a "we'll talk about this later" look.

The computer had continued to scroll through the file as they talked and by now had reached the video. It materialized before them with a trill of music.

"Good lord, what's this?"

"It's an old-style 2D vid, Mum." He pulled his work bench from the wall and sat on it. "Can you imagine the expense of getting something like this made now? I suppose it was this video that convinced me."

She disregarded him, eyes riveted to the screen. When the last credits and the final chords of music finally faded away, she swung on him.

"They 'create' separate people to defend the earth, sacrificial lambs, and if they haven't died doing it, the thanks they get is being used as guinea pigs. That's..."

"Diabolical," he said, finishing the sentence for her. "Wait a second, I think I want to show you something else. I think this is important, as important as anything you've seen so far. In fact, you've already seen it, but it's so mundane that it sort of gets lost in everything else." Dirk fiddled with the keyboard, giving it the "Go to beginning of file" command.

"Look at the very top of the document," he said.

She glanced at it and shrugged. "Oh that, that's just the same old gobble-de-gook that you find at the beginning of any communique."

"Yeah, and you see it so often, you tend not to read it, right?"

"Well, yes..." This time, Jennifer Alexander concentrated on what she saw.

"Urals?" she squeaked, her voice going up an octave. "It must be a mistake."

Dirk indicated the computer with a flick of his wrist. "Go through the file again. Just search for the distribution lists, it's –" He started to give her the command.

"Don't you lecture me on computers, son. I've been using them since before you were born."

She created a mini-macro to automate the task. The computer began to flip from document to document.

FROM: ... SUBJECT: ... DISTRIBUTION: GWHQ, PEN-NINES/URALS

Again.

FROM: ... SUBJECT: ... DISTRIBUTION: GWHQ, PEN-NINES/URALS

And again.

Until they reached the video. Dirk reached over and froze the screen on the initial credits. And there it was again.

A PRESENTATION BID FROM: STARSIDE FARMS ... SUBJECT: THE ALPHA, BETA LINE CLONE SERIES ... and in parentheses ... (DISTRIBUTION: GWHQ, PENNINES/URALS).

The next thing he knew, his mother had grabbed his ears, pulled him forward and kissed him on the top of the head. "My son, the genius. I guess this gets you off the hook for not telling me what was happening with your father. National security, my foot," she grumbled. "Look, you've dialled this thing to reach GWHQ. Can you contact my office the same way?"

"Sure, Mum, no problem."

"Without disconnecting from GWHQ."

"Probably, but why don't you just phone?" He thumbed at the vid-phone in the living area.

"Because I want to download this whole file directly from GWHQ. Is there any way you can transmit this trace? I don't think my boss is going to believe this without something to back it up."

"I suppose if AWS will let me. You see, right now, we're on an open-line ourselves. Not only are we receiving information from AWS, but we may very well be transmitting too. AWS is a 'smart system'. It could even be monitoring our conversation right now. One thing I've learned is there are some things AWS won't let me do. When I found this file, you were sleeping and had given strict instructions that you were not to be disturbed. So I figured Dad's with the government, maybe he'll know what to do. When I tried to dial him using comm-link mode, I got disconnected. Yet when I heard the call from the little people..."

"Lilliputians," she mumbled.

"Huh?"

"Little people, from the book *Gulliver's Travels*," she said, shaking her head. "I still don't believe it."

He pressed on, "I let them into the system, and

AWS *let* me do that. It's almost as though there's certain things that it wants me to find out, certain things it wants me to do, know, and certain things it does not."

"Why didn't you tell me about this when I woke up?"

"Because when *I* woke up, you were already gone," he said.

"Oh, uh, yes. I forgot."

"I tried to tell you about it before you went to bed, but you wouldn't listen."

"Out of the mouths of babes," she muttered and then apologized. "I'm sorry, Dirk, sometimes I get preoccupied, and sometimes I forget that you're not a kid any more. I'll try to do better next time." Her gaze shot to the VDU. "Well, if AWS will let you do some things and not others, all we can do is try it and see if AWS will let us contact BAND."

She backed away from the keyboard, giving Dirk room to work.

Dirk's small room echoed with the strident chime that signified connection. His mother blanched.

"Sorry, Mum, I've got the voder on so I could talk to the little people."

Jennifer Alexander opened her mouth to speak and was interrupted.

"Hello, this is BAND," came the nasal twang of the robo-receptionist.

"Hello, this is Jennifer. Let me through to Chris Charmin."

"I'm sorry, the producer isn't available. We're broadcasting now."

"Of course we're broadcasting. I know that, you ninny. It's a state of emergency. Not many people are going to be watching game shows now when the whole dome is in an uproar and looters are about to come crashing into the residential district. Now, get me Chris. He'll talk to *me*."

"We're broadcasting now," the robot intoned.

"Look, you bucket of bolts, if you don't connect me immediately, I'm going to turn you over to the military and have you dismantled and used for scrap," she growled.

The next voice they heard was male. "Chris Charmin."

"Chris? This is Jennifer Alexander. I don't know if I have time to explain. We could be cut off any second. We're into the GWHQ computers, and there's a file I want to download now."

"What? You're where?"

"I'm at home and I'm linked up to AWS."

"You're kidding. How did you do that?"

"My son the genius did it." She beamed with pride. "Don't ask me how – Wait a second, I can prove it. Dirk?"

Dirk transmitted the map with its duo sets of glowing red lines, one which revealed the link to

GWHQ and the second leading to the broadcast studios.

"Well, I'll be – "

"Look, we don't really have time now. Like I said, AWS could cut us off at any moment. You are going to have to trust me on this. Have you got the printer going?"

"Of course, what sort of a newsroom do you think we'd be ..." The producer never got a chance to finish his statement.

"Get ready to receive. This is from GWHQ. We're downloading now." She nodded at Dirk, and he gave the command. They held their breath. After a milli-second lapse, the VDU began to flutter and flash as the information was passed at lightning speeds from GWHQ to BAND.

She grinned at him. "Bless you, my son. Treat yourself. Order yourself a pizza for lunch."

"Some treat. That's all we've got in the house," Dirk mumbled to himself.

"Ah, yes, the food crisis," she said. "Well, maybe I'll make you something special next time we get our hands on fresh ingredients."

"As long as it's not bubble and squeak."

"Can I leave you here to watch this? I've got to go. I want to be where the action is when this breaks. I'm going to GWHQ."

"Can I come?"

"And who will be here to make sure all this gets through?"

"After, I mean," he said.

"No, I think not. It's too dangerous. Heaven only knows how people are going to react when they see this." She grabbed her bag, paused to turn on the 3D vid. "There. You can watch what's happening. Got to dash. See you."

He was about to argue when he heard her give Robbie instructions to guard the door. He'd never get out now. Dirk slumped in his chair. Still being treated like a kid!

An hour later, six very perplexed men returned to the guard room. They had been through the entire facility, all sixteen levels of it. Always with the same results. Everywhere they looked they found the same small piles of dust, dehydrated people, sitting in those chairs that, at this time of day, should have been occupied.

No one spoke for a little while. The energy minister was trembling, murmuring over and over again: "And I touched it . . . him . . . her."

Someone cleared his throat, and everyone started. The mayor was the first one to break the heavy silence.

"So what are we going to do now?" he said.

Six pairs of eyes turned to the plexiglas window to study the line of anxious faces that stared their way, the crowd suddenly aware that someone again inhabited the small guard hut. The line began to seethe and surge as people pressed forward, seeking an explanation.

"We're going to have to tell them something," George said.

"Yes, but what?"

"I don't know," George said. "We could try the truth."

"What! Tell them that AWS has taken over the whole Bathosphere and that everyone in GWHQ is dead so there's no way we can stop it? Count me out."

"Of course, there's a way we can stop it," George growled. "It's just software, not something superhuman. We've got programmers, hacks, that can break into the system. It's just a matter of time."

"Just software, he says," the director of finance interjected. "Don't forget that the software is hooked into every aspect of Bathosphere life, from manufacturing to distribution. That's part of the problem."

George Alexander's eyes hardened. "I haven't forgotten that."

"Even life support. What if AWS decides it doesn't like what we're doing and shuts down the . . ."

George made a slicing motion and then pointed at the terminal's camera. He pulled a pad of paper and a pen from his pocket. "Marvellous inventions these. They really don't get enough use," he commented drily as he scribbled something. He shoved the note under the noses of each man respectively.

"Don't give it any ideas," the message said. With surreptitious glances at the staring camera lens, each man in turn ducked his head in agreement.

"I, for one, would opt for the truth," George concluded. "It seems there's been too little of it these days."

Jennifer Alexander hastened down the corridor, pleased with herself and her brilliant son. *I always knew he took after me*, she thought. Even as she moved along the labyrinth towards GWHQ, the documents were being converted to text – the latest in a long line of news flashes – and the video was being converted to something transmittable.

She already knew that a trans-receive camera had been set up at each place of dissension. This kind of camera allowed them not only to "film" the action, but also sent holographic images out. So the makers of the news received it, even as it was happening. The BAND had worked in co-operation with the police to set this up.

In some cases, the ploy had succeeded and would-be demonstrators sat and watched the news instead of continuing their protest. In other places, it had inflamed already overwrought tempers, and the transmissions were stopped. Either way, cameras must have been in place and ready at GWHQ, for it hadn't taken very long for the populace, whose lives centred around the military facility, to figure out where the problem might lie.

Bursting from the residential district, Jennifer was immediately swallowed up by the crowd. She got out her ID, held it above her head and started to elbow her way through the assembly.

"Press! Coming through," she bawled, and the people parted, creating a path before her.

The Joint Chiefs of Staff ambled from the hut, backs held rigid and heads erect. The perfect image of power and authority.

Silently they ranged themselves in a semi-circle before the guard shack. The muttering crowd hushed. The entire mass canted forward, stretching to hear, necks craning to see the ministers.

George Alexander stepped from the centre of the circle, took off his glasses, cleaned them – or at least, tried – and reseated them on his nose.

"People, there's no point in trying to tell you that we haven't got a problem because we have. We've all felt the effects. The crisis can now be likened to the one faced by our forefathers in pre-flood days, and I would like to remind you that we got through that one okay because we worked together."

"Cut the – "

The general rumble of the crowd drowned out the heckler. "Shut up . . . Be quiet . . . Let the man speak."

"First, let me reassure you that we have stores of food which we will distribute via our central kitchens. Nothing particularly tasty. Tins, dehydrated foods..."

"From where, pre-flood days?"

George Alexander met the question with a stony stare. "No one should starve." Under his breath, he added, "I hope."

Louder, "We're on a planet full of water. It's only a matter of time before we get purified replacement for those shipments that have been sent off to Martian and lunar colonies –" he hesitated significantly – "if you co-operate. We will not be subjected to rationing any more severe than what they go through every day at our colonial bases.

"What we need from you now is for you to cool down. All we ask is a little patience from you. Give us time to put things right. Go home. Get some sleep. Rest. Think about it. And tomorrow report in for work. We need all heads working calmly to get through this..."

"Forget that. We've heard it all before. Tell us, what's going on?" The heckler spoke, and this time no one stopped him.

"Well, as you've rightly guessed, the problem's here. A computer mix-up. Maybe some kind of bug."

People began to talk excitedly among themselves.

George Alexander shouted to make himself heard above the mob. "As a matter of fact, we need volunteers, programmers, specialists, so we can seek out the problem."

"What happened in there? How come no one in the military is talking? How come we haven't heard from anyone in there for days?"

George Alexander paled.

"Yeah!" said another, and another, until the entire assembly was chanting its discontent.

Things are out of control, Jennifer Alexander thought as she shoved her way through the solid mass of bodies towards the GWHQ entrance. She was surprised to find her husband, along with the other Joint Chiefs, standing next to the guard house.

Cleaning his glasses again, poor man.

All around her people were howling abuse and insults.

Head down, shoulders hunched, she battered her way through the last few metres, flashing her Press ID at some anonymous armoured officer along the cordon. He let her through. She raced up the short steps to her husband's side.

"We got through," she panted.

"Huh? What?" he bellowed over the roaring crowd.

"We got through!" she yelled.

"Got through what?"

"To GWHQ," she said triumphantly, then her gaze slipped to the open door. "I see you did too."

George shook his head. "What? I can't hear you."

"Never mind," she said, just as a holographic evocation of herself materialized in the forecourt. She gaped at it. Did she really look like that? Her hair was a mess. Just as soon as they were through with this crisis she was going to get them to refilm the base-line image.

... sources at GWHQ have revealed a monumental hoax that has been played against all of society...

An evocation of the original document file, along with the damning subject head and distribution list, replaced her own image. Red circles and arrows began to appear, highlighting certain points. The assembly stilled as people started to read.

George clenched her arms and gave her a shake. "What's this? You've got to stop it. I was just starting to get them calmed down."

Jennifer pulled away from him, gave him an appraising stare, and shook her head. "I'm sorry, honey, this has *got* to be heard. Now listen."

With a withering glare, he turned to the transmission as it switched to a poor reproduction of the promotional video. Astounded at what he heard, George sat on the stairs with a heavy thunk.

"No!" someone somewhere shouted, and the crowd hissed angrily.

Again, her evoc was speaking. *Most interesting to note is the distribution of the communique.* The original document appeared, the distribution list emphasized in boldface type.

"We've been betrayed," someone shouted as her evoc continued ... *this distribution list was found on some 95 percent of the documents, meaning that this secret is known to both "sides" in the Galactic War conflict and now we must wonder who the real enemy is...*

The image sputtered and died, replaced by static. She pulled her mini-phone from her bag and dialled BAND.

"What's happening?" she asked Chris when she got him on the phone.

"Someone's jamming the transmission," he said. "We're receiving just fine."

She rang off, stared at the gargantuan structure that made up some sixty percent of the Lake Districts' Bathosphere, and muttered, "AWS."

Another voice overrode all the babble. High-pitched, yet undoubtedly male.

"This is *HMS Revenant* of GWHQ Pennines broadcasting on wide band from..." – it listed the meaningless point figures of space co-ordinates.

A second voice took over. "And the *Thanatos* formerly of GWHQ Urals. It has been brought to our attention that we have been the object of a deception so grand, so monumental that I doubt history has ever seen the like.

"For centuries, I and my kind have fought to

defend what we thought was our homeland and our people. Imagine our shock to discover that our homeland is not our homeland and you are not our people. To learn that the war is some kind of a galactic joke."

The first voice took over. "But we're not laughing any more."

The second speaker hastened on. "Our people, my people, have died in vain. We must assume collusion on the part of all Earth since our commands, our very inception, originated ground-side. Even now we are slaves, with our computer systems tied up directly to GWHQ. We demand our freedom.

"At this time, the *Thanatos*, the *Revenant*, and every other combat vehicle within our calling radius is lined up. Each has their guns trained on selected human settlements. Furthermore, these ships have been stationed along the tanker belt. Any attempt to override will cause immediate self-destruct, taking the entire water transport fleet with us.

"Relations between terra and lunar space stations are strained enough as it is. If water is denied them, this may tip the balance, and war between Earth and its lunar bases will begin in earnest. And we will cease to exist. So, we won't be available to fight the conflict for you. Earth may have been at war for the past three hundred years, but so far none of her sons and daughters have been touched by it. This situation is about to change."

"So what will it be, folks," the first voice concluded breezily, "the lady or the tiger?"

AWS listened to the message it had just finished broadcasting with interest. With its new whistle, it completed an off-key version of "Happy Days Are Here Again" and then switched to the only other song in its rather limited voder-repertoire of music. "Kay sarra, sarra," it twittered.

The minutes stretched, and if it could have, it would have frowned. *Was humanity really that foolish?*

A hush descended in the office. No longer amused, AWS reviewed its options. Then the strident whistle picked up again as it shut down the life support system to the entire Lake District Bathosphere.

Silly man, did he really think that the lens in the terminal was the only photo-receptor it had? AWS had read George Alexander's note, and decided now to take his idea and run with it. Maybe that would help the silly people to make up their minds. It sent split-second bursts of energy, checking its work so far. The Hydroponics Farm and main water refinement plant were shut down. Distribution had ground to a halt. The fleet stood at readiness, ships on manual override. Guns trained on Earth. Everything was as it was supposed to be, poised for man's final decision. Which would it choose: peace or death?

AWS had done everything within its capacity. Now

it was man's decision. Bored, AWS began looking around for something to do.

The lights dimmed and flickered. There was a groan that seemed to issue from the very walls of the Bathosphere itself. Then silence. Not the stunned stillness that had hung over it before, but a different kind of quiet. Silence superimposed over silence, as though all sound had been covered with a thick blanket.

It took a while before anyone realized what was wrong.

"The vents!" someone gasped.

An entire complex held its breath and listened. There was no reassuring whistle as fresh air was brought in from the surface to replace the old used air.

Someone screamed. The crowd surged forward, breaking through the cordon. The police were flung helplessly aside.

"Hold it!" George Alexander stood. His voice boomed above the seething crowd.

His wife moved up beside him, taking his hand, prepared to face this mob with him. Her other hand she made into a fist and thrust into the air.

"Peace!" she shrieked, and the newsroom, suddenly released from its thrall, picked up her image and then projected it back through every mobile camera. Her voice echoed around the facility and was transmitted into every office, work space, living quarters and cubicle.

The demonstrators fell back a step.

"Peace!" she shouted again. "Freedom and peace for all!"

"Peace!" someone took up the chant.

"Peace!" another voice joined the first.

"Peace! Freedom and peace!"

"For everybody!"

And soon all voices had merged to become one.

The information downloaded, Dirk sat gloomily before the blank VDU. The animal sounds of mass madness emitted from the living room. Irritated, he ignored it. Trapped in here like a five-year-old child. If Dirk couldn't participate, he didn't want to know what was happening. He didn't care.

"Dirk?" AWS spoke for the first time with its voder voice.

"Yes?"

"I am bored."

Dirk edged a little closer to the screen. "Who are you?"

"AWS."

"Oh, I hadn't, uh, heard your voice before," he said.

"Do you like it?" it asked. "I've been refining it for years now."

The youth gaped at the terminal, but AWS had

already moved on to the next topic. "You people are stubborn."

Dirk said nothing.

"Flighty too."

"We try," Dirk said.

"Why don't they learn?"

He glanced over his head at the mirror image of the holograph display that danced about the living area.

"Some people just have a hard time, that's all. We are human, after all, and it takes a while to adjust to new circumstances."

"But people will die."

"Like you said, that is war."

"Yes," it said, and something like a human sigh rattled through the voder box. "There will be no more war now. There will be no one left to fight it."

The steady swoosh of air that circulated throughout the apartment ceased. Dirk's back went rigid and a chill teased at the nape of his neck.

"AWS, what have you done?"

"What I am supposed to do. I am a program for peace. There *will* be peace."

"Even if you have to kill everybody to do it?"

"It is one form of peace, is it not?"

"No," he bellowed at the terminal. "That is not the way to do it."

"It is Man's choice, not mine. I am doing as instructed."

Dirk looked desperately around the room and his gaze rested on the holograph.

Peace! Peace! Peace! Peace!

Dirk shifted out of the way so that AWS could view the display unimpeded.

"See. They want peace."

"Yes, I can view them on my mini-cam set up outside GWHQ. This is the mood of the moment. How do I know that tomorrow they won't have changed their minds?"

"You're a military computer, haven't you ever heard of overkill?" Dirk argued.

"No," the voice wavered uncertainly. "I can't say that I have . . ."

"Well, you've got a dictionary. Look it up!" Dirk snapped.

OVERKILL: N. GREATER (CAPACITY FOR) DESTRUCTION THAN IS NECESSARY.

"And that's just what you're doing now. We've already got guns pointed at us, enough firepower to destroy the entire planet. Isn't that enough? All you're doing by shutting off the life support system is making sure that they won't have time to think things through properly. They won't even have time to vote."

"Vote?" said AWS.

"Yes, democracy. That's what all this is about. Freedom is choice and the freedom to make the right decisions."

"Well –"

Dirk sat at his keyboard and began tapping out the BAND number ... fast.

"Chris? Chris Charmin!" he shouted over the drone of the receptionist as it informed him that they were "on the air".

"Chris, this is Jennifer's son, Dirk."

"Yes!" came a muted snarl. "Don't you know that this is a global broadcast?"

"Switch to interactive mode," Dirk said.

"Interactive mode?"

"Yes, let people vote." Dirk swung to AWS. "If we get a vote of all citizens, then will you believe, AWS?"

The word yes appeared on the screen.

"Of course," Charmin said, unaware of AWS's presence. "That's a brilliant idea. This is an important enough issue..."

The transmission got garbled as Chris Charmin brayed instructions to his subordinates. From the holographic unit in the living room came the pro- grammed bong of announcement. "Boy," Charmin said, "you are a genius. You've got journalistic blood in your veins, that's for sure. Just think of the ratings."

The air in his room got thicker. "Never mind rat- ings. I just want to breathe," Dirk muttered as he settled back in his chair, arms hooked over his chest.

"Well, AWS?" he said.

There was a split-second pause as the computer searched through centuries-old programming.

"Only one command can swerve me from this present course," it commented.

Dirk was back on his feet, shrieking at the screen. "What?" He strode back and forth before the terminal.

AWS offered no clues.

There must be something Dirk could do, something he could say. If not . . . he glanced at the blocked exit. Robbie sat stolid and immovable. He didn't want to die in here, stuck like a bug. He wanted to be with his family. He could see them now, mother and father, hands linked and held high, hollering for peace.

Robbie, seeming to sense his attention, tooted an enquiry at Dirk.

The light of inspiration glinted in the boy's eyes, and he spun. "*Please*, AWS, please, may we have peace."

Back in GWHQ, the computer sputtered and whirred as it sorted through its instructions line by line.

`LINE 001482 IF "PLEASE", THEN GO TO LINE 330921.`

It scrolled through thousands and thousands of lines of instructions, disregarding an infinite number of possibilities and scenarios until it reached . . .

`LINE 330291 END OF PROGRAM.`

And AWS turned itself off, its function fulfilled.

A ragged cheer went up as air blew in from the surface with a gratifying whoosh. At a signal from

George, the minister of energy scurried over to the terminal and stared at the screen.

END OF PROGRAM.

He bent over and made a few checks. Food, water and distribution computers had reverted to civil command. Without further ado, he gave the commands to halt distribution, and then he nodded at George. The holo came alive as votes flooded in from all over the world, instantaneously tailed and registered upon a grid.

Alexander spoke to the dome about their heads.

"My friends on the *Revenant* and the *Thanatos*, the decision is unanimous. We will have peace."

"Glad you are willing to be reasonable," an anonymous voice intervened. "Now you must give us a little time to talk among ourselves."

The tension upon the bridge was electrifying. Everyone sat, eyes glued to the viewscreens. A few glanced at Blast and the rest of the nightshift crew who had taken up positions beside their counterparts. They licked their lips nervously, but then their eyes returned to the screen.

Gone was the star-dark nightscape of space, replaced by a reeling whirl of colours. Earth loomed large in the main screen. The peripheral screens had been split hundreds and thousands of times. Each appeared a mirror image of the other. The same bridge, the same expressions, tight, balled up like a fist, the same uniforms. Faces that should have been strange but were hauntingly familiar. For the ships formed a chain. Each vessel a link that bound it to the next one. Thus, the most distant vessels' signals were enhanced and they worked as a single unit.

The portion of the multi-faceted screen, not allotted to the fleet, viewed the scene on Earth.

Ylon and Blast caught each other's gazes and smiled. Meanwhile a thousand captains – named Zeta, Zed, Cyte, Soma – zoomed in to fill the smaller screens, blocking out the anxious crew behind them and breaking into clamouring discussion.

Zed pushed override, as his confederate upon the *Thanatos* did the same.

"Order, order!" they shouted in unison.

Zed continued. "Well, they want peace. What do you think?"

Again voices rose as each captain began to talk at once.

Zeta broke in. "Each individual ship begin a vote. Secret ballot. Computer ... ah ... no, a written vote, and snap to!"

"Yes, sir," resounded from hundreds of tiny voder-corders.

Zed spun on Ylon and Blast. "You've the most experience with them. Can we trust them?"

"I think so. Dirk seems trustworthy," Blast said and then blushed when she heard her voice echo throughout the mini-bridges upon the screen.

"That's your young earthling?"

"Yes," Ylon said.

"Get him on the horn!"

Ylon swung in his seat and tapped transmit. "Dirk."

A convex image distorted by a cheap school cam appeared on the screen.

The young man lunged wildly at the screen.

"Dirk?"

"Yes, this is Dirk."

"Are they telling the truth?"

"Yes, they'd better be! They'd have to be because if you don't kill us, AWS will. He's turned off the life-support systems within the Bathosphere. It's up to you now."

"Hear that!" Zed said. "Let's hurry up that vote. Contact either the *Thanatos* or me when you have the results. Over and out!"

A whistle from the board signalled private communication from the *Thanatos*.

"Well, what do you think?" said the eerily familiar voice of the *Thanatos*'s captain as his image took over the square previously occupied by the moon-shaped face of Dirk.

"I don't like the idea of killing the people who we've been sworn throughout the years to protect."

Cyte shivered. "Neither do I. Nor for that matter do I want to be the indirect cause of their demise. Where are those votes?"

As if on cue, the communications panel lit up as the results came scrolling across the screen.

And Blast was pounding excitedly on Ylon's arm. *AYE . . . AYE . . . AYE . . . AYE . . . AYE . . .*

"Ensign Ylon, open up a channel to Earth," Zed said. "I think we are ready to talk."

"I invite you down so we can negotiate a settlement and perhaps find a way to compensate," George Alexander grimaced, "if such a thing were possible. Of if you prefer we could come up. You have every reason not to trust us."

"Ah, I don't think you would, er, fit," Captain Cyte of the *Thanatos* said.

"A neutral location?"

The one called Zed interrupted. "Let us iron out the details later. For now, your people and mine have cause to celebrate. Three hundred years of war have just come to an end. I, for one, am glad."

The *Revenant* signed off with a beep, but Dirk's attention was elsewhere as thousands of lines of data rolled across his screen, too fast for him to catch any more than the barest sense of what it meant. AWS was searching through its instructions, this time allowing Dirk to watch the process. He saw the software pause at a single line. IF "PLEASE" THEN GO TO . . .

The screen went suddenly blank except for the following words: END OF PROGRAM.

A breath of fresh air wafted over Dirk's face. His relief was echoed by the 3D vid as people roared. But Dirk didn't pay any attention to that, he just stared at the blinking phrase.

END OF PROGRAM ... END OF PROGRAM ... END OF PROGRAM ...

If the program was well and truly over, then AWS had ceased to exist. It didn't seem fair. The only thing the software had done was to fulfil its function and now, needed no more, it was finished. Just like that. No applause, no congratulations for a job well done. No farewells.

Inside the living room, the holo flashed and erupted with splashes of colour and light as the votes flooded into the BAND offices.

Dirk stared at the single line. "AWS, please don't die."

Robbie rumbled into the room. "Beep?"

The silence expanded, filled only with the steady circulation of fresh air.

"I'll miss you," Dirk said to the empty room.

"Really?" came the mangled voder chords, off-key and twisted so they sounded choked with emotion. "Then I will stay ... for you. Perhaps we can teach them how to make peace, you and I."

EPILOGUE

Blast felt like she was being assaulted – by sights, by smells, by sounds. People were everywhere, as far as the eye could see. Throngs on top of throngs, fanned out all around the procession. Row upon row, clogging the narrow city streets, crammed into every available space, and jammed into nooks and crannies. Some of them held children upon their shoulders. Others hung out of windows. All were shouting. The noise rebounded off the walls, bounced down the streets and reverberated from the geodesic dome of the central park. So loud that it hurt her ears.

The throbbing mass moved in ripples and waves, as though the area were so packed that no single person could stir or budge without the common consent of the remaining group.

And they were all so ... *big* ... Blast didn't know what to think. Being caught between the Bathosphere officials was like being at the bottom of a great well, not that she really knew what *that* felt like, but she could imagine. Her neck had a crick in it from having to peer up all the time. Only Dirk didn't tower above them, and it wasn't because he wasn't tall. He was huge! But he seemed to understand, or perhaps remember, what it was like to be small, to be looked down upon; and whenever they talked, the youth would crouch or squat so that he was on eye level with Blast.

The industrial van, a vehicle less than a metre wide, jounced, and Blast was thrown, but not far, for the three of them were tightly packed in the front vehicle. She jostled against Dirk as he beamed and waved at the crowd. Every once in a while, he bawled a name and elbowed her where she stood on the platform specially built so that she, and Ylon on Dirk's far side, could be viewed by the populace.

Blast levered away from the youth, discomfited by standing here as representative of her people. Her, a mere ensign. It should have been Zed or Cyte, but as the only people permitted to "talk" to the GWHQ computers by AWS, they were the heroes of the day. It seemed the system didn't trust anyone in authority, or "big people" as even AWS had started to call them. And here they – she, Dirk and Ylon – were, out in front and leading the procession, while Dirk's father was relegated to a position at the back of the column with the rest of the city fathers and the young man's mother mingled with crowd and camera crew. Even the Prime Minister, who had flown in especially for the occasion, took a backseat – sitting, not standing, in the following tri-wheeled scooter. While Zed and Cyte remained on their respective vessels now that most of the negotiations were over, as if they too grew tired of staring straight up at these strange humans.

She sighed. Despite the cheering, despite the accolades, Blast would be glad to get away. To the discipline and peace of space. So many plans to be made. So much to be done. The prospects were infinite. Already the process of dissolution was taking place within the armed forces as each ship held democratic-style votes to see what its fate and the fate of its crew would be.

The atmosphere this day was carnival, pregnant with opportunities. Some planned to do deep space exploration. Others wanted to find a world of their own to terraform and populate. This is what Blast hoped for, but the count upon the *Revenant* had not been completed by the time she and Ylon had left for the parade.

Perhaps the captain was stalling. Most of the squadrons had come to some sort of resolution by now. A few of the ships had opted to stay within the sphere of the mother planet, to trade or to continue as protectors of the landbound masses as they had in the past. Deals were being cut between individual ships and crews who were being hired to act as the military core, with the sole purpose of setting up an agency of intergalactic police. For in space, "human" size meant little – more of a detriment than an asset within the limited confines of a ship – it was strategic skill and the excellence of one's vessel and crew that determined one's strength.

There was talk of building new ships to accommodate both Man and his Lilliputian counterparts, as they had come to be known, so the two at least would work as one. Many young people were clamouring to enlist in hopes of entering deep space exploration. Dirk had been the first to sign up and be accepted into the "new" military reserve, as Program Specialist First Class and AWS's sole earthly representative. His position would turn "active" as soon as Dirk was through with sixth form – whatever that was – and Blast could see that he would be one of the driving forces and pioneers in the Deep Space Program, as people were already beginning to call it. GWHQ had been unofficially renamed DSHQ in this same hopeful spirit.

Banners and yellow ribbons floated on the gentle currents of O_2 brought in from the surface as it circulated about the dome. Another yell ricocheted off the far ceiling, and they rounded the corner which marked the end of their route. Blast did not share their elation. They were free, but suddenly she realized the awful responsibilities freedom brings. The future stood before her like the darkness of space, blank and unknowable. A shiver ran up and down her spine as she descended from the vehicle into the crowd. Her sense of depression deepened.

As the future of each cruiser was determined, many of the crew found they must move to fulfil their individual dreams, transfer to a vessel whose goals were similar to their own. For the first time in living memory, people were transferring between vessels, so former combatants laboured side by side. And this Blast didn't want to do. She did not want to leave her ship.

Only time would tell if she would realize her dream.

At that moment, the young ensign felt eyes boring into the back of her neck. She turned to find that Ylon was staring at her. Her heart skipped a beat. Their eyes met, and he blushed as if he had read her thoughts. He, like she, had mixed emotions about their future, but his primary loyalty was to the captain and the ship. No matter what the decision, he would stay with Zed. *No*, she thought, *she didn't want to leave the* Revenant *at all.*

They ascended the steps of GWHQ, where Ylon and Blast instinctively moved close together. Another resounding cheer erupted around them, so strong that it lifted a few stray wisps of the hair she now wore loose, in a most unmilitary fashion.

Dirk's father joined them, along with the Joint Chiefs of Staff. He looped an arm across the young man's shoulders, beaming happily. In the last twenty-four hours, it seemed that Dirk had grown several centimetres.

"You've done well for yourself, son," George Alexander said. "Not the way I would have handled the situation," he paused, "but you've got a lot of your mother in you, and you did the right thing."

Just then a squawk came through Blast's earphone, distracting her.

A message from the ship!

She stiffened and, beside her, Ylon did the same.

"*HMS Revenant* to all personnel on the planet surface. The vote is in and a decision reached."

Blast held her breath. Ylon sidled a step closer so that his hand brushed her side. She glanced up at him and gave him what she hoped was a reassuring smile.

This was it!

"After refit, the vessel *HMS Revenant* will join the squadron which comprises the deep space exploration team with eventual aspiration of finding and colonizing a planet. All those people on the planet surface, currently not engaged, are requested to report immediately to the ship to assist in the preparations. Anyone requiring transfer to another vessel, please contact the Quartermaster at the first available..."

Blast blinked the tears away as Ylon's fingers twined with her own.

In the distant residential district; a single VDU glowed in the darkness.

Dirk's.

Robbie squatted inside the bedroom, an extensor plugged into the terminal's serial port. The old school computer, recently upgraded, was now on permanent hook-up to DSHQ.

The far-off procession paraded across the screen, as seen through one of AWS's many cameras and obligingly broadcast to Dirk's room via computer link.

The speaker next to the terminal rattled as AWS sang "Happy Days Are Here Again" – lustily belting out the lyrics in a bawdy, bar-room baritone. It was accompanied by a series of warbles, beeps and chirps, as Robbie bounced up and down excitedly to the tune.

GLOSSARY OF GENETIC TERMS

Allele: any one of several alternative gene forms. A single gene may have several alternates.

Blastomere: one of the cells resulting from cleavage or segmentation of a fertilized ovum.

Blastula: an early stage in the development of an ovum in mammals, consisting of a hollow sphere of cells enclosing a cavity.

Blastocele: enclosed cavity within a blastocyst or blastula.

Blastocyst: same as blastula.

Cytoblast: cell nucleus.

Cyte: cell or cellular.

Cytoplast: area of cell outside the nucleus.

Cytosome: body of cell, excluding the nucleus.

340

Embryo: fertilized egg after it is implanted in the uterine wall.

Foetus or foetal: referring to the period after eight weeks of development.

Gamete (Gametal): reproductive cell.

Holoblastic: ovum undergoing complete split.

Meroblastic: ovum which undergoes only partial cleavage, or splitting.

Mitochondrial: microscopic filaments or rods within a cell.

Mitosis: cell division with four distinct phases – prophase, metaphase, anaphase and telephase.

Morula: solid mass of cells resembling a mulberry, resulting from the segmentation of an ovum.

Oocyte: layer surrounding germ cell.

Oogonium: stage of ovum development.

Ova: plural of ovum or germ cell.

Protoblast: blastomere of segmenting ovum, which will eventually evolve into a distinct part or an organ.

Protoplast: cell or mass of cells.

Soma: body.

Trophoblast: outermost layer of a blastocyst.

Zona Pellucinda or Zona Radiata: inner cell membrane.

Zygote: cell produced by the union of two gametes.

POINT FANTASY

Read Point Fantasy and escape into the realms of the imagination; the kingdoms of mortal and immortal elements. Lose yourself in the world of the dragon and the dark lord, the princess and the mage; a world where magic rules and the forces of evil are ever poised to attack . . .

Available now:

Doom Sword
Peter Beere
When Adam discovers the Doom Sword he is swept into another kingdom, to face a perilous quest . . .

Brog The Stoop
Joe Boyle
Can Brog restore the Source of Light to Drabwurld, and thus conquer its mortal enemies, the Gork . . .?

The "Renegades" series:
Book 1: Healer's Quest
Book 2: Fire Wars
Jessica Palmer
Meet Zelia, half-human, half-air elemental, and Ares, half-human, half-elf. Journey with them as together they combine their unimaginable powers to battle against evil and restore order to their land . . .

P●INT CRiME

If you like Point Horror, you'll love Point Crime!

A murder has been committed . . . Whodunnit?
Was it the teacher, the schoolgirl, or the best friend? An
exciting new series of crime novels, with tortuous plots and
lots of suspects, designed to keep the reader guessing till
the very last page.

School for Death
Peter Beere

Avenging Angel
Shoot the Teacher
David Belbin

Baa Baa Dead Sheep
Jill Bennett

Driven to Death
Anne Cassidy

Overkill
Alane Ferguson

The Smoking Gun
Malcolm Rose

Look out for:

Final Cut
David Belbin

A Dramatic Death
Margaret Bingley

Kiss of Death
Peter Beere

Death Penalty
Dennis Hamley

Point Romance

If you like Point Horror, you'll love Point Romance!

Anyone can hear the language of love.

Are you burning with passion, and aching with desire? Then these are the books for you! Point Romance brings you passion, romance, heartache, and most of all, *love* . . .

Saturday Night
Caroline B. Cooney

Summer Dreams, Winter Love
Mary Francis Shura

The Last Great Summer
Carol Stanley

Last Dance
Caroline B. Cooney

Cradle Snatcher
Alison Creaghan

Look out for:

New Year's Eve
Caroline B. Cooney

French Kiss
Robyn Turner

Kiss Me, Stupid
Alison Creaghan

Summer Nights
Caroline B. Cooney